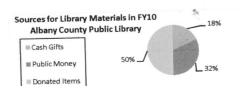

Sources for Library Materials in FY10
Albany County Public Library

- Cash Gifts
- Public Money
- Donated Items

18%

32%

50%

Wildwing

EMILY WHITMAN

Greenwillow Books
An Imprint of HarperCollinsPublishers

I am indebted to the authors of the following books, which I consulted for research: J. A. Baker, *The Peregrine* (New York: New York Review Books, 2005); Frank Lyman Beebe and Harold Melvin Webster, *North American Falconry and Hunting Hawks* (Denver: North American Falconry and Hunting Hawks, 1989); John Cummins, *The Art of Medieval Hunting: The Hound and the Hawk* (Edison, N. J.: Castle Books, 2003); Casey A. Wood and Florence Marjorie Fyfe, editors, *The Art of Falconry, Being the De Arte Venandi cum Avibus of Frederick II of Hohenstaufen* (Stanford: Stanford University Press, 1943); Nancy Goldstone, *Four Queens: The Provençal Sisters Who Ruled Europe* (New York: Penguin Books, 2008); Marcy Cottrell Houle, *Wings for My Flight: The Peregrine Falcons of Chimney Rock* (Reading, Mass.: Addison-Wesley Publishing, 1991); Margaret Wade Labarge, *A Baronial Household of the Thirteenth Century* (New York: Barnes & Noble, Inc., 1965); and Robin S. Oggins, *The Kings and Their Hawks: Falconry in Medieval England* (New Haven: Yale University Press, 2004).

Wildwing

The text of this book is set in Times Roman
Book design by Sylvie Le Floc'h

Library of Congress Cataloging-in-Publication Data

Whitman, Emily.
Wildwing / by Emily Whitman.
p. cm.
"Greenwillow Books."
Summary: In 1913 England, fifteen-year-old Addy is a lowly servant, but when she gets inside an elevator car in her employer's study, she is suddenly transported to a castle in 1240 and discovers that she is mistaken for the lord's intended bride.
ISBN 978-0-06-172452-7 (trade bdg.)
[1. Time travel—Fiction. 2. Social classes—Fiction. 3. Mistaken identity—Fiction.
4. Peregrine falcon—Fiction. 5. Falcons—Fiction.
6. Great Britain—History—1066–1687—Fiction.] I. Title.
PZ7.W5924Wi 2010 [Fic]—dc22 2009044189

10 11 12 13 14 CG/RRDB 10 9 8 7 6 5 4 3 2 1
First Edition

 Greenwillow Books

For my parents,
Warren and Gerda Rovetch

The spotted hawk swoops by and accuses me, he complains
of my gab and my loitering.

I too am not a bit tamed, I too am untranslatable . . .
— *Walt Whitman*

Tell all the Truth but tell it slant—
Success in Circuit lies
— *Emily Dickinson*

Miss High-and-Mighty

It's the same old cobbled street through the same old town, but for once I barely smell the cakes from the tea shop, don't even pause to stare in the windows. I'm floating along, another me, in a dreamworld. Thanking God for sending a teacher so new, she hasn't learned yet that there are somebodies and nobodies in this town, and that I'm one of the nobodies.

She's gone and made me the queen!

I smile, remembering Caroline's horrified gasp. She's to be nursemaid in the play. Caroline, who tells the other girls not to talk to me, who pretends I don't exist if we're in the grocer's at the same time. She turned so bright red, she looked like a furnace about to explode.

I imagine Mum's face when she comes in the door tonight. I'll say, "You know those costumes you stitched for the theatrical society? The ones you kept telling me not to touch? I'm to wear one even grander!"

I think of the old woman who led us down the stairs to the costume room, lit by one dim electric bulb. There were pantaloons and billowing skirts and green silk shining like the river in sunlight, and a big furry bear's head grimacing on a shelf, and a pile of wings fluttering in a corner. The woman pulled out a gown, all red and gold and sparkling glimmer, and slipped it over my clothes.

"The length is good," she said in a scratchy little voice. "We'll shorten the sleeves a bit. And the neck doesn't need to be quite so low, now does it?"

Caroline whispered something to Jane in the corner, and they burst out laughing, but I didn't even care. I just kept looking at the yards and yards of rich fabric cascading down around me, the stones sparkling at neck and cuff.

Now, as I walk home, the street disappears, I'm so deep in imagining how I'll walk in that gown. How I'll hold my head. How I won't stand aside all meek and quiet for anyone.

Suddenly a voice jabs through my thoughts like a bad cobble edge under my shoe.

"There she is," says Caroline. "Miss High-and-Mighty."

Jane and Mary are with her; they stare at me and laugh. I

put my head down low and keep walking. It's the best day of my life; I'm not going to let them pull it to shreds.

"A queen?" Caroline sneers. "Doesn't she look it, though!"

"In that old dress?" says Mary, smoothing her own well-tailored gabardine.

They snicker. Their bright new shoes click out the same rhythm as my mended pair. I walk faster.

Caroline's voice gets harder, tactical, like a hunter closing in on her prey. "Queens come from good families. They know who their fathers are."

"Right," says Jane. "It's all about how you're born."

"Who's going to believe *her* in that role?" Caroline raises her voice so I'll hear her over a passing motorcar. "They'll take one look and walk out."

"Who's *your* father, then, Addy?" says Mary.

My feet slow as I try to repeat Mum's words, try to think them loud enough to drown out their taunts. *Don't let them get to you again. Don't even look in their eyes. Just disappear into yourself. It's the only way . . .*

"That part should have been yours, Caroline," says Jane, the toady. "You hold yourself like a queen."

"It's easy for me," says Caroline, tossing her head. "*My* mother isn't a slut."

"Look at her dress! The same she's worn all month."

"Ragtag queen. Secondhand queen."

I won't, I think. *I won't.* But I feel my fingers closing into a fist in my pocket.

"Can't be a queen without a father."

"Like mother, like daughter."

Their voices get louder and louder, drowning out the quiet words in my head, until that familiar black anger comes surging through me, drowning out all Mum's words, and I swing.

The door opens. Mum comes in and sees me, my needle slipping lightning fast through the rip in my skirt, neat little stitches I'd hoped to have finished before she came home, so tiny she wouldn't notice them.

She shakes her head, sighing, and there are years of disappointment in that sigh.

"I tripped." My words come out too fast. Even I wouldn't believe them. "On my way home, the curb, I didn't see it and—"

"Mrs. Miller saw you through the grocer's window. She told me."

I know better than to say anything. My only hope now is to look meek and obedient. I turn back to my stitching, but inside I'm praying as hard as I can, *Let her forget what she said last time. Please let her forget.*

God isn't listening.

"So I've found you a place, Addy. It's time you left school."

Her words are a seam ripper, slashing through everything that holds me together.

"Not now!" I cry. "There's to be a play and—"

"Yes. Now." She takes off her hat and slaps it down on the shelf, hangs her coat on the hook. "I heard Mrs. Beale is leaving to care for her sick daughter in London. She does for Mr. Greenwood. He'll be needing someone."

"Mr. Greenwood! But he's—"

"So he's a little batty." She sinks into the other chair. "There's no harm in him. A place like this won't come along again soon, not in this village. We couldn't hope for better."

Here's the thing. Mum makes her way by disappearing into the woodwork, becoming small, invisible, a mouse who tiptoes in and gratefully nibbles the crumbs that great folks leave behind. She's always cutting out fabric, always stitching, so I can stay in school. And I work hard, I do; but I keep hearing the other girls whisper, *"Bastard bastard bastard."* Then there's trouble. And it's always my fault.

Mum is looking at my face. "What is it, then?"

How can I tell her what it means to me, the chance to be in this play? To be someone people look up to for once, even if it's only onstage? But to explain, I'd need to start with what they say about me—and about her. What it was like when I was young. The teasing. The names. No one to play with because, as they were only too happy to explain, their mothers warned them away from me, as if whatever taint I'd inherited were catching. What it's still like. The raised eyebrows, the cold wind as they swerve to avoid me in the halls.

But I can't tell Mum that. So all I say is, "Two months, until the performance, please! And then I'll go wherever you tell me."

She shakes her head. "He'll have found someone else."

"But *you're* the one kept me in school this year, said I should stay as long as we could manage it."

"And so I did," she says, softer. "And so I did."

Something flutters in my chest. One more sigh from her and I'm safe!

But then her voice turns bitter. "Now I see I was wrong. What good has it done, tell me that? Making you dream of things you can't have. Because no matter how quick and bright you may be, you'll still wear a maid's apron when all is said and done. A maid in a good house if you're lucky, a scullery slavey if you're not. You won't do better than this place. For God's sake! I was ten years old when I went into service, and you a great girl of fifteen!"

She stands and walks a few steps to the side of the room that counts as our kitchen, opens the cupboard, rummages for the potatoes, an onion. "You've been getting above your station. Not watching your words with your betters. Let alone your fists." She reaches for the knife and now its steady *chop, chop* underlines her anger. "It's their money puts this roof over our heads. Puts this food on our table."

Something rises inside me, fighting what she says, and I cry, "But I'm to be the queen!"

"The queen?" she exclaims, turning to stare at me. "That's the problem right there! Exactly *who* do you think you are?" For a moment the knife is pointing right at my heart; when it resumes chopping, her back is to me again, a solid wall. "Why must you keep drawing attention to yourself? Holding your head up so high. Wearing your hair loose down your back, calling every eye to you—the boys stare enough as it is! It's no wonder the others tease you."

The acrid sting of onion fills the air. Mum wipes the crook of her elbow across her eyes. For a moment I think she's crying, but her voice is steel as she says, "Get your head out of the clouds, Addy. This is the life you were born to." The knife thunks down. "This is the life you have to live."

I Become a Maid

Mum gives me a quick once-over, twirls her finger to make me turn around so she can check my braid, the back of my dress. Opens the door without a word. Steps out into the street.

I'm starched and ironed within an inch of my life. My shoes are polished bright. My cuffs and collar are scratchy new. Any specks of dust that come near take one look at my brilliant white apron, then turn and run shrieking in fear.

Which is what I want to do.

Instead of walking down Market Street on my way to meet Mr. Greenwood, with everyone watching me, knowing where I'm going, and why. I hear them in my head, the women in Mrs. Miller's shop, buying their bits of folderol, chirping to one another in their high little voices. "Order! Obedience! Organization! That's what service will teach her. High time she learned her place." And then they'll waddle off to lunch, delighted their world is safe and no little upstart of a fatherless girl will steal the role of queen away from their well-bred daughters. . . .

I realize everything is quiet. I come back to myself. I'm still in the doorway. Mum has stopped a few doors down and is turning back to look at me. I expect her to give me a tongue-lashing, but instead she sighs, "Coming, then?"

I pull the door shut behind me. The click of finality. As if I'm leaving this life forever.

Which is silly, I think, as I walk through the crisp morning air. It's not like I'm leaving home. I'm only going to be a daily. *If* I get the position.

"It's a good place," says Mum again. "You'll stay busy doing it all yourself, cooking and cleaning. But at least there's no strutting pigeon of a housekeeper finding fault with all you do, like in the big houses. No screaming children grabbing at your apron strings, adding to your work."

She talks us down the street, the words a lifeline to keep me from drowning under what everyone must be saying. Like the girls at school, and the new teacher. I see Caroline leaning over to whisper to Mary, laughing, and my desk so empty, it's like I never belonged there in the first place. Like I never even existed. . . .

"Are you listening to me?" asks Mum again, and I see I've stopped and she's stopped, too, and she's shaking her head. We start walking again, more briskly now, as the road twists away from the shops and climbs uphill toward the edge of the village.

"You're lucky to be coming home every night"—the church bells start to strike: *bong*!—"and not sleeping in some closet in an attic with"—*bong*!—"scullery work your only task all day, turning your skin raw up to the"—*bong*!—"elbows, and ladies' maids and valets and cooks"—*bong*!—"lording it over you. No, as I said, it's lucky I ran into Mrs. Beale"—*bong*!—"when I did, before Mr. Greenwood could even post"—*bong*!—"the position, or believe me it wouldn't have lasted, so you be"—*bong*!—"sure to work hard and be respectful and quiet and obedient because"—*bong*!—"you don't want to mess *this* up."

As the last reverberations fade, I hear her sigh again. Reminding me how much I've messed up so far.

"Patience," she says for the thousandth time, "is a *virtue*."

All those *bong*s have carried us up the hill, across the bridge, along an isolated road to a house nestled at the edge of the woods.

Mum sighs again, but for once it isn't about me. "The poor dear man," she says, shaking her head slow and sad. "How he can stand to live here after what happened, so close to these woods and the cliffs down to the sea. Knowing those little bones are out there."

She opens the gate and waits for me to step through. "Well, come along then," she says, all brisk again. And she's knocking at the door.

There's a long wait.

Nothing.

Maybe she heard wrong. Maybe he isn't expecting us. Maybe he doesn't want me after all. Maybe he died in his sleep. Maybe—

There's a slow rattling as the door unlocks and swings inward. Mr. Greenwood is all bent over, looking far older than his sixty years or so. He'd be tall if he stood up straight. That's what Mum said: how tall and handsome and proud he was when his wife was alive and the boy was born. How his gaze was bright and sharp, how those brows—now a tangled gray thicket—were as bold as an eagle's brow, and his hands were the cleverest hands you ever did see, with long fingers as nimble as his mind, always coming up with new inventions. Before the tragedy. Before he gave up and stopped doing anything but wandering the woods. Still looking.

A shiver runs through me.

But Mum is standing right next to me, and she gives me a quick whack on the backside, and I remember. I curtsey all polite, bob my head, and say, "Addy Morrow, at your service, sir."

He nods, opening the door wider. Then without a word,

he turns and creaks down the hallway. We follow, Mum shutting the door firmly behind us. With the door goes the sunlight. The hall is paneled top to bottom with wood so dark, it's like walking into a cavern. Thick carpeting swallows our footsteps. We pass several closed doors before Mr. Greenwood leads us into a sitting room with a great padded chair in front of a meager fire, and windows with curtains so heavy, the velvet obscures all but a sliver of light. Everything feels obscured, the walls behind jumbled bookcases, the floor beneath a dense oriental carpet. But over the mantel there's one spot of brightness: a painting of a beautiful young woman with that swooped-up hair they used to have, and one of those high lace collars. She gazes out warmly from eyes that are the most remarkable bright blue.

"Won't you have a seat?" His voice is rough, as if he's not accustomed to talking much. Then he's looking around, and we're all realizing there aren't any more chairs.

One chair. For one old man.

"No, thank you, Mr. Greenwood, sir. We prefer to stand," says Mum.

She waits for him to speak, but there's only an awkward pause, stretching out longer and longer. Finally, she says, "With your permission, sir, I was wondering if we might discuss Addy's hours."

He nods.

"I understand Mrs. Beale comes in at eight, but Addy would prefer to start earlier, if it please you."

Again, only a nod.

"As for cooking, Addy can't do anything fancy, but she's fine at the basics, and she's a quick learner. A simple breakfast, lunch, tea, and she'll leave you your dinner. Is that right? Now, when you entertain—"

"I don't entertain," he rasps. "And no lunch. I am out much of the day."

I almost sigh in relief.

Now the two of them are talking wages and uniform and days off, and before long it's all passing over me in a wash. There's a sadness in this house, no matter how thick the carpet or crowded the shelves, a sadness so deep, it could swallow you whole.

In my head I hear Mum's voice again from last night, and I'm seeing not the drawing room but woods, and wild, wind-tossed branches.

"They searched everywhere for that boy," she'd said. "Mr. Greenwood, he looked like a madman, eyes wild and darting, hair practically standing on end. Kept saying how the boy was all he had left in the world, with his wife dead and gone, and how he'd never forgive himself for giving the nurse the day off. The maid was busy in the kitchen, you see, and the boy was supposed to be napping, but they discovered the back door wide open, and the boy nowhere to be found. Barely two years old, he was. You were but a few months yourself, and everything to me, and it cut me to the core knowing how Mr. Greenwood must be feeling. Then, on the third day, when they'd mostly given up hope, they come across Mr. Greenwood atop the cliffs not far from those old castle ruins, staring down at the sea where it crashes onto the rocks like doom itself. A good place to jump and end your anguish. They talked him back from the edge, with gentle voices and soft moves, and him still calling, 'James! James,' as if the child could hear. Oh, it was enough to break your heart. The doctor sedated him, kept him sleeping for almost a week, and he's never been the same since. . . ."

Silence pulls me back to the room. Mum and Mr. Greenwood are both looking at me, waiting. I have no idea what they just asked, so I bob another curtsey and say, "Yes, sir."

That seems to do it. Mr. Greenwood shuffles up the hall and opens the heavy door.

"Tomorrow morning," he says, his voice like rust. "Good day."

The fresh air hits me with a wallop. What just happened? Where have I been?

The Back Door

Mum walks through the gate. "We'll make one more stop before we go home," she says.

"Where?"

"The Whittingtons'. They're expecting us so you can apologize to Caroline."

"What?" I stop dead. My feet have forgotten how to move. Leaving school and losing my part in the play: I thought that was the worst thing that could ever happen to me. I was wrong.

"But I told you," I say, with a growing sense of desperation. "I didn't even start that fight!"

"It doesn't matter who started it. You took part in it. And if Mrs. Whittington stops asking me to make her dresses . . ."

She doesn't need to finish the sentence. I know what she means. We can't spare a single coin. And yet I try one last time. "She'll be at school, you know."

"Her mother said she'd be home for this."

I drag one foot forward, then the other. Mum nods and starts walking again.

So here I am, lagging four steps behind her as we turn down River Road and cross the bridge to the good part of town, where the bigger houses shout out their importance to the world, trying to pretend they're as grand as country estates. Their trim front gardens boast, "We have a gardener!" and their large front windows demand you look in so they can proclaim, "We have fancy furniture!" My face feels hotter and hotter. My footsteps slow.

Mum stops in front of a house. *Her* house.

"Are you coming?" she says. So I open the little gate and start down the path to the door.

"Not there!" cries Mum, aghast. "What *has* that school been teaching you?" She leads me around the side of the house—every window staring at me with dark, accusing eyes—to the servants' entrance. She knocks.

A grim gray-haired woman opens the door, plump and pasty-faced in her ruffled apron, her snow-white cuffs, her frilly fluff of a maid's cap.

"They're expecting you," she says.

I take a step forward, but she stops me with a look.

"Wait here," she says sharply, closing the door in our faces.

I can hear my breath heavy in the still air. Everything inside me is screaming to run and keep running forever. I struggle to keep my feet in place.

I look at Mum. She's staring straight ahead, unreadable, impenetrable.

Steps approach from inside, and the knob turns. The maid pulls the door open and then stands aside as *they* fill the frame: a vast battleship of a woman awash in gray silk, and Caroline in a purple dress, a new one she's never worn to school before. I recognize it anyway; Mum was finishing the hand stitching just last week. I know without a doubt Caroline put it on specially to meet me at the door. The back door.

"Well?" demands the battleship.

"Thank you for seeing us," says my mother in a little, disappearing voice. "Adelaide has something she would like to say."

She looks at me. I take a breath, trying to steady myself. Trying to ignore the anger and humiliation building in me like trapped steam.

As I lift my eyes to speak, a victorious smile slashes across Caroline's face. I can't look at her; I look at the battleship, forcing the words out through my teeth.

"I'm sorry for the trouble I caused."

There's a pause. "Well?" she demands.

I haven't said enough.

"It won't happen again, Mrs. Whittington."

"Don't tell *me*. Tell *Caroline*." She turns to her smirking daughter.

I'm gritting my teeth so hard, they feel ready to crack. Each word comes out tighter than the last as I look up at Caroline and say, "It won't happen again."

"That's better," says Mrs. Whittington, taking an imposing step forward. "A girl like you should know her place."

Before I can answer, Mum jumps in. "Beg pardon, ma'am, but Adelaide is leaving school to go into service."

"Oh!" exclaims Caroline with relish. "That means she can't be in the play! *Too bad*."

I can't even look up anymore. All I see are the stone pavers beneath my feet, my clenched hands. The air reeks of Caroline's exultation.

"And the green gown," says her mother, taking a step back again. "Will it be ready next week?"

"I'll bring it for a fitting in a few days, if it please you," says Mum.

"Fine," says Mrs. Whittington, as crisp as a new-ironed pleat. She turns and walks away.

Caroline lingers for a moment. "Yes, fine," she echoes, a perfect imitation of her mother.

The maid steps forward and shuts the door.

The Safety of Stone

"Addy! Come back!" cries Mum.

I keep running. I don't even turn my head, not after what she's done to me. And now she's standing in front of the Whittingtons' house calling my name. . . . The bridge cobbles blur. Market Street rises up around me. A motorcar screeches to a stop. A shop boy, his arms laden with boxes, turns to stare. They're all staring, everyone in the whole bloody village. At me: Addy Morrow, girl in disgrace.

I keep running until the streets of Little Pembleton are far behind me, and the cobbles turn to packed earth, and the bricks give way to trees. I'll never live this down, never. I can hear Caroline at school, her high-pitched voice boasting how she's made the halls safe from bastards and upstarts. Imitating Mum shouting in the middle of the road. Gloating as she describes my head bent before her all meek and subservient.

I feel as hollow as a pitcher, the life poured out of me.

The trail grows steep and narrow, and I slow to a walk. The air here is brisker, saltier, and I take gulping breaths as if it could wash the wounds inside me clean. I round a bend, push through a last tangle of trees. And there it is: the castle. Or what's left of it.

It's been more than a year since I last came, but the call is as strong as ever, a magnet pulling me around the pond, past the remnants of walls, across the dips and ridges that hint where smaller buildings once stood, and up to the tower.

I used to come here all the time, before there was so much work to do. I never told Mum, with her fears of the steep cliffs plummeting down to the pounding surf, her warnings of men lurking behind trees to snatch away any young girl so foolish as to be out alone. But I couldn't help myself; I was drawn here by the sound of the sea, the stubborn stones. I came because I found early on that *they* never did. Couldn't be bothered to walk so far in their fancy shoes. Didn't think it worth their while, a pile of old rock buried in moss and lichen.

At the base of the tower, I stretch out a hand to touch an ancient stone, waiting for the familiar chill. And then my feet are climbing the few remaining stairs, up to where they collapse into rubble. My fingers remember every handhold. I haul myself up to the gaping hole that was once a grand doorway, and step through into darkness.

I inch along the inner wall, watching each time I place a foot to make sure there's stone enough to hold me. Through the arch, to the twisting stair, and now I'm spiraling up, higher and higher, freer with every step, as if, when I reach the top, I could fly away.

But there is no top; the tower lost its upper stories long ago. I step into a chamber where the only roof is sky.

And there's my window seat, nestled in a wall so strong, no catapult could ever destroy it. I've measured with my steps. These walls are thicker than our rooms at home are wide. Outside the castle, people must have lived in a state of constant fear, like sparrows glancing up after every bite, watching for the danger that's always about to pounce. But here there was power aplenty to protect them. I step up into the nook and sit. Gray-green rock above and below me, before and behind me—here, in the safety of stone, I can finally breathe.

I slide over to look out the narrow slit of a window. Caroline's voice crashes into the wall like a brittle arrow; it shatters and falls. Her purple dress blocking the servants' door, the waves of shame tugging me under as I stood there apologizing for what wasn't my fault: the castle resists it all.

I lean my cheek against cool, chiseled stone. This is how thick my skin will be from now on. When Caroline's obedient flock caws like scornful crows, when their mothers glance at my cap and apron before turning and whispering to one another: that's when I'll remember these walls. How they let nothing in. And nothing out.

I sit, and sit, and sit. Mum will have long been back at her stitching, expecting me at her side. Let her worry. I'll stay here until the sun goes down. I've no classes to attend, do I? No play to rehearse, and only this one last day until my new position is pasted on me like a label.

A hawk swoops by. I follow its flight down to the pond and its fringe of trees, each one stuck wherever a seed happened to land. Then the sun bursts out from behind a cloud, there's a patch of blue—and all at once the pond is a shimmering mirror. It holds the same trees I was just looking at, but for once there's nothing to imprison them, and they float free.

My breath catches in my throat. That's the world I want, the one in the lake, the one without roots or rocks or soil to hold me down.

A fish breaks the surface of the water. From that small spot, circles start to spread, and the bigger they grow, the more they waver, losing whatever force once held them together. Suddenly the circles are gone, and there's nothing but ripple. Then the mirror is gone, too, blurred by a gust of wind, as if a mighty hand is dipping down to stir the waters. What was trees shimmers into a green-gold haze, and then even that disappears.

The brief brightness is gone, and I'm left with a yearning so strong, it hurts. An ache for a land somewhere between rooted trunks and shifting water, between the bound world and the dream.

But not here, I think bitterly. An alder tree can't become an oak at will. A maple can't pick up its roots like legs, and stride, step by powerful step, along the shore to find the sun. And everything that ever said otherwise—all those years of school, and the plays and moving pictures that promise you can be someone else, something more—they were all lies.

A Strange Old Bird

"First we'll lay the fire," says Mrs. Beale, thrusting the cinder pail and a metal box toward me. "I assume you know *that* much."

I nod and follow her out the kitchen door.

"I shouldn't even be here," she grumbles, huffing and puffing down the hall like an overworked locomotive. "Lord knows I have more than enough on my plate as it is, leaving for London tomorrow. I can only spare you an hour, and I won't explain anything more than once, so pay attention." She's speeding up, gathering a full head of steam. By the time she reaches the room with the portrait, she flings the door open, surging in without so much as a knock or a by your leave!

I freeze, tensing for the blast of Mr. Greenwood's anger.

But after a moment of silence, Mrs. Beale appears back in the doorway, hands on her wide hips, and exclaims, "Don't stand there big-eyed like a rabbit, girl! We have work to do."

"But Mr. Greenwood . . ."

"Out rambling the woods, like he does every morning. And a good thing it is, so you can do your work without getting in his way. Now, are you coming or not?"

She waves toward the hearth. I walk over and set down my equipment, then kneel and open the box. But it's full of so many brushes and bottles and cloths, you could stock a shop with them. I pick up a bottle at random. My confusion must be written plain on my face, because Mrs. Beale sighs in exasperation and creaks down to her knees.

She starts by pulling out a clean cloth, and makes a great to-do of laying it on the rug. "You don't need any more dust in *this* house," she grumbles, handing me the cinder brush. "This, at least, you recognize?"

I sweep up the ashes neatly and quickly enough to win a nod of approval.

"Now your black-lead," she says, taking a brush from the box. "You use *this* brush to lay it on"—a few dabs— "and *this* one to brush it in"—her hand spins in circles—"and *this* one for your polishing." Only then does she arrange the paper, then kindling, then coal, and most particular about the amounts, she is. Out comes a leather, and she polishes the grate. Finally she leans back, nods in satisfaction, and lights the fire. She motions me to put everything back in the box as she struggles to her feet.

"He likes the drapes closed," she says, walking to the window. "The fire and the one electric light, that's all he wants. Like a tomb it gets, in here. But I say a person needs proper light for vacuuming." She pulls the velvet roughly aside and sunlight streams in, illuminating a swirl of dust. "And dusting. That will take you long enough, with all this nonsense around." She picks up a small metal object and flips a switch on its side. Tiny stairs start to move up; when they reach the top, there's a blur and then a spark—

She turns it off and bangs it back down on the table. "Inventions, he calls them. But does he ever use them for anything? Or even make new ones? Dust traps is what I say, cluttering up the house and making more work for the likes of us. I'd tell him about it, I would, but I stay out of his way. If you know what's good for you, that's what you'll do as well. A strange old bird, he is."

But her voice is becoming a dull drone in the background as I look around the room. Why didn't I notice them before? Odd bits of wood, wire, and steel are everywhere, scattered atop piles of books, shoved into shelf corners. My eyes linger on miniature gears connected to a tiny clock, on a cylinder sprouting wires that for some reason makes me think of a castle tower flying a misshapen pennant. A crumpled trail of papers starts at its base and meanders across the shelf, as if Mr. Greenwood was about to throw them away and then couldn't quite let them go. The more I look, the more magical it all feels, almost ominous, as if I'm peering into a wizard's lair and the wizard himself is about to walk through the door and find me out. And yet there's something oddly tempting about it as well. My fingers reach toward a brass box, flicking a miniature handle to open a miniature folding door—

"Good Lord, girl!" cries Mrs. Beale, snatching the box up harshly. "Mr. Greenwood may not look like he notices much, but break one of his gewgaws and he'll give you a tongue-lashing you won't soon forget! So watch your hands." Her eyes narrow, as if she's remembering something. "And your temper, I daresay."

I feel my face grow hot. She's been hearing about me. Her, and everyone else in town. She walks out the door, but I have to wait a moment, swallowing my humiliation, before I can follow.

She's standing outside the drawing room, staring at the

far, dark end of the hall. As I approach, she lifts her hand and points. Now I make out another door, almost lost in the shadows.

"Whatever you do, don't go in that room," she says. "It's locked. Always locked. Do you hear me?"

I want to ask what's inside, but she's already chuffing back to the kitchen. She sighs down onto a stool and starts ticking off on her fingers.

"Let's see, then. Laundry. Electric iron, plugs in over there. Breakfast and dinner. Tea, if he's home for it. Likes ginger cake, he does. Remember, you're a daily with light cooking, not a cook with cleaning, so nothing fancy. The vacuum is in there—nasty, heavy, unwieldy thing. Woodwork. Dusting. Polish. Oh! That's right. The grocer's. You'll have to walk to town to place your orders. Mr. Greenwood can't be bothered with a telephone. Never talks with anyone himself, so he can't see why others would need to." She sighs, making sure I appreciate the hardships she's suffered. "Have I covered it all, then?"

Oh, she's given me a clear picture, right enough: a tomb of a house, with odd creations lurking in every corner, and a fierce old man who hates people and is likely to explode if I do anything wrong. Lovely.

She comes to her feet, rummages in her pocket, and

hands me a great clanking ring of keys. "A chance like this doesn't come along very often," she says. "You're a lucky girl."

I rise in the dark and have a quick swig of tea to brace myself. As I tie on my apron, Mum nods at me in approval. "Not so bad, now, is it?" she asks, as if she can't see the way I set my jaw. I slam the door behind me, and then I'm dashing through town, quick as I can, before the other girls have a chance to wake. Past the shops, still shuttered, and the funny old church with its squat tower, the bird heads carved around its arched door peering at me in the first glimmers of light. I let myself into the house ever so quietly and put the kettle on.

He only takes tea and toast for breakfast, and I can do that right enough, though I have to search for the bread knife and the marmalade pot. By the time I've got it all on a tray and carry it to the dining room, he's already sitting at the table, those fierce eyebrows pulled low. I don't say a word, just set things out before him, pour the tea, drop a curtsey, and dash out as quick as I can.

Back in the kitchen, I draw a deep breath, then start filling the sink for breakfast dishes. But when I turn for the soap, my elbow knocks a cup off the counter, the elegant cup

I chose for my own morning tea, and I reach out—too late! There's a terrible crash as the cup strikes the floor, shattering into a thousand pieces.

My head jerks up and I stare at the door, my chest so tight I can barely breathe. But there's no shout from the dining room, no clomp of angry footsteps down the hall. He must not have heard.

I gaze down at my disaster. Shards of china jut up like blue and white cliffs from a sea of white specks.

Do I tell him? That teacup probably cost more than my week's wages.

I think about it for a long moment. Then I tiptoe to the closet and take out the broom and dustpan. I sweep up every grain. And when I empty it all into the dustbin, I bury the evidence deep under scraps of paper and soggy tea leaves.

Not long after, I hear Mr. Greenwood shuffling down the hall. The front door opens and closes again. He'll be out for hours, now; that's what Mrs. Beale said.

After I've washed and dried his breakfast dishes and put them away again, after I've mopped the kitchen, I decide to start a cake for his tea. Ginger cake, that's what she said he likes. I start opening drawers in search of a cookery book, but all I find is a jumble of papers and bits of string. In frustration, I jerk open a small drawer near the window. And there, right on top, sits a stack of well-thumbed cinema fan magazines.

Well! So much for the virtuous, always-working-too-hard Mrs. Beale!

I pick one up and start leafing through. All those actresses with their pouty little mouths and their huge wide eyes, their transformations from picture to picture, not one of them stuck being someone she can't stand to be.

I slap the magazine down on the counter. If Mrs. Beale could take time for herself now and then, so can I.

Into the drawing room I march, bold as you please, right up to the shelf. A forest of books rises before me: red, brown, green, black. I should choose something worthy of the risk I'm taking. An elegant leather volume catches my eye, gold glinting from the tops of its pages, and a kind of greedy determination fills me. I may not have a part in the play, but as long as I'm working here, at least I'll have this.

The play . . . Now I know what I'm looking for. Not the school play, but something much better. I start skimming the titles, shelf after shelf, working my way deeper into the room. Finally, near the heavy drapes, I find them: slender matching volumes bound in deep blue, gilt letters sparkling on their spines. The works of Shakespeare.

Romeo and Juliet, Two Gentlemen of Verona—and then there it is. *The Tempest.*

The moment I slip it into my apron pocket, I feel eyes on my back. Slowly, sure I'm about to be sacked, I turn. But it's only the lady in the portrait looking at me, amusement sparkling in her sky-blue eyes, as if she knows something I don't. I sigh in relief. *She* won't mind! And she certainly won't tell.

I'll learn to do my work well enough that I can do it quickly, and there'll be a half hour now and again to sit with a book and a cup of tea. A half hour when I get to be part of a different world.

Love's Telephone

As the days go by, I learn my way around, the rhythms of Mr. Greenwood's comings and goings, how he likes his tea. It's been almost two weeks now. I'm setting a fat slice of pound cake on a plate just as the clock strikes in the drawing room. Perfect.

I carry the laden tray down the hall, careful not to slosh the tea or the pitcher of milk. The thick carpet muffles my footsteps. As I near the drawing room door, I hear a strange sound, somewhere between a lilting melody and a rusty hinge crying out for the oil can. I stop and listen, trying to make out the words as they speed up and slow down:

"My sweetheart's the man in the moon
I'm going to marry him soon

'Twould fill me with bliss just to give him one kiss
But I know that a dozen I never would miss . . ."

I didn't know there was a gramophone in the house! I
tiptoe to the door and peer in. To my amazement, it isn't a
gramophone at all, but Mr. Greenwood singing. Yes, singing! His hands rest on the mantel, and he's gazing up at the
portrait with a tenderness that tells me she was his wife. I
stand there, gaping, while he croaks a few more lines:

"Last night while the stars brightly shone
He told me through love's telephone
That when we were wed—"

I'm so astonished, I forget to hold the tray straight, and
the saucer slides into the teapot, chiming like a bell. Mr.
Greenwood looks over with a start, his brows lowering, and
he takes a step toward me like an old bull about to charge.
My hands tense around the tray.

But then his eyes focus on my face. "Ah, Addy," he says,
giving his head a shake as if coming to himself again. He
walks to the table and sinks into his chair. "She used to sing
that song."

I don't know why, but I answer, "It's beautiful."

He nods. "A silly old song, but she loved it." His voice is wistful.

It's more words than I've heard from him since I started. Looking at me and speaking, both in the same day: is this actually Mr. Greenwood?

I spread the china out on the table. As I pour his tea, I'm not thinking and I lean forward too quickly. The book in my apron pocket bangs against the table's edge.

"What is that?" demands Mr. Greenwood, staring at the offending rectangle outlined so clearly against the thin white cotton.

My heart starts pounding. How could I have been so stupid? Why didn't I leave the book in the kitchen drawer, as I always do, or put it back on the shelf? I've just been reading it over and over! And why, oh why, did he have to start noticing me today, of all days?

I know what's coming.

"I'm so sorry, Mr. Greenwood." My voice is quivering as I set down the teapot and reach into my pocket. I draw out the slender blue volume. "Truly, I am!"

"My Shakespeare," he says, ominously quiet.

"It won't happen again, sir," I plead.

What am I saying? Of course I won't have another chance, not after something like this. He'll say it's theft.

And there are no other places open in this town. Mum will send me off to be a live-in for sure. A scullery maid, bottom rung of the ladder.

He stares at me. "Go. Go and—" A cough stops him; when it subsides, he draws in a deep, gasping breath. I brace myself for the shouting, the raised hand to come. The blood is pounding in my ears so loudly that I miss his next words.

"Beg pardon?" I whisper.

"I said go and get a chair. Bring it here."

I walk slowly to the dining room and pull out a straight-backed chair, wondering how it will figure in my punishment. My steps are even slower as I walk back.

"Here," he rasps. "At the table."

I put the chair where he shows me. Whatever is coming, I will not cry.

He motions me to sit down, and I do. Waiting.

"*The Tempest*." He turns the book over in his hands, opening it to a random page, shutting it again. Finally, he says, "Why this one?"

I look up from the book to his face, and the gleam of interest in his eyes surprises me so much I find myself saying, "It's all storm and magic. And freedom at the end."

"Ah, yes," he says. And then, to my amazement, he recites from the play:

"Full fathom five thy father lies;
Of his bones are coral made;
Those are pearls that were his eyes . . ."

He stops there, leaning back with a sigh.

But it can't be left like that, unfinished, the words unsaid! And so I whisper the next lines:

"Nothing of him that doth fade
But doth suffer a sea-change
Into something rich and strange."

"Exactly!" exclaims Mr. Greenwood, slapping the book on the table so hard, the china rattles. "That's exactly it!"

And that's how it started, this strange arrangement. Now I know he's batty, because no sane gentleman would act this way. He had me leave the second chair in the drawing room. Every afternoon, when I bring the tea tray, it has two cups and saucers, and two plates for the cake. And heaven help me, I sit down with him and we talk. That's right. A gentleman like him, sitting at the table and chatting away with a girl like me. It might as well be something out of the cinema, it's that unlikely.

I could never tell Mum. She'd say I'm walking a danger-ous line, that people who step above their stations get beaten back down, and hard. She'd say it isn't my place. But it's get-ting difficult to tell my place with Mr. Greenwood. It's as if a switch turned inside him and he started to come alive again, like one of his inventions, after years of stillness. He sees me now when he passes me in the hall, nods, says hello. His voice still creaks like an old gramophone, but the more he uses it, the easier the words flow. He tells me about plays he saw on the London stage, and what that stage was like in Shakespeare's own day, and what England was like even earlier, in the time of castles and knights in armor. It's wonderful what he knows. And even more wonderful are the books he puts in my hand and tells me to read, and the discussions we have about them after: Shakespeare and Marlowe, Sir Walter Scott and Dickens.

Sometimes there's a shift in him, like the sky begin-ning to lighten after a thunderstorm, and I think I catch the glimmer of a smile. But sooner or later, he glances up at his wife's portrait, and another bank of gray clouds moves in. He goes back where the world can't reach him, and I clear the tea things.

And he never—no, never—mentions his son.

Nobody

As I pull open the door, the bell jingles and Mr. Wentworth glances up, gives me a nod.

"Afternoon, Addy," he says. "What can I get you today?"

I look down at my list. "Potatoes and carrots. Beef, enough for a stew. And a pound of sugar. And butter." I'll get the stew and pound cake going for Mr. Greenwood's dinner before I start the ironing this afternoon. "And Mr. Greenwood asked special for some of those chocolate biscuits he likes."

"I know the ones," says Mr. Wentworth. "Won't be a moment." He slips through a door into the back, and I hear his feet tromping downstairs. I reach over to the bread and pick up a loaf for a sniff: is it as good as mine? I'm about to put it back when the doorbell jingles behind me and I hear two pairs of shoes prancing in.

"Look. Somebody's here." It's Mary's voice, as snide as ever.

I freeze in place. I will not turn to look at them. I feel my face burning above my starched collar. I'm acutely aware of my apron, the white maid's cap perched on top of my head. The one Mum makes me wear. The one I forgot to take off to come marketing.

"That's not a *somebody*," says Caroline. "It's a *nobody*. Nobody at all!"

They both laugh like it's the funniest thing they ever heard. I still don't turn around. Where *is* Mr. Wentworth? How many storage rooms can he have down in that cellar?

"You were wonderful at rehearsal yesterday." Mary says it to Caroline, but I know each word is directed at me. "Lucky thing it's *you* playing the queen. *Some* people aren't meant for more than scullery work."

"Maybe she could clean up for us after the performance," says Caroline, each word dripping scorn. Then, louder, "Where's your bucket, Addy?"

My hands clench the loaf so hard, they squish right through.

"Addy," says Caroline. "Where's your—"

The back door swings open again.

"Oh, there you are, Mr. Wentworth," says Caroline, suddenly bright and cheery.

"Out of school early, aren't you girls?" he says.

"It's a half day," says Caroline. "We wondered if you'd post this flyer in your window. It's about our school play. We want everyone to come." I feel her eyes on my back. "And I'll take a pack of those sweets. No, the lemon ones."

Coins clink down on the counter, and the door jingles open and shut.

There's a long silence.

"Addy?" says Mr. Wentworth. "Addy?"

The Locked Door

I bang the lid on the stewpot, toss the big spoon into the
sink with a clatter. Finish the washing up, the water boiling,
so I can pretend it's the heat and not shame making my skin
burn. Oh! I'll never live it down! Putting that mangled loaf
on the counter to pay for, and Mr. Wentworth's eyes lifting
from the tortured bread to my face, and that look of *pity* . . .

I grab the broom and start in hard enough to sweep the
tiles away. Caroline, the queen? I heard her reading for that
part; she'll destroy the play. I throw the broom back in the
closet. The stew is bubbling, so I turn to give it a stir, a taste,
add a pinch of salt, then the lid back on and the heat as low
as it will go. I plug in the iron and pull over the big basket of
linens, but they just sit there as Caroline's words sneak back
into my thoughts.

It's a nobody. Nobody at all.

I stare out the window, across the fence to the trees in the distance. If I could, I'd shed the girl I am like a snake slides out of a ragged, outgrown skin. I'd change my hair, my clothes, my name. And if anyone asked me about Addy Morrow, I'd deny she ever existed. One day . . .

Oh, Lord, the iron! I grab it, but no harm done; it's just getting hot enough now. I take a napkin from the basket, sprinkle it with water, and run the iron across so steam rises, leaving the napkin smooth. That *one day* isn't here, is it? I try to remind myself of all the things I should be glad of. An afternoon off every single week, and evenings off, and Sundays, too. How many working girls have that? And Mr. Greenwood telling me to take home slices of the cakes I bake him, giving me books to read, asking me what I think of them. Isn't that worth something?

I fold the napkin and set it down. Reach for another.

And the money is good. I remember Mum's face when I put the coins in her hand the first time, and her saying there'd be enough in a bit for nice fabric to make me a new dress, and *not* a maid's navy blue. Isn't that worth something?

I pull a heavy red tablecloth out of the basket and start across the edge with long, even strokes, trying to match my breath to the rhythm. The fabric softens under the iron. At first glance it looks plain, even boring; but then the light catches it at a certain angle, and suddenly I see roses, nothing but roses, that were hiding there all along.

One last stroke and the tablecloth is perfect. I fold it several times and start to place it in the basket, but then I stop. This one should go right into the linen press so there's no chance of a crease.

I unplug the iron, drape the cloth over my arm, reach in my pocket for the jangle of keys, and start down the hall. Past the dining room (I'll dust in there tomorrow, maybe bring in some flowers) and the drawing room (must wind that clock, and light a fire before I leave so it will be cozy when he comes home) and . . .

And then I stop in front of the next door as if I'm seeing it for the first time. The door that's always locked.

I've seen how Mr. Greenwood looks the other way when he walks past, as if he can't even bring himself to admit it exists. It's his son's room. It has to be. I can picture it so clearly, I might as well be looking through the door: a small bed, blanketed with fifteen years of dust; toys scattered across the floor as if the boy just ran out for a moment (a train, perhaps, its wheels mired in gray snowdrifts); and cobwebs draping everything like shrouds.

All of a sudden, I want to see the mysterious room for myself.

Whatever you do, don't go in that room. That's what Mrs. Beale said.

But I'm sick of rules and restrictions. Sick of everyone telling me where I don't belong.

I hold the keys up in the dim light, searching for one I've never used before. There's the key to the front door, the back door, the linen press. A heavy bronze clunker is too big. What if he's gone and thrown the key away? But no sooner do I think that than the next one feels different in my fingers. The top is all old-fashioned curlicues; the teeth, long and jagged. I wiggle it into the lock, and it turns with a loud complaint.

The door creaks open into darkness. The air is so musty and stale, it's hard to breathe. Light, that's what I need, and the window will be against the far wall. I walk over carefully, because the room is full of large, looming shapes, and I don't want to knock anything over or trip on the toys. My outstretched hand finally touches velvet, and I pull.

Sun bursts into the room, lighting great flocks of dust as they swoop from the curtains like frightened birds. I inhale a lungful of the stuff, and next thing I'm coughing and sneezing, my eyes watering so I can barely see. I rub my face on my sleeve, and rub, and rub—blast! The tablecloth! Streaks of gray run across the red field like a muddy river. I'll have to wash and iron it all over again.

With a sigh, I lift my eyes to look at the room.

In the light I see there's no train, no toys, not even a bed. There's no sign a little boy was ever here at all. The room is some kind of library. Books line the walls from floor to ceiling, their titles hidden by a whitewash of dust. More dust rimes a desk where papers are scattered like flotsam after a storm. The lions carved on the feet of the desk try to glare at me, but cataracts of dust dim their eyes. Spiderwebs dangle from the ceiling in tangled sheets; I had that right at least. But they're drifting down to a huge crate plunked right in the middle of the room.

It's like that Roman town I read about in school, the one buried by volcanic ash. In one instant people froze into eternal stillness, until they were no more than statues.

If this wasn't his son's room, why did he lock it away?

I walk over to the desk. A journal still lies open as if he'd just put it down. I blow the dust away and read, *Archaeological Investigations into Medieval Village Structure*. I pick up a bit of yellowed newsprint; it crackles in my hand. BOY STILL MISSING, blares the headline. "Two days of exhaustive searching have failed to provide . . ." Fifteen years this room has been locked in silence.

But my impatience won't let me read for long. Ribbons of dust are sparkling in the light, eddying into the cobwebs that drape the oversized crate. What could it be? The table-cloth has to be washed again as it is, so I snap it at the crate like a bullfighter's cape. Dust goes swirling in great arcs, tracing the path of my cloth. Again and again I snap, until I see it's no wooden crate I'm uncovering, but the metal, fili-greed sides of . . . a *lift*?

Yes, a lift. Not attached to anything, just the box itself, the part that carries you up and down. I should know. I've been in a lift once, when Mum and I took the train to the city to buy my school things.

I wad the fabric up like a big red dustcloth, and I scrub, revealing open metalwork on the upper half and solid metal on the lower. Under my hand, the door folds partway in, as if inviting me inside. What is it doing here? Was Mr. Green-wood using it for one of his inventions? I think of the tiny brass box in the drawing room, the one Mrs. Beale grabbed from me when I first came, and I realize it was a miniature model of this lift. What could he want with the real thing?

I open the door the rest of the way, remembering that glorious day in the city, and the boy who operated the lift, how his eyes looked me over even as he bobbed his head and called me "Miss." How he slid the door closed behind me, like this; how it clicked shut, like this; how he reached over to a row of buttons—another swipe of my cloth reveals a complicated panel with knobs and numbers and dials—and pushed the button for our floor, like this—

The lift rattles and creaks. The floor starts vibrating under my feet. I've gone and started something! How do I make it stop? I grab for the handle, but a sudden lurch throws me backward, and then the air is filled with a gigantic whirring, and the dials on the panel are spinning, floor numbers rushing by faster and faster—too many floors!—until they disappear in a blur. The lift is shaking like an earthquake and a tornado rolled into one, and my hands are searching for something to clutch, and I'm thrown back on the seat, my eyes squeezed shut against the force of it, and there's a tremendous crash—

And then stillness.

Her Ladyship Has a Taste

My eyes are still squeezed shut. I hardly dare open them. What kind of a mess has that banging and rattling made? I take a deep breath. Instead of dust, I smell fresh air. A breeze brushes my arm.

Oh, Lord, I've broken the windows. How long will it take me to earn enough to replace them? I'll need to sweep up the shards, get someone to fix the panes, look for a new position. . . .

Something rustles in the breeze, probably the papers on the desk, and then—*chirrup!*

My eyes fly open at the unexpected sound. But when I see what's around me, I squeeze them shut again, and my heart starts beating like a drum corps on parade.

It can't be! It's impossible!

Just slow down, Mum is always telling me. So that's what I'll do. I'll begin again, slow as can be, and when I open my eyes this time, everything will be normal. I take a few seconds to breathe deep, and then, looking straight down, I open my eyes the smallest bit. There are my feet in their sturdy black shoes, the same as ever. I lift my gaze inch by inch. The solid lower walls of the lift need a polishing, just like before. Thank God. Another few inches and I'll be looking out through the filigree at the dusty library. One more inch—

But going slow hasn't helped at all. Outside the lift, there's no broken glass to clean up; there isn't even a window, or walls to set a window in: just a field of waving grass, long and autumn gold. Around the field, trees dance in gowns of crimson and orange and green. Morning sun filters through the ironwork in bright patterns, splashing my skin with gold. Like I'm in a church painting.

Like I'm in paradise.

Now there's no slowing my breath, or my heart. Paradise? All those times I said I hated my life, that I wanted something different, I never meant this! I'm not ready to be dead! And what kind of way is this to die? I run a finger up and down the curving strips of metal. Whoever heard of a lift to heaven?

As if in answer to my question, that warm *chirrup* comes

again from above and behind me. An angel, calling me out.

As I push down the handle, a message flips into place over the door: RETURN PRECISELY AT SUNDOWN. Paradise seems to come with instructions. What does that mean, "return"?

Oh, but the air smells bright and alive! The grass is dry and springy underfoot, and so long it tickles my ankles.

Chirrup!

I turn. There, not ten paces behind the lift, towers a dead tree, and at the end of a long, bare branch perches not an angel, but the most magnificent bird I've ever seen. It must be as tall as my forearm is long. It has a rosy tan breast stippled with black, and a warrior's broad shoulders; the head is steel-gray, so it looks like it's wearing a helmet. Huge black eyes seem to take in the entire world at once.

Now it tilts its head with an inquiring look, as if eyeing me bird to bird.

That look fills me, and suddenly I don't feel confused anymore. Why, this is a dream, is all! A hallucination. I conked my head good and proper, and I'll wake up soon enough, with a huge mess to clean up, and Mr. Greenwood and Mum staring at me all disapproving and disappointed, shaking their heads. I'll be miserable enough then. I might as well enjoy my dream while I can.

The bird nods approvingly, spreads its wings out wondrous wide, and all at once it's soaring. How did it get so high, so quickly? It circles the field a few times and then flaps off over the trees. Almost as if it wants to lead me on. All right then, I think, not even stopping to put down the tablecloth. And I follow.

The forest welcomes me in. Soon thick branches are rustling overhead, dimming the light and hushing sounds, so it's almost like being underwater. I can't see the bird, so I stop, hoping to catch the sound of its cry. Instead I hear a soft burbling. Another minute brings me to a stream, and now I let it be my guide as I walk along the bank and, when it narrows, leap from stone to stone. The trees grow thinner.

A voice calls out from somewhere up ahead. There must be people in my dream.

I peek around the trunk of a wide oak. The stream banks climb to a bridge, and in the middle of the bridge stands an old horse, resting in front of an even older wagon, and in the back of the wagon there's a large crate of clucking chickens.

"Come on, then! We haven't all day!" calls the driver.

At first I think he's talking to me, or even the chickens, but then I see there are more people coming up the dusty road. And it's the most wonderful thing: they look like they've stepped from the pages of *Robin Hood*. There are men and a boy in earth-colored tunics, belted at the waist, with leggings snugged to their calves and funny little nightcap hats. A handful of women chatter along in browns and greens, their headdresses strapped like bandages across their foreheads and under their chins, hiding all their hair, so their faces shine out like the centers of daisies. A straggle of children brings up the rear. Once they reach the bridge, the old horse jerks back into motion, the chickens squawk in complaint, and the parade winds its way on down the road.

As the last person passes, I clamber up the bank, staring after them. I take a step to follow. But then I glance down and see my apron, a maid's apron, and I've a maid's cap perched on top of my head, and I'm clutching a smudged tablecloth. I don't look right at all. Unless . . .

I give the tablecloth a good shake, sending a last flurry of dust flying, turn the smudged side inward, and toss it around my shoulders. The sun blazes the cloth into a beautiful field of red roses. I pull off my cap and shove it in my pocket, only to be pricked by a pin. That will be the brooch for my crimson cloak. Finally, I pull off my apron and wrap it around my head, looping the ties under my chin. Now I look as if I belong.

I hurry down the road. My feet seem to know which

direction to take before I even see the turns, almost as if I've been here before.

But when I round the bend, I gasp at what's before me: a perfect little walled town, its gate open wide, colorful pennants flapping in the breeze. The wagon has just passed through the gate, and I run to catch up with the crowd flowing in its wake.

Half-timbered houses crowd the narrow street, their upper stories jutting out overhead. I'm in a river of people, surging past shop fronts and whitewashed walls, past shutters thrown open to display bread or cloth or meat inside. The street spills out into a marketplace crowded with carts and stalls, laughter and music, people in homespun and others in silks. A fair! And me with nothing to do but enjoy myself.

Oh, the air sings to my senses, with the scent of meat pies wafting from laden trays, a rainbow of fabrics spilling out across tables, the lilting strains of a flute! A man looks at me and gives a little bow as he calls, "Keep those fine fingers warm in my soft fur-lined gloves!" Dogs growl and tug over a stolen bone; a peddler holds up a dangling ribbon strung with charms; a man walks about with a monkey on his shoulder, and the monkey proudly sports a red embroidered cap. Ahead of me there's a bright tune and a circle of onlookers. As I come closer, they part, making way, and there in the middle is a bear galumphing about on its hind legs! People clap at the awkward dance, and a boy passes a hat for coins.

An old woman with a basket of apples gives me a gap-toothed smile. "Would your ladyship care for a taste? The best you'll ever eat." She cuts a fat slice, handing it to me with a nod and a deferential smile.

A lady? Me? Well, then! I try to look noble as I bite into a fruit almost as sweet as her respectful gaze. A few drops of juice land on my rose-covered cloak, the one that's convinced her I'm worth her while. But as grand as I look, I've no money for more, so I thank her and wander on.

My steps lead me to a stone church with a short, squat tower. There's something oddly familiar about its shape and that big wooden door, the stone arch carved with triangles. I walk closer. Like a blurry cinema reel coming into focus, the triangles sharpen, and all of a sudden I realize what they are: three rows of birds' heads, their beaks pointing worshipers inside. And there, along the doorjamb, stands a familiar dragon, a bold knight on his horse—why, it's my church, the one I pass every day on my way to Mr. Greenwood's house! But here in my dream, each bird's beak ends in a fine point, and each eye is bright, as if they were carved only yesterday.

My church. And so this is my town, but as it might have been in the Middle Ages. Now I know why my feet knew every turn of the road. I might as well have been walking from Mr. Greenwood's to the grocer's!

I hug my cloak about me in the gathering chill. Those fur-lined gloves would feel wonderful now. I turn to look for the glove seller, but he's nowhere in sight. The crowd has thinned. How long was I standing staring at the church? Shutters are closing; people are packing up their stalls; the bear, on all fours, disappears around a corner. The sun slips behind the rooftops, casting the square into shadow.

And then I remember the sign in the lift: RETURN PRECISELY AT SUNDOWN. With that sense of absolute certainty that comes in dreams, I know I must do as the sign says and reach the lift before night falls.

I follow a few stragglers back between the houses, out the gate. The town doors slam shut behind me. There's still a wash of sun on the treetops, but it's fading. I hurry down the road, feeling more anxious with every step, and when the last people are far behind me, I break into a run. I'm filled with a growing sense of dread, an eerie feeling that if I don't get to the lift in time, I'll never see my own world again.

The sun is a mere sliver on the horizon when I reach the bridge. I swerve off the path at full tilt. But the bank is

steeper than I expected, and I trip, tumbling down, rolling over and over until I crash up against a tree. Dazed, I look up at the same massive oak that hid me before.

My knee throbs, my head spins, but I can't stop—the light is almost gone! I jump up and dash along the stream, trying to remember my way, terrified I've taken a wrong turn. I want to wake up one day! I want to live more than a dream! Finally, the trees open onto the field—thank God! The lift is there where I left it, shining in the last long rays of sun, and I leap in, slamming the door behind me. The sun sinks, the light dims, and something clicks. The floor numbers start flipping, faster and faster, until they're blurring together, swirling into the colors of golden grass and green metal until everything turns a rattling, shaking shade of black.

For My Own Good

I come to in the library, exactly where I started. The door to the lift is slightly ajar. I look around, steeling myself to face whatever disaster I've created with all that whirling and shaking.

Except there isn't one. The windows are intact. Books still line the shelves, papers still litter the desk. There's only one difference: a clear circle surrounds the lift, as if a tornado had blown the dust outward and away.

I raise my hand to see how big a bump I've given my head and if there's any blood. My hand touches not hair but my apron. And the tablecloth is pinned at my neck.

I sink down on the little bench. I must have been delusional, swaddling my head in an apron, acting out my dream like a sleepwalker! It's a wonder I didn't go stumbling blindly about the house, falling down stairs or setting the kitchen afire. In a daze, I take off the tablecloth. Imagine, using a tablecloth for a cloak! Quite the grand lady *I've* been. I unwrap the apron from my head and then, slowly, in case I'm still dizzy, stand to tie it back on.

How long was I dead to the world? Hours and hours, most likely, to have a dream like that. And today my day off early, and Mr. Greenwood probably about to walk right through that door and find me here! How long do I have to set things straight before he's home? I jerk the metal door open and run into the hall, down to the drawing room, to look at the clock.

At first I think it's stopped, because the hands have barely moved since I glanced in before. I reach down to wind the key, only to hear the familiar *tick, tick, tick*. I step back, staring; if the time on the clock is right, I can't have been unconscious more than a few minutes. Stranger and stranger.

At least I have plenty of time to vacuum the dust from the hall and finish the rest of my work before I leave. I walk slowly into the kitchen, but instead of pulling out the vacuum, I find myself sinking down on the stool and leaning back against the wall. There's a tune in my head—ah! It's the one that played for the dancing bear! And then I'm lost in my dream, trying to remember everything before it fades. The smell of the meat pies, the church with its sharp new carvings, the sounds of the harp and calling voices—I want to keep it all inside me forever. And the glove maker bowing his head as he offered me his wares, the old woman calling me "your ladyship," people making way for me everywhere I walked . . . I close my eyes, trying to recall the embroidery on the little red hat the monkey wore. . . .

The next thing I know the clock is chiming five and I wake with a start. I've never done that before, falling asleep at work! Never! Mum will be wondering where I am. I hurry to lock the library back up tight, praying the hall is dim enough to hide the dust. Quick as can be, I set things out for Mr. Greenwood's supper and wash up a last few dishes in the sink.

What a strange day this has been, I think, pulling the gate shut behind me. And then, because I'm so late, I run down the road toward home.

I'm out of breath when I come in the door. Mum is setting the teapot on the table.

"What kept you so long?" she asks.

Well, I'm not about to tell her I fell asleep on the job, am I? "The stew needed attention," I say, taking off my apron and hanging it from its hook on the wall.

I turn to the table. Mum is staring at me aghast, her

eyes as wide as they'll go, and then her brows slam down. "Adelaide!" It's an accusation.

"What?" I say, bewildered. "What have I done?"

I follow her gaze to my skirt. There's a great gaping rent down the middle of it, and streaks of dirt as wide as my hand. It looks just as if—

"Fighting again!" cries Mum. *"How could you?"*

"But I haven't! I don't know where that rip is from. I haven't been fighting, I swear!"

"Then you tell me what happened to your skirt," she says bitterly, as if she knows I'm lying. I'm too stunned to answer.

I hear the medieval town gates closing behind me, feel the road under my shoes as I run in the last pink rays of the sun. . . .

"The best position in town and you're throwing it away like rubbish!" Her eyes are somewhere between tears and rage, but rage has the upper hand.

The stream bank drops down before me, and I fall. . . .

"I was wrong to think you'd make an effort," says Mum, almost shaking, as if it's her life she sees in tatters before her. "Didn't you hear a thing I've said? Keep up like this, and you'll end up in jail, or"—she pauses—"or *worse*! Our livelihood! Your reputation! Your future! Don't they mean anything to you?"

After all these years, after this strange day, it's suddenly too much. Something snaps. "*My* reputation?" I shout. "What about *yours*?" Her mouth drops open, her face goes ice-white, but the words keep pouring out of me. "*Or worse—* you can't even say the word, can you? *Pregnant!* You're the one got pregnant without bothering to get married first, not me! You're the reason they call me *bastard*—"

I stop, but it's too late. My words ring horribly in the room. I see every line on her face. The pain she's always worked so hard to hide is laid bare.

She draws in a deep breath, and her eyes go hard. "Something has to change," she says. "And soon, before your headstrong ways ruin your life. I'm finding you a place as a live-in."

"A live-in! But Mr. Greenwood—"

"I'll go with you tomorrow to give your two weeks' notice." She holds up a hand. I wish she were yelling; this cold anger is worse. "No! Not one more sound from you. Go to bed. I can't even stand to talk to you right now." The words catch in her throat. "Go. Go!"

Later, much later, I think I hear sobbing. Her bed stays empty all night.

I don't sleep either. My head is awhirl, Mum's words jumbling up with images from my strange dream. I reach for my skirt and finger the rip, run my palm along the broad streaks of dirt.

No, I think again. *It's impossible.* But how could I get stains like these inside a library? That's not dust; it's dirt, ground in like you'd get from tumbling down a stream bank.

What if it wasn't a dream?

I see the tiny model of the lift in the drawing room, and the lift itself standing like an oversized packing crate in the middle of the library. . . .

And then, in spite of everything, I find myself gasping with amazement. He made a time machine, that's what he did! Mr. Greenwood, who everyone thought was mad, invented a machine that took me right back to the Middle Ages! Why, if people knew, he'd be the most famous man in all of England. To think, all these weeks I've worked in a house that holds a time machine, chatting with its inventor over cake and tea.

But tomorrow Mum is coming to announce my two weeks' notice. I'm leaving Mr. Greenwood and his magical house for good.

The brief excitement seeps away, leaving me hollow. When you're a live-in, they don't even bother to learn your name, that's what I've heard, just call you Elsie or whatever it is they've chosen for the girls in your position. Because you're not a person then, are you? I sink my head in my hands. How can Mum think that's going to give me a better life?

There's no point trying to convince her. She's beyond

listening, even if I came up with the best lie in the world. And the truth? That would sound like the biggest lie of all.

In jail . . . or worse. All she can see is me on the same path she took, into the arms of a lad who promises the world but runs off as soon as your belly is showing. She'll do anything to save me from her fate, no matter how much life she bleeds from me in the saving.

But I can't live like she wants me to, all meek and squashed and sorry, crumpled into a corner like a worn-out blanket. I can't shrink myself into what she wants me to be! I think again how I felt in the grocer's, that loaf of bread smashed in my fist. That's how I'll feel every day when I'm a scullery maid, sleeping under the eaves in a shoddy maid-set bed, up and scrubbing the grates before dawn, gazing down reverently when the great ones pass so we can all pretend I don't exist. Disappearing into the woodwork. Like I believe what Caroline thinks of me.

"Why must you be so headstrong?" Isn't that what Mum always says? "Take the hand you're dealt and make the best of it."

And then, in the black middle of the night, I sit up in bed, stifling a cry of wonder, as I realize exactly what cards I'm holding.

Going

Of course I listen at the door, but Mum's voice is only a wordless murmur, and I have to settle for the moments when Mr. Greenwood's mumbled responses rise into outraged clarity.

"Two weeks!" he cries. "A live-in? That girl? . . . Smart as a whip . . . she can think circles around . . . and you're sending her to do work the dullest drone . . . Insanity! Let her . . ."

Their voices come closer, and I rush to the kitchen just in time as the drawing room door swings open.

Now Mum's words are clear as can be. "What kind of mother would I be otherwise? It's for her own good. Two weeks, sir. Good day."

I open the front door for her. She sighs at me, shaking

her head, but I look at her straight on, not a tear in my eyes. Yes, I feel sorrow, and anger, but more than anything else I feel excitement rising in me like a great wave.

Mr. Greenwood comes out of the drawing room soon after, grabs his coat, and throws open the door. The chill air surges in; I pull his muffler from the shelf and thrust it in his hands.

"I must think," he says, lifting his head to look at me. "There's a way around this, if only I can think of it."

"My mother has made up her mind, sir," I say. "You can't change her when she gets like that."

"I'll help you," he says, briefly reaching out to touch my hand before he steps outside. "I'll find a way."

My heart catches. In that moment I almost tell him he's already found a way to help me, that he found it years ago. But I bite my tongue. I won't endanger my plan with any-one's ideas of what's safe or proper or wise.

I force myself to wait, washing the breakfast dishes and dusting the drawing room, until I'm sure he's truly gone for the day. Then I pull out my keys and walk down the hall to the library. For the second time in fifteen years the door opens.

The lift rises in the center of that circle blown clear of dust, like a tree inside a fairy ring, or a stone for ancient rites towering on an altar. Something sharp and strong shivers through me, and for a moment I'm frozen on the threshold. An invention, I tell myself. Not magic, but science and math, knobs and dials. I take a step forward—and there's that shiver again, almost an electric shock, as if some tremendous power waits in those bits of steel and wire, reaching out to me. I need a minute before I touch it again.

I turn my steps to the wall where an oval frame tells me a mirror is hiding. I wipe it off and stare at the girl looking back at me: her hungry green eyes, her stubborn mouth.

You, I think. *I know what you want. You want to start over, like this breath, the one you're breathing now, is the first you ever took. And the step you're about to take is the first time your foot touched the earth, and the word you're about to speak is the very first time you ever heard the sound of your voice ringing in the just-born air.*

And all you have to do is go in that lift and shut the door.

I tie the door to the lift open with twine so it doesn't slip shut and whirl me back before I'm ready. Then I step inside and start examining the panel with its dials and labels. On the top row, the word TODAY is engraved on a small copper plate, followed by boxes for day, month, and year, looking for all the world like the board in a railway station where the numbers flip over as trains arrive and depart. The date reads, 11 OCTOBER 1913, still accurate after all these years. A small clock ticks away as if it were the most ordinary thing in the world.

Next come dials for how many days or years you wish to travel into the past. I'll leave it the same as it was yesterday, 673 years. I do the numbers in my head. It's the year 1240 I'll be living in soon.

There's one last row on the bottom, but the print is so small, I have to sit on the bench and lean forward to read it. MANUAL ADJUSTMENT, it says. RETURN TIME PLUS, and then the dials. It seems you can choose to stay in the past a week—or a year—before you return. That could be useful, I think, coming to my feet.

I walk to the desk and start sorting through the typed pages, the scribbled notes, the books and journals. An ancient map shows Little Pembleton, the road, and the bridge; a circle of ink outlines the empty spot where this house stands now—the exact spot where the lift waited in the past, as if it always stayed in one place and the years whipped by around it. There's a calendar labeled "Julian" and another labeled "Gregorian," and a paper on determining the age of trees, and page after page in a scrawling hand with mathematical equations and sketches of the lift and wiring diagrams. I thumb through books on medieval manners, clothing, farming, battles.

I throw the last book down with a bang, sending up another cloud of dust. I could read for weeks and not learn a fraction of all there is here. Don't I know enough already? The lift will take me to the past, where all I need is one nicely woven cloak and I'm a lady. And that was just a tablecloth. There's a red and gold gown hanging back in the costume room, and it fits me just right. I wonder how people will treat me if I go back dressed like a queen.

I clean the room until the lions are bright-eyed and the books stand proudly at attention on the shelves. I'm not sure why I do it. Perhaps so I'll have a fitting sendoff when I go. In some strange way I feel it's for Mr. Greenwood, though he'll never even notice.

He doesn't come home for tea.

As the light fades, I lock the door behind me and head down the road into town. But I don't go right home, not just yet. Everyone must be at dinner; the streets are empty, and there's no one to see me turn the corner to the theatrical society. The door is unlocked. Inside, everything is dark.

I feel my way down the stairs and to the wall with the electric light switch. The room shimmers into life, the pile of fairy wings glittering as if they're rising in full flight, the great shaggy bear's head growling down at me from its shelf. But there's no time to stop and look. I need to be home in a few minutes.

Where is it?

The hangers are a jumble of possibilities. The flounced skirt and crook of a saucy shepherdess, a nurse's sturdy uniform, a bottle-green Elizabethan gown with a wide ruffed collar.

Where is it? Did the old woman take it away to alter it for Caroline? The thought makes me feel almost sick to my stomach, and I pull the next hanger so roughly, a robe falls to the floor. I bend to pick it up. Something brown-skinned brushes against my hand and I startle, drawing in a quick breath. But then I see it's only an old leather glove, oversized and rough, like something a hunter might wear. For some reason I slip it on. The sturdy leather rises to my elbow, and cords dangle from it like little leashes. I twirl my hand to see them swing, and they snag a bit of fabric, red and gold—

The queen's gown! I toss the glove back down. My heart pounding, I pull the dress from its hanger, fold it up small enough to fit in my satchel, and run out the door.

The Ocean

I look out from the drawing room window, watching Mr. Greenwood shuffle stoop-shouldered through the gate, and I see he's forgotten his muffler yet again. I grab it and run out the door after him.

"Mr. Greenwood!" He stops and sets down his old leather valise. "Didn't want you getting cold," I say. Which I'm saying instead of good-bye.

He wraps the plaid wool around his neck, then surprises me by reaching for my hand and giving it a warm squeeze. "I won't be back for a few days," he says. "I have matters to sort out with my solicitor." He lets go of my hand to peer at his watch. "My train!" he exclaims, grabbing the valise. And then he's gone off down the road.

Gone for days, so I have all the time in the world.

And yet I feel the need to hurry as fast as I can.

I dash back to the kitchen, finish the dishes, shove them in the cupboard. Scrub the kitchen counters. Run into the drawing room and polish the table where we've shared books and tea. It will be hard enough for Mr. Greenwood, getting used to someone new; I won't have him coming back to a mess.

I glance at the clock. Fifteen minutes have passed. I open the door and peer down the road. No, he isn't coming back. The house is mine.

My heart flutters as I open the cleaning cupboard, reach down into the dark, and pull out my satchel. I set it on the table, unbuckle the straps, and pull up the flap. And there it is, all sparkle and silky flowing wonder: the queen's dress.

I pull off my sturdy navy blue, right there in the kitchen, and tug the red and gold gown over my head. It shimmers down, and I take a few steps, feeling the luxurious fabric swish around my legs. It barely sweeps the ground. The belt drapes around my waist, its long ends hanging down, proclaiming what a very grand lady I am.

The one thing I don't have is a proper covering for my hair. But there was that other picture in the costume book. I undo my thick braid, spreading the strands across my shoulders. Mum can't make me hide my hair away now.

Underneath the gown are my much-mended shoes, my only pair. Well, there's nothing to be done about that. These skirts are long enough to hide them. I start to gather up my navy blue, and then I realize that with any luck I won't need it ever again. I toss the dress back on the table.

With any luck, I say, because Mum may call me head-strong, but I'm not stupid. I've got a plan in case things don't work out in the past. I'll set the return dial to read, 15 DAYS. That's long enough to know if I can make a life for myself there. If not, the lift will be waiting for me at sunset. But I don't expect to need it. And I certainly don't want it. I've a new life to live.

I grab the key ring and hurry down the hall. The black key clicks into the newly oiled lock. Now everything is dusted and mopped; there won't be any cobwebs draping across *this* dress. The desk shines under its stacks of neatly arranged papers. I pull open the curtains; not a speck of dust flies out. In the light I turn to look. There it stands: the lift to the past.

I push the handle to fold the door inward, and step in. I turn the dial, and then I slide the door shut. Something clicks, the numbers start whirling and the cage rattling and the room spinning and everything turning black. . . .

Things are different this time. I can tell before I even open my eyes. Wind weaves through the metal filigree, teasing my hair; great gusts toss the tree branches, sing through the grasses in a long, low dirge.

I open the door, step across the threshold, and breathe in a salty ocean tang. Across the steel-gray sky, darker clouds sail to the east. That always means the tail end of a storm. The air is so brisk, I almost wish I'd brought the tablecloth cloak again. But it wouldn't have been grand enough with this dress, and I'll warm up once I get moving. I have a town to visit.

I turn toward the woods. Rising before me like a church steeple is the same dead tree, and there, on its outstretched branch, sits the same magnificent bird, almost as if it had been waiting for me all this time. It stares right at me with piercing black eyes, then lifts off with great easy flaps of its wings, like oars rippling through water. But this time it's flying away from town, toward the cliffs that tumble down to the sea. And something calls in me to follow.

I hesitate. I'd been planning to retrace my steps from last time, right up to the church, and pretend to have hurt my head so badly, I don't remember who I am. They'll have to take care of me since I look so grand, while they search for where I belong, and that will give me time to figure out how to live here. That was the plan. But after a storm, the ocean is so wild and free. . . .

All right, then! I'll take the long way around. It will be the perfect start to my new life. I'll fill myself with the waves' surging, shouting voice, and then I'll head over the lowlands and back into town by the river.

There's no path on this side of the field, but I know where Mr. Greenwood's house stands in relation to the shore, and I make my way into the murmuring trees. The land starts down a familiar slope, then opens up at the top of the bluff. I look down on the river, white-capped where it meets the sea. The wind itself is flowing through my veins.

It's lucky I know the way down, because I don't find the broad path I'm used to, just a thin deer trail. Now the wind shifts direction, pushing me until I'm running—no, flying!—my arms spread like wings, the long skirt flapping behind. Down I run, around the curve, and down, my ears filling with the roar of the surf and the shriek of gulls, until I reach the place where the hill butts against the cliffs, and boulders loom out of the water like something giants hurled from above. I don't care if it's cold, I want to feel the sand with my feet, so I take off my shoes and stockings and set them atop a large rock. Then I follow the strip of shore under the cliffs, heading out to the point.

But as I go farther, it turns out I have to watch where I step. The beach is littered with tangles of seaweed and piles of branches—even a whole tree, roots and all. What a gale it must have been! I lift my skirt as I edge past great clumps of flotsam and jetsam, long jagged boards, the curve of a cask, an oar.

And the wind is still singing, whipping foam from the crests of the waves!

From the depths of a glistening green tangle, something glints as bright as silver. I bend to pull the slippery strands of seaweed aside, and gasp as I pick up the most amazing little treasure box. The sides are patterned silver, and the top is ivory, carved into the funniest mermaid with two tails, one pointing to each side, as if she can't decide which way she's heading.

I feel joyful and smug and shivery all at the same time. Not here thirty minutes and I've already found treasure! This must be valuable indeed, worth enough to sell or trade for something to get started in my new life.

The box is heavy for something the size of a small loaf. My fingers trace the clasp, turn it; I lift the lid. Staring up at me is a gold cross as big as my palm, inset with stones so red they look like fresh-spilled blood. Like rubies.

Could it be?

The cross is on a heavy chain. I place it around my neck.

Next I find a chunky ring with a snarling bear's head, surrounded by a circle of glittering little stones. I put it on my finger. Rubies, gold: I can live on this for years!

As I close the box, a tumble of boards catches my eye. Maybe another treasure is hiding in there. As I clamber closer, I see the boards are curved like a boat's hull, and I remember the tales of shipwrecks on this shore, long, long ago. Was it smugglers? Yes, that's it, and now I've found their riches!

I'm in luck again. Rich purple fabric peeks out from under the boards. It's bound to be too wet to use for a cloak, but maybe I can clean it once I've got myself a place, and make another dress.

I bend to pick it up . . . the surprisingly heavy fabric . . . wrapping an arm, a limp arm . . . heavy with death.

I leap back, the cross banging against my chest like a fist on a door. I breathe deeply, then lean forward and gingerly lift a board away. It's a man all right, dead and drowned and newly gone. No smell, no rot, just a beautiful young man with dark hair, a sodden tunic clinging to his body, jewels at neck and sleeve, caught in a snarl of splintered wood.

My head jerks up, and I stare at the pounding sea. A boat crashed on the rocks last night! And I'm the only one here to help.

I whirl around, searching for any movement, a sign of life. A pile of seaweed shivers, and I run over, but it's only a crab scuttling around a barrel. Another barrel bobs up and down in the water as waves wash it near shore only to snatch it back again. Something else is floating, too. Another body. Is it moving? Could this one be alive?

I run into the surf, the water wrapping my heavy skirts around my legs. When the waves bring the body close, I grab a handful of velvet, and tug, and tug, until I pull it clear of the water—a torso without any legs.

I let go, leaping back with a scream.

A shout answers me from the cliffs above.

A Miracle

I swivel around. Three men on horseback are pounding down the trail.

Relief surges through me like a flood tide. Thank God! They'll search and find anyone who can still be saved.

They leap from their horses. One strides across the littered beach, splashes up next to me, hoists the half body, and tosses it ashore. Then he takes my arm, guiding me back from the grabbing, sucking surf.

"It's a miracle!" he says, staring at me, at my dress, as if I'm an apparition. He whips off his cloak and flings it around me. I realize I'm shivering from head to toe.

"Hurry," I say through chattering teeth. "Someone may still be alive."

"Oswald!" he calls. "Robert!"

The two men rush forward, and he gestures with his chin along the beach. Without a word they stride off in opposite directions, peering into piles, lifting boards, scanning the waves as the wind snaps their cloaks. Green cloaks, yellow tunics, green leggings: they all match, like some kind of medieval rugby team.

The man in charge towers a full head over me. He studies the beach, sharp-eyed, then turns back to ask, "How many were on the boat, my lady?"

"I . . . don't know."

"Not the crew, then, but your party—how many accompanying you?"

"Accompanying *me*?"

He looks at me piercingly. "Ladies-in-waiting? Attendants? Men-at-arms?" Seeing the confusion on my face, he continues, more slowly, as if he thinks I'm having trouble hearing. "If we know who accompanied you, we'll know how many bodies we're looking for." He pauses. "That you live, it is a miracle indeed. But seeing this wreckage, chances are slim that others survived. Forgive me being so direct, Lady Matilda."

Now I see! He thinks I was on that boat. And he thinks he knows who I am. "Lady Matilda?" I shake my head. "I'm—"

But the intensity in his eyes stops me as he stares at my dress, at the great cross dragging down the chain around my neck, at my hand and the ring with the bear's head, all teeth and fury. Then he glances over at his horse. I follow his eyes; there, stitched in bright yellow on the green saddle cloth, snarls the same vicious bear.

I hide my hand quickly behind me. He'll think I stole it! And the cross—oh, Lord, it's too big to cover.

But he's not accusing me of anything. He turns toward one of the men. "Oswald!" The man comes running, stands alert beside us. "I'm taking her ladyship to the castle at once. You and Robert continue searching. I'll send more men, and a wagon to carry back what you find."

"But I'm not your Matilda," I insist. "I merely took a wrong turn. I'm going to town."

"To town?" Now there's a different kind of concern in his eyes. "My lady, I'm afraid his lordship would not think it wise, not in that sodden kirtle, or with that shiver threatening fever. Or your head so—"

He stops suddenly, as if he's gone too far.

I reach a hand up and start patting my hair. What does he see up there? Did I get something tangled in it?

"Careful, my lady!" says the tall man. "Wait for someone at the castle to look at your head. You must have suffered a mighty blow. Small wonder you're confused."

The castle. Of course: they've come from the ruins atop
the cliffs. But it won't be ruins now, will it? There's a real
castle up there, all moats and jousts and knights in shining
armor. My castle, come alive.

"She can take my horse," says Oswald, looking at a huge
beast. I step back in alarm. That enormous thing? And me
never on a horse in my life?

"Not with that head. She'll ride with me," says the tall
man, and then he and Oswald aren't waiting for me to agree,
but are bundling me up on his steed, and he's leaping behind
me, and before I've taken another breath, we're hurtling up
the hill, pebbles flying out from the horse's hooves.

What am I doing? This is all wrong! I've just been pulling dead bodies out of the surf—dead bodies without legs—
and more dead people are lying there under the debris or
floating offshore. Again I feel the clammy touch of water-
logged skin against mine, and a shiver runs from my spine
to my toes. I shouldn't be doing this!

But under the shivering, and the horror of the bodies,
and all the confusion, there's . . . excitement. Me, taken for a
grand lady! Me, the one they worry about and rush to help!
Me, on my way to the castle!

Up the rise, under the wind-whipped trees, flashes of

gray sky flickering through branches like seabirds' wings. Back the way I came, but so fast, I barely glimpse the clearing as we skirt its edge—can't even see the lift or the dead tree—and we're plunging into the forest, paths twisting and branching like a tangled maze. A startled stag crashes away. Then we burst through into the open and—

Oh! My heart almost stops! It's my castle, but mightier and more beautiful than I ever imagined: a shining white citadel, imposing towers piercing the sky, flags whipping in the wind like battle pennants. Someone is peering over the wall, and then there are shouts, and we're clattering across a drawbridge, through massive walls. Now I'm being lifted down, and there's neighing and barking and clanking and shouting, and the smell of a wood fire, and people running from every which way, and the tall man calling out orders.

Suddenly there's stillness inside me as I sense someone's gaze. There, to my left: a boy a few years older than I am, with gold-blond hair and high cheekbones. His arm is bent at his side, and on his wrist rides a small speckled hawk. They're both staring at me, hawk and boy, and the boy's eyes are a piercing shade of blue, as if he's got the summer sky trapped inside him.

A plump older woman rushes toward me with a blanket, and then she's wrapping it around me, her arm circling my shoulders.

"Poor lamb," she's saying. "You poor, dear lamb!"

I hear horseshoes clattering back over the drawbridge as she bundles me up the stairs, every step solid and sturdy and new, and through a mighty door strapped with iron like it's wearing its own coat of armor. Then I'm being pushed up a winding staircase, *my* staircase! I reach the familiar arch and start to step through, but she's urging me on, because there's another story above us, a level I never even knew existed. I don't have time to watch my feet as I turn and turn, driven by the woman behind me, up to another door.

Beatrix

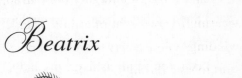

"Here we are, my lady," she says, as warm and comforting as a hearth fire. "Your chamber. How lucky we prepared everything early! His lordship is still away, I'm afraid. But that's not so bad, now, is it? Because it means we've got more space for you, and nice and quiet, which is what you're going to need."

She reaches to my neck. "If you'll allow me, I'll put your cross over here." She lifts the necklace off, clanks it down somewhere, then walks behind me. "Now, off with this lovely kirtle of yours—will you look at the weave of this fabric! I've never seen the like!" She starts untying and loosening laces, and then the sodden weight of the gown is lifting off and I'm standing there shaking in my cold, wet underwear.

"Well, don't they do things different where you're from,

my lady!" She's eyeing my underwear as if she's never seen such things before. I cross my arms firmly across my chest. "Where is your shift? And what are *these* flimsy things? Well, no matter; they're sopping, and you're as wet as a drowned cat." She reaches a hand to my underwear, and I leap back.

"No!"

"But you're all ashiver, my lady," she says, shaking her head firmly. "His lordship will never forgive me if you take ill. We need to get you into that warm bed."

She leads me toward a gigantic wooden box of a canopy bed, so high it has its own little set of stairs up to the mattress. Red, embroidered curtains are pulled back to reveal a coverlet of silky white fur.

"In you go," she says. "You need nothing but the skin the good Lord gave you, and the warmth of those covers."

"Please," I say. "Could you turn around for a moment?"

"I surely don't know *why*," she mutters, but she does, and I pull off the rest of my wet things and climb the stairs and slip under covers so thick and warm, they'd keep you toasty at the North Pole.

It's the softest, coziest thing I've ever felt. And yet here, in this big bed, I feel more vulnerable than before. Now that I'm not tugging at dead bodies, or clinging to a galloping horse, or being pushed up the stairs, I'm starting to have time to think. And those thoughts are making me uneasy. These people have decided I'm their Lady Matilda, come from afar. But what if someone knows the real Matilda, and cries out that I'm all wrong? What if the lady herself shows up, dripping and furious? Or they find her body washed ashore?

It's a delicate line I'm walking, and I'll need all my wits about me.

Clutching the fur to my neck, I try for my noble voice, the one I was going to use in the play. *Confidence*, I think. *Command.*

"Verily, I would that you bring me dry vestments to wear," I say. "Prithee."

She raises her eyebrows slightly, but then she nods. "I'll have to round something up," she says. "Oh, to think of all your beautiful kirtles and cloaks lost to the sea! What a tragedy! And what a tremendous cost to replace them. Though of course that's nothing to you."

Right, I think. Nothing to me.

"Though it may take me awhile," she goes on. "But no matter, as you'll be resting in bed for at least a day or two."

I almost agree, she sounds so certain, but then I take in what she's saying. A day or two! I could be long gone by then, if they find their real lady. I want to see my castle, all of it, while I have the chance. I want to learn how to play my part, find clues about who I'm meant to be.

She's standing there, all respectful, waiting for me to respond. Well, she's my servant, isn't she? And I'm her lady. I get to do what I want for a change.

In my best regal tone, I demand, "What is your name, wench?"

She straightens up. "Beatrix, at your service, my lady."

"Well, Beatrix, I do not wish to wait. Verily, I desire dry clothes, and I desire—I mean, I want them *now*." There's a questioning look in her eyes. Don't I sound medieval enough? I search around for words, and a line from *The Tempest* pops into my head. "Do not infest your mind with beating on the strangeness of this business."

"Infest my . . . ?"

Oh, that wasn't right at all! Her eyebrows shoot up so high, they disappear beneath her headdress; her mouth is agape. I clamp my teeth together so no more wayward lines can sneak through.

Slowly, very slowly, Beatrix closes her mouth, and a different, thoughtful expression comes into her eyes. "Yes, my lady," she says, with a curtsey. "Indeed, my lady. I'll go and see what I can find. In the meantime, if it please your ladyship, do stay under the covers until you stop shivering and talking so odd. Let me care for you, as your lady mother would do were she still alive to see this day. I'll send for a good hot drink to warm your blood and soothe your poor bumped head. And then I'll find you something to wear just as fast as ever I can."

My teeth are chattering. A hot drink *would* feel good, and I suppose it won't take long. I find myself nodding and sinking back against the pillows.

Once she's out the door, I look around. The walls aren't bare stone, like I expected; they're painted a cheerful gold and green. A long tapestry hangs on the far wall, with horses and hounds. And— Oh! There's a window seat tucked into the wall's thickness, but it's brightened with a scattering of richly embroidered cushions and a shutter pulled back from the window.

"Here you are then!" Beatrix bustles back in with a steaming cup coddled in a cloth. She pulls back the curtain enough to stand by the bed and sits me up, the covers wrapped high around me. As if helping a toddler, she holds the cup to my lips and tilts it as I drink—something hot and slightly bitter—and I can't stop, because she's still tilting, and a drowsy warmth starts flowing through my veins.

"One more sip, now," she's cooing. "That's right. Feels lovely, doesn't it? So relaxing. So restful. Just what you need. . . ."

My eyelids are growing heavy, my limbs loosen, my hand lets go of the side of the cup. . . .

To His Most Excellent Lord,
Sir Hugh of Berringstoke,
From His Faithful Servant Eustace

My lord, greetings and faithful service. It is with great concern that I write to urge you return with all possible haste. Following a storm the likes of which I have never before witnessed, the winds strong enough to bring down a great number of valuable trees in your lordship's forest, I sent men to investigate the damage. It was God's will that I did so, for they discovered Lady Matilda wandering the shore, stunned and confused, amidst the shattered remnants of her vessel and the drowned bodies of her men. She stood in the carnage immaculately clad in a finespun kirtle, a substantial gold cross studded with precious stones draped around her neck. Father Bartholomew believes the cross protected her. All are calling it a miracle.

There were no other survivors. The lady's traveling

party, attendants, and men-at-arms have all perished. I regret to inform you that Bertram and Gawyn, whom you sent to accompany the lady, were among those whose bodies were recovered.

You will recall, my lord, that we did not expect the lady so soon. Her party must have made remarkably good time in their travels, setting sail earlier than planned. Their very speed proved a curse as they sailed into the fury of the fatal storm. We are not yet prepared for Lady Matilda's presence, let alone the guests and banquets to follow. The cloth for the household's new attire is still being cut and sewn; the buttery remains almost bare of wine; I have yet to purchase sufficient wheat after the failure of your last crop. Moreover, in terms of household economy, we can no longer count on what the lady was expected to bring with her. All that could be found or salvaged were seven barrels of wine, a single kirtle of Lincoln scarlet, a cloak lined in miniver, and the lady's jewel box. As for the remainder of her valuable clothing and worldly goods, the sea has swallowed them whole.

I have taken the liberty of engaging the cook's sister Beatrix to attend her ladyship until such time as more suitable companionship may be arranged. She is a woman of middling age, not given to drink, and though lacking in refinement, she provides practical ministrations in addition to accompanying the lady as modesty requires. Such service is all the more essential as it is feared Lady Matilda's mind may have been affected by her ordeal. When found, she was speaking oddly, apparently unaware of her own name, as well as the fact that she was bound for Berringstoke.

Given these developments and the possible risks to her ladyship's health, not to mention all that hinges on her presence, I beg you, my lord, to return at the earliest opportunity.

The trees downed by the storm will at least provide a sufficiency of wood for burning. I pray you inform me if I am to take venison in your park against your arrival. I suggest we purchase wine in the amount expected but lost in the storm as soon as a good price may be arranged. I await your approval on these as on all things, that your business may prosper.

I remain, my lord, your most obedient and respectful servant,

Eustace, Steward of Berringstoke

Waking

My limbs are so heavy I can't move. I drift in and out from the ocean of sleep to the shore of day, still clutching a dream full of hoofbeats and barking dogs and woodsmoke. Each time I start to wake, another wave tugs me back out into the vast darkness. I give in. There's no morning sun on my eyelids, no need to leap up and put on the kettle, or iron my dress and apron before I head off to work. And I don't want to wake, with my bed more delicious than usual, and the covers under my fingers as soft as fur. . . .

Fur?

I sit upright, feeling around in the dark. Yes, that's fur under my fingers, and heavy curtains around me, sheltering a womb of a bed.

It wasn't a dream. I'm in the castle.

How long was I asleep? I peek out the curtain and blink in the sudden brightness. It was midday when I climbed into bed, but this is morning light. I must have slept all yesterday and through the night. It was that drink, that warm bitter drink she poured down my throat! *My lady*, that's what she called me. They all think I'm some lady they expected to arrive on that boat.

I yank the curtains open the rest of the way, breathing fast. They were expecting a lady—where is she, then? I stare at the door as if soldiers were about to fling it open with cries of "Imposter!" I look around frantically for my dress, so I'll have something on when they hurl me out the gates. It's nowhere to be seen, but a long linen shift hangs from a peg on the wall. That must be what counts as underclothes here. I clamber down and slip it over my head.

The feel of it on my skin stops me. It may just be linen, but the hand is wondrous soft and fine. The best, no doubt, that money can buy. I hug my arms about me, running my fingers up and down the fabric, the movement slowing me down enough to think. I look again at the monumental bed, the soft furs, the tapestries, the embroideries.

There's no army surging through that door at the moment, is there? A day and a night have passed, and I'm still here. There must have been men searching everywhere.

Wouldn't they have found their lady, if she's still alive? And if she's dead . . .

I stand up straighter, determination filling me, spreading all the way down to my toes. If she's dead, there's a place open in this castle for a lady. And I've waltzed right into it. All I have to do is learn the part.

"Lady Matilda," I say out loud.

I turn to the bed, my hands automatically reaching to straighten the sheets.

But what if someone knows what she looks like, and sees I'm all wrong? What if her body washes ashore, or her parents come searching, or—

I shake out the fur coverlet, then settle it down again neat as can be. Then I'll deal with that when it happens. I've got the chance of my life, more than I ever imagined, and I'm not going to throw it away—I grab a pillow and give it a good hard shake to fluff the down—because of a mere *what if.*

I lay the pillow in place, and I'm shaking out the next one when the door opens. In bustles Beatrix, a tray in her hands, a blue gown draped over her arm. She kicks the door shut before turning to the bed.

She stops dead. "My lady! Whatever are you doing?"

"Just making my—" And then I stop, too, because I

realize what she's seeing: a grand lady who's used to being waited on hand and foot, making her own bed. I jump back like a child caught doing something naughty.

But if I'm a grand lady . . .

I put my hands on my hips. "How *could* you?" I demand.

"How could I what, my lady?" She walks to a chest and sets down the tray.

"You drugged me! You made me pass out!"

"I didn't *drug* you, I *dosed* you, as any caring person would. And you with no mother or lady-in-waiting about to think what you need." She clucks like a mother hen. "You needed sleep. And it's done you good. You should have seen yourself yesterday, all wild eyes and shivers. And look at you now! Such rosy cheeks, and your green eyes so bright, they're a wonder against your chestnut hair. Indeed, they were mistaken when they said you were—" She stops suddenly, putting a hand to her mouth, then continues, flustered, "That is to say, their descriptions didn't do you justice."

I look up sharply. What descriptions? What am I supposed to look like?

A wonderful smell of warm bread wafts through the air. My stomach growls; I'm starving, and everything on that tray must be for me. I reach for a fat buttered slice, and take a huge bite. It's delicious. I grab the mug, take a gulp—and almost gag on a thick alcoholic brew. I start coughing.

Beatrix comes over, takes the mug from my hands, and pats me on the back.

"Oh, Beatrix," I say. "I *do* need your help!"

She looks pleased. "Indeed you do. Why, you've put your shift on backward, trying to dress yourself! Oswald was right. That must have been a fearsome blow you were struck."

"A blow?"

She nods, then motions me to pull my arms from the sleeves and twirl the shift around to face the right direction. "That's why you're so confused and all, talking so oddly and forgetting simple things." She holds up the blue gown for me to slip my arms through the sleeves. "Though when I came to poultice it last night, I saw no bump." She sighs. "Alas, the wound must lie deeper, and such wounds are harder to heal."

Excitement flutters through me. That's it! I could hug her! I'd completely forgotten my plan to pretend amnesia in town, and it will work even better here in the castle. It's the perfect excuse for not knowing how to do things like a grand lady. Whenever someone looks at me strangely, I'll just clasp my head and moan a little.

Beatrix starts tying and lacing and adjusting things on the dress. She stands back and gives an approving nod. "Not as fine as you're used to, of course. We thought you'd be bringing your own. I'll do some stitching later. The sleeves aren't right. But you're such a beauty, you could wear anything!"

A beauty, me? Oh, I've seen how some of the boys stare, but I thought it was because they were assuming . . . I look up at Beatrix, wondering what to say, and then I notice her head. "Don't I need something to cover my hair and neck, like you have?"

"Why, no," she says. "Enjoy your beautiful hair until you're married. So thick and such a rich brown, though a bit of a tangle, isn't it? From the wind and the sea and all your disasters. We need to do something about that."

She glances around. There's almost no furniture in this gigantic room, except for the bed, some benches, and a few trunks. She walks to one, opens it, shakes her head, and opens another. She rummages around and comes up with a comb.

"Let us sit in the window nook, and I'll do your hair," she says. "What a glory it will be when I'm done with it!"

She motions to me, and I step up into the window seat, scooting to the far end so I can look out while she combs my hair. The storm disappeared with the night. A few small clouds are just escaping over distant treetops, and the sky is crisp and blue, a perfect autumn day.

Below me, a hodgepodge of thatched buildings nestles inside the great stone walls. It's like a city down there, a whole world, abustle with people shoeing horses, stirring cauldrons, turning spits of meat—

The comb catches a knot. "Ouch!"

"Begging your pardon, my lady." Beatrix gently works through the tangle and starts on another section. She's found my secret: I *am* proud of my hair. Mum makes me wear it hidden away in a long, tight braid, dangling down my back. "You don't need the young men looking at *that*," she always says.

A banging noise rises from below as a smith pounds a hammer, muscled arms bulging from rolled-up sleeves. A man is leading a huge black horse; the beast tosses its head, and the man stops, stroking its side. A skinny boy turns a handle at a big stone well as a bucket rises from the depths. A flurry of movement turns into wings flitting in and out of a tiny tower at the top of a building, and now my ears sort out the cooing of pigeons. I'm so entranced, I hardly feel the comb plying my hair.

And then I see him. The lad with the eyes.

He stands tall and slim. The sun shines on straight golden hair; on his wrist he carries that same small hawk. As I watch, he lifts his arm, bringing the bird closer, and seems to whisper something in its ear. With his other hand he strokes its back.

"Beatrix, who is that?"

She stops combing long enough to peer over my shoulder and follow my eyes. She gives me a knowing glance before sitting back and taking up the comb again. "That would be William, the falconer's boy. Not such a boy anymore, though. Getting to be quite the young man, and such a way he has with the birds. Almost better than his father, or so they say. But don't you be getting any ideas." She gives a sharp tug, and I wince.

"Me? Ideas?"

She sighs. "We all know why you're here, my lady."

"Oh?" I ask, hoping she'll say more.

But instead she stands and proclaims, "There! You're a vision! Now eat your bread and drink your ale, and then if you feel well enough, the steward wonders if you will grant him a moment."

Eustace Steps out of a Tapestry

Beatrix leads me down to a huge room with a towering timbered ceiling. Smoky candles spread wavering circles of light, but there are so few windows, much of the room disappears into shadow. The floor is strewn with rushes. A boy is pushing them into piles and lugging them out; a stench trails after him. Just yesterday that's the sort of work I was doing, keeping things clean for those above me.

There's a raised platform at the far end of the hall, and on the platform a table, and behind the table a thronelike chair, and behind the chair a life-size tapestry of trees, a leaping stag, and hunters clad in green.

And then the shortest hunter peels away from the fabric, turning to stare at me with penetrating eyes.

I gasp, grabbing Beatrix's hand. He takes another step—

why, I could almost laugh, I'm so relieved! It isn't the tapestry come to life, just a green-cloaked man, and one with a paunch and a mincing walk at that.

And yet, as he comes closer, my sense of unease returns. It's not that he's short and overweight, or that he has a bulbous nose; it's more the calculating look in his eyes that puts me on edge. The stingy set of his mouth makes me think he's the one who watches the castle's purse strings. But he clearly doesn't stint on himself: his cape is lined with fur so fine, it ripples as he walks, and at the neck he sports a sparkling jeweled pin.

I'm just about to curtsey when, thank God, I remember and catch myself in time. He stops a few steps away and bows deeply, his cloak sweeping the dirty rushes.

He rises. "Lady Matilda, in the absence of Sir Hugh, allow me to bid you welcome."

A confident tone, that's what my role calls for. Almost hoity-toity. "And you would be . . . ?"

"Eustace, Steward of Berringstoke, and at your service, my lady."

He pauses, waiting, while I search for another line. "What a charming castle," I finally say.

He bows again. "As you see, we did not expect you so soon. You find us somewhat unprepared." He glares at the boy sweeping rushes. "Look sharp there! Can you work no faster? Sir Hugh will hear of this!"

A panicked look crosses the boy's face, and he starts moving in double time, like one of those books of pictures where you flip the pages to make the characters leap.

Eustace turns back to me as if expecting congratulations for keeping things in line. "But you shall see us at our best anon."

Anon. That's a good one to stash away.

He takes a deep breath, and his tone becomes one of studied concern. "We grieved to hear of your losses, and yet we rejoice at your survival. I am sending a messenger to Sir Hugh today, requesting that he return as soon as possible."

"Oh, there's no need," I say. "Verily."

As far as I'm concerned, the longer this Sir Hugh is away, the better. Isn't the lord of the house likely to know his guests? I can use the time to think what to do if he sees I'm not Lady Matilda. And until he returns, I don't have to be so careful. Servants are always more relaxed when the head of a household is gone.

Or they would be, I think, watching the steward's face, if this sharp-eyed man weren't ferreting about every corner.

He reaches a hand under his cloak and brings out something that glitters in the candlelight. "His lordship wished you to have this as a token of his regard."

He hands me a small flat case. It's covered in green silk, heavily embroidered in gold. I step closer to a candle to make out the picture: a lady sits in a bower, and a unicorn approaches as if to lay its great horned head in her lap; her hand is raised, not to ward off the beast, but to welcome it.

"I've never seen such needlework," I say, and that's the truth. I sew all the time, but practical things like seams and hems and buttons. Nothing like this.

Eustace bows his head. "Word of your talent precedes you, my lady. Perhaps plying the needle will soothe you in your grief."

Oh, right. Grief. I lower my eyes and sigh.

"Perhaps you would care to open it?" he asks.

There's a little latch. Inside are compartments with needles and pins, an elaborately etched thimble, and colorful skeins of silk.

"It's lovely," I say.

He bows low, and then starts to back away. Why, I'm so grand he doesn't dare turn his back! I try to restrain my smile, but once he's scooted out the door, I find myself breaking into a grin. That went rather well! This man, at least, seems quite certain of who I am. I turn to Beatrix—and clamp my mouth shut as I see, from her expression, that grinning isn't the thing for a lady.

She leans forward and surprises me by whispering, "You'd be wise not to take that one lightly, my lady. Keep your eyes open." Then she straightens and, as if I'd imagined the moment, says in a normal voice, "I do beg your pardon, but I'm afraid I have a few things need doing. May I leave you for a time? You could look around the great hall, if it please you."

I'm glad to have the chance to be on my own, go where I want to go, with no one looking at me too closely.

"Take your time," I say. "I'll walk around in the courtyard."

"The court—" She follows my glance to the door. "Oh! You mean the bailey!" She clucks again. That's right, me and my poor hurt head.

"Verily, I'll be fine," I say. "I'll see you anon."

With raised eyebrows, she bobs a curtsey, and then hurries away.

The bailey. That's where I'll start. Not in this echoing room where the boy is still sweeping and spreading new rushes. I give him a smile on my way to the door, and he almost drops the armload he's lugging, he's that surprised. I *must* start being more condescending.

I step out into the beautiful autumn morning and pause for a moment at the top of the stairs, smelling smoke and fresh bread, hearing hammers and horses. I'm a lady, I am, and I can go anywhere I want! I'll make a round of the thatched buildings against the walls, and find out what each is for. That one, so clean and neat, between the dovecot and the kennels. That's where I'll start.

My Falcon

※

I'm standing outside the door when I hear a funny little whistle, a fragment of a tune that sounds out of place and just right at the same time. In my eagerness to see what's making the sound, I push the door too hard, and it goes slamming into the far wall. Someone whirls around: William, his eyes blazing with anger. And on his arm, with its feathered helmet, my greeter, my guide—

"My bird!" I cry, all loud and excited.

There's a frantic flapping of wings as the bird leaps off backward. The next thing I know, William is settling it again on his glove. He seems to look inside himself and go still; without a word to me, he lowers his head and speaks to the bird as if there's nothing in the world but the two of them. "There, now. Don't worry. There."

He must be a few years older than I am, seventeen or so. Slim, but with strong shoulders and a way of standing that shows how easy he is in his body. His eyes are as blue and untamed as the sky.

He lifts a pouch from his side, takes a sip—and then he's spitting it out at the bird's face! A fine mist coats its feathers. I'd laugh, but a look comes over the bird, a look that if I saw it on a person, I'd say was happiness. William sprays again, and it opens its beak to catch some of the water as it mists that fine head, those wings.

What a magnificent creature! The tilt of its head, the bright gleam in its eye, like a candle shining in a deep cavern . . . Caught up in the vision before me, I forget, for a moment, where I am. Who I'm pretending to be.

"There now," William says again, sounding strong and gentle, all at the same time. The bird relaxes before my eyes. Its feathers fluff out, and for a second it looks almost vulnerable, but then it gives a little shiver, and instantly every feather is once again sleek and in place, molded to its body like armor. Except for that alert eye, the bird is still.

William flashes me a glance, warning me not to say a word. He reaches to his side and comes up with a strip of meat. The bird bends its head to take it, and he whistles those haunting notes again, like an incantation floating in the air.

My heart is in my throat. I can feel the power he just calmed with his gentleness.

He lifts his hand to a perch, and the bird steps over, one yellow, taloned foot and then the other. He ties a line rapidly with his free hand, then steps away, nodding at me to follow him out the door. The bird chirrups after him as if it wants him to stay near.

He closes the door softly behind us. I blink in sunlight so bright, it blazes my thoughts blank. There's nothing in my head but sun. It's as if I've been entranced.

Finally he speaks. "I beg your pardon, my lady. That's my fault, Pilgrim bating like that. I thought you were the boy come to clean, as should know better." His voice is low, his words respectful, but his gaze has borrowed its intensity from the falcon.

Then I remember. "You found my bird!" I cry. "The one I saw when—" I stop as fast as I started. I nearly told him about the lift! That won't do. I smooth my skirt with my hands. "When I was riding back from the shore. From the . . . disaster."

"You saw a peregrine?" he asks, a quick, interested look coming into his eyes. "Where?"

I don't want to mention the field, so instead I say feebly, "I don't remember."

"It wasn't Pilgrim," he says, glancing back at the door. "She's been in the mews. You saw another, a haggard, mayhap."

"Mayhap," I say, pretending to know what he's talking about.

Suddenly a smile lights up William's face. "I'm glad you're here," he says. "I was going to ask for an audience. You see, I've been training one special for you."

A magnificent falcon for my very own! I imagine carrying it on my fist, stroking its breast with a gentle finger, seeing what those feathers feel like on my skin.

He indicates another door with a tilt of his head. "His lordship asked me to have her manned for your arrival. You'll have to be quiet and gentle when we—" He stops suddenly. "I beg your pardon, my lady. Forgive me if I overstep my place. I forget what you . . ."

"You forget what I've forgotten," I say, filling the empty space. "I do, too. I can't even remember being near falcons." Lord, is that true! "So just tell me everything. Pretend I know nothing at all. That's the best."

It's how I'll learn.

But he doesn't go on about how I'm to act with the bird. He pauses and looks at the ground, long eyelashes close to high cheekbones. "If you don't mind my saying"—he looks up—"you're not how I expected."

Now those brilliant eyes are gazing right into mine, and

suddenly I realize I'm talking with a lad, a handsome one at that, and for once I'm not lowering my head and rushing in the opposite direction. I feel my cheeks flush. I can't look away.

There's a long moment of silence. He's standing there, waiting. As if he expects me to say something.

Then I blush again, hotter, as it comes to me. Not how he expected? He must mean I'm being too familiar for some-one of my rank. How could I have let myself slip so soon? If I'm to convince this castle I'm their lady, I need to be as dignified and demanding as everyone expects.

I gather my grandeur back around me like a cloak. "And why, pray tell, are we standing here? Bring me my falcon."

He gives a slight bow. "Do you mind waiting here? I'll bring her out on the glove."

I stand in the sun, almost dizzy from the unfamiliar feel-ings swirling around inside me. Apparently, when Lady Matilda wants something, people listen. I want that bird on my arm, that strength, that power. I want—

The door opens. William steps out, and on his arm—

My heart plummets. On his arm is the little chirp of a bird he was carrying when I rode through the gates. It can't be even half the size of Pilgrim, and those brown feathers remind me of an old speckled hen.

"Where is my *falcon*?" I say.

"Right here. She isn't named yet; that's for you to do, of course. The calmest little merlin you ever saw. Doesn't get upset about anything."

With his free hand, William reaches into that pouch at his side, pulls out a strip of meat, and offers it to her. She gobbles it up, like a lady gulping cakes at a tea party. She's got that kind of body, too: small and soft and round. Like she never flies anywhere, just sits around all day, eating. Why does he even bother with a glove for this bird?

He strokes her brown breast gently with a finger, then lifts his head, smiling. Until he sees my face.

"Don't you like her?" he asks, a note of worry creeping into his voice. "I've trained her carefully, so she'll be sweet for you. Beautiful markings. But of course, if you want a different one . . ."

"I want Pilgrim."

My words ring out around us. They surprise me so much, I almost jump.

"Pilgrim is a peregrine," he says carefully. "I've been manning her for Sir Hugh. This one will sleep in your room, come with you to town, to church. Not all edgy and particular, like Pilgrim. And you know the saying: A merlin for my lady."

A saying, as if the rule were etched in stone. Mum was always telling me I should be happy with what I have. And yet, my *wanting* is still there, delicious, demanding. Well, I'm not with Mum, and this isn't *always* anymore.

"I want Pilgrim," I say again, clipping off each word.

William's jaw sets. That's not what I expected. "It's true Sir Hugh hasn't met Pilgrim yet. But you don't expect me to give *him* the merlin, do you?"

He's getting that stony feeling. I can sense it in the air. This doesn't feel right at all, not with him. So, even though it may not be wise, I drop the ladying. "I'll discuss it with Sir Hugh when he comes," I say. "Until then, I'd like to be around Pilgrim. Not say she's mine, just be near when you care for her. Perhaps learn to work with her, like you do. That will be all right, won't it?"

William looks thoughtful; his face eases. It's like his feathers got smoothed back down. "It's time she was getting used to more people," he says. He tilts his head, about to say more, when Beatrix comes panting up.

"Where have you been, my lady?" she says, all red in the face. "I've been this worried about you! Couldn't find you anywhere, and here it is time to eat almost, and you making your appearance at the high table, and we want you at your finest, don't we?"

She turns and bustles me toward the castle, herding me like a sheepdog. I let myself get pushed upstairs.

To His Most Excellent Lord,
Sir Hugh of Berringstoke,
From His Faithful Servant Eustace

M̲y lord, all greetings and due respect. Your affairs progress as well as could be expected. I have arranged to purchase sufficient wheat to cover our losses at a most reasonable price. Hops are now brewing for beer.

The reason for my writing after such a brief interval is not, however, a happy one. Lady Matilda made her first appearance at table this day, and it is apparent that the travails of her journey have affected her grievously, resulting in the loss of the most basic knowledge and etiquette.

The household was forced to wait for some time before she rushed in late. After staring about like one dazed, she sat, not at the high table, but at one of the lower trestle tables, until the woman Beatrix approached, whispered in her ear, and led her to the appropriate seat. When the boy brought the pitcher, instead of holding her hands over the basin for washing, she raised a goblet as if expecting it to be filled for drink. I was forced to wash my hands before her, in spite of the breach of etiquette, to demonstrate the method as tactfully as possible. Her eyes were as wide as if she had never seen such a thing.

As for the trencher of bread we were to share, she placed it firmly before her, tore off a segment, and proceeded to actually eat it, as if it were finely milled white bread. I feel it is my duty to inform you that, as I lifted my eyes in shock, I espied other members of the household staring, aghast. I glared at them in silent communication, and none disgraced your lordship with laughter.

The lady acted as though the goblet was for her use alone, compelling the lad to run and fetch another for me, and I forced myself to drink singly. Halfway through the meal, she noticed those at other tables sharing trencher and goblet and, in sudden comprehension, grabbed the goblet newly brought to me and took sip. I barely know how to mention this, my lord, but she neglected to wipe the rim.

Her speech is likewise somewhat odd. Her manner alternates between an overfamiliarity with those beneath her and a tone that is so formal as to be almost stilted. It is much like a closed tap on a barrel of ale, opened full to flow with sudden force.

I can only surmise that, in addition to the shock of her losses, the lady suffered a fearsome blow to the brain. We must pray that she will improve with time. I assure you I will keep a close eye upon her until your return.

In a positive light, I report with relief that her ladyship's bodily health appears robust. She eats, while with few manners, with great gusto. She rushes about as if seeing everything for the first time, and appears to prefer outdoor activity to the comforts of the solar. It is to be hoped the fresh air will encourage her return to full awareness.

May I again urge you to consider returning as soon as possible? Haste is of the essence. The string of missives from Sir Giles continues unabated, and we must prepare for a possible escalation in his approach, particularly should her ladyship's state imperil your plans. The constable has raised the subject of increasing the number of men-at-arms, but funds for this, as for all else, are not yet in your coffers.

Striving diligently for the furtherance of your estate, and thinking only of the safety of Berringstoke, I remain yours obediently and respectfully in this as in all other things,

Eustace, Steward of Berringstoke

By the Fire

Beatrix and I are sitting by the fire in the solar, each with our stitching in our laps. Beatrix picks up a linen napkin from a basket at her side and starts hemming. Her stitches are nice and quick. Me, I'm staring at the swath of forest-green silk spread across my lap, wondering how to go about embroidering something like the lady and unicorn on my needle case. I knot my thread and make a first pass through the cloth.

"That bread you set your food on," I say. "Remind me what it's called."

My first meal in the great hall didn't go nearly as well as I'd expected. I have a lot to learn, and Beatrix, tut-tutting about my poor muddled head, is helping.

"That's the trencher, my lady. You share one with your

table partner. After the meal, the boy collects them, laden with sauce and drippings, and gives them to such as are poor and hungry. Alms, it is, as the good Lord wishes of us."

Lovely. I've been eating the plates.

I start outlining a castle with tiny stitches. "And the goblet?"

"Shared as well, my lady. Your partner will offer you platters of meat and other fine dishes, and you, likewise, offer them back to him."

"But if we share a trencher, how do I know whose bit is whose?"

"Well, you don't take that much at a time, now, do you? You just learn to keep track. And you must not"—she clears her throat, takes a stitch or two—"simply must not eat the meat off your knife! Hold it in your fingers, there's a proper lady."

"It's hard, without a fork."

"A fork? At your seat? Why, what would you do with a great long thing like that? A kitchen tool, that is."

I start on a pennant for the top of my slightly lopsided tower. Just plain, straight stitches again. I don't know anything fancier: no little knots, or flowery shapes, or raised bits. The flag is halfway filled in, and already it bores me. I toss the green silk aside, rethread my needle with some of Beatrix's white, grab a napkin from her basket, and start hemming.

Now *this* kind of stitchery I can do in my sleep. I did it with Mum often enough. I picture us sitting late at night, Mum and me, as I help her finish up the hemming, hardly a word between us, but there's a quiet ease in the air, and our needles practically fly through the cloth until we stop for a sip of tea. . . .

But then the cozy feeling around the picture starts to twist, and becomes something darker. That was all coming to an end, wasn't it? I stitch faster to close up the memory, before pain starts sneaking through.

Beatrix looks at me and smiles. "Aren't you a dear to help me so, instead of your own work! But there's no need, now, really."

"Oh, I want to do things for the castle, too," I say.

She nods appreciatively. "An eye out for everyone. That's a lady's role, true enough." She stops to work out a snag in her thread. "Now, the man who cuts the bread is the pantler. The one with the wine is the butler. In the absence of his lordship, you must keep the conversation flowing with the wine, so the spirit is lively. Ask the harpist to strike up a song now and then."

"Doesn't Eustace do all that?"

"He did today, because you're poorly, but once you're well, it's more your place."

Exactly who is this Lady Matilda, that she's so important to the castle? I'm about to prod Beatrix for more information, but she's still talking.

"At meal's end, you must wait for the ewer and basin to be brought again. Your dining partner will pour water over your hands, as you do for him. You left Eustace in a bit of a spot today."

The truth is, I couldn't leave the steward soon enough. There's something in his sharp eyes that makes me feel exposed. Something in his voice, no matter how flattering, that sounds like a threat.

"I'd rather he weren't my partner," I say.

She ties a knot. "Things will all change soon enough."

She looks up with a look of such understanding, it's almost as if she *knows* about me. My needle slips, pricks me through the cloth. A bright spot of red appears on the linen, and I gasp. I never slip in my stitching!

Beatrix gently takes the cloth from my hand. "There, you see? Back to what you know, my lady. That will be best." And she hands me the shimmering silk with its misshapen outline of a castle.

The Bailey

A dozen slavering dogs strain at their leashes: bloodhounds as big as colts, and brindled beasts that are all long legs and fangs, and smaller dogs that stare at me with fierce intelligence in their eyes, working the air with their muzzles, memorizing my scent.

"No sudden moves, if you please, my lady," says John, the master of the hounds. He's a stocky, bearded man with a hunting horn slung over one shoulder. "They don't know you yet."

"But they will soon enough!" declares Father Bartholomew, the castle chaplain. He runs a pink hand across the fringe circling his bald dome, but it springs right up again, a most unruly halo. He's taken it upon himself to show me around the bailey.

"His lordship is particularly proud of his lymers, and with good reason." John nods at the legs with teeth. "You can expect excellent hunting when he returns."

"And venison for the table," chortles the chaplain. "Does your ladyship enjoy the chase?"

The chase? Am I supposed to know how to do that, too? I decide not to say anything, because I'm having a hard time trying to figure out what Lady Matilda should know about a castle, and what would be unfamiliar for her here, in this place. It's all new to me, a tumult of sights and sounds, not to mention the smells: dogs and cooking and sweat and fresh wood, all jumbled together. I'm trying to absorb as much information as I can, without saying anything stupid.

Luckily, Father Bartholomew doesn't wait for me to answer, but starts walking away from the kennels. "Now, if you will allow me," he says, "I'll show you the perfect place to sit when you want privacy and a touch of fresh air."

We pass a small shed, just big enough for the single man sitting at a table with a pot of glue and a stack of wooden shafts. There are dozens of arrows leaning against the wall to dry, and yet there's a frenzy to his motions as he trims and glues on feathers, as if he has more to finish than he can possibly manage.

"Does he always work that fast?" I say.

"The fletcher?" My guide shakes his head. "They must be stocking up. A bit of an alert, I hear."

"And why is that?" I ask, as we near the stables.

Instead of answering, he stops, distracted, and points to a gleaming black steed, half again as large as the other horses. It snorts as a man cinches a saddle on its broad back.

"That must be the new destrier they're sending his lordship," says Father Bartholomew. "To replace the horse he lost in the jousts."

"Lost?"

He nods. "Broken leg this time, I heard. Not forfeited like the last one. Oh, you should hear the stable master go on about it!"

I glance back at the horse, somewhat concerned about its fate, as we start walking again. A red-haired boy pitches hay from a loft, its fresh scent competing with the ripeness of dirty sweepings at the side of the building. Half a dozen horses stare at us with eyes as dark and deep as mountain pools.

Past the blacksmith's shed with its hammering and heat; the carpenter's, where men are working a two-handled saw back and forth across a log—"Lots of wood down in that storm," says Father Bartholomew; past the well and the skinny boy hefting two full buckets on the yoke across his shoulders; past the gatehouse—"Where the men-at-arms live, of course, though they're too busy training to introduce you to the constable"; past chickens and pigs and bake sheds; until finally we reach the far wall and come to a stop.

"For your ladyship," says Father Bartholomew, nodding and smiling at a small wooden door, just the right size for me. After all the clamor and bustle, it looks welcome indeed. This must be my own private entrance! I'll be able to slip out quietly and walk in the woods whenever I want time to myself.

"How lovely!" I say. He reaches toward the door, but my hand is there first. He stands back, looking pleased that I'm so pleased, and I lift the latch. The door opens.

But it's only a garden, nestled inside yet another ring of impenetrable castle walls. I sigh in disappointment, but luckily the chaplain doesn't notice.

"The perfect place for your needlework," he says, plumping with pride. "They've been readying it for your arrival. Such sweet-smelling herbs. And look, roses!"

Yes, there are rosebushes with a last few autumn blooms, the sweet, simple kind with a single ring of pink petals. And a pear tree with a stone bench beneath its laden boughs.

"A place of peace away from the frenzy of the bailey

in times such as these! And with all the preparations afoot, you'll be glad of it, I daresay."

"Preparations?" I ask, assuming this time he'll tell me.

"Exactly," he says. "Quite private!"

He pulls the door shut again. "Now I'll show you the chapel. I want to be certain you know where it is because, that is, you see . . ." He pauses, wringing his hands in embarrassment, then goes on all in a surge. "That is to say, we've missed you at matins, and I assume it's because you weren't sure where to find us, or perhaps it's because of your head, or—well, in any case, you'll be joining us, of course, now that you're feeling better."

It's clearly been quite the oversight on my part. Another thing I've been doing wrong.

"Why, certainly," I say.

As we start back, I hear the drawbridge clanking down, and my breath catches. I turn to look. Each time someone rides across the drawbridge, I wonder: Does *this* person know the real Lady Matilda? Will *this* be the one to find me out?

Father Bartholomew is still rambling on. "Unless you prefer morning mass to matins? I could start doing morning mass, if that's what you're used to. A much bigger production, of course, and people around here tend to be so busy."

A wagon rolls into the bailey. I recognize the men following on horseback: the tall man and Oswald and Robert, who brought me from the shore. I start to relax, but then I notice the grim set of their jaws. They see me and freeze for a fraction of a second, as if they don't like what they're about to do.

They dismount. The tall man hands his reins to Robert, and then he's walking over to me with that long-legged stride. His eyes are too serious by far.

They've found me out.

"Dear God!" Damn, I've said it out loud. Father Bartholomew nods in response, then lowers his head and raises his hands in prayer.

The man reaches us and bows low and long. Too long. He's reluctant to rise.

"What is it, Edward?" asks Father Bartholomew impatiently. He, for one, can hardly wait to see what's about to unfold.

Edward—so that's his name—straightens and looks down into my eyes. "Several bodies have been found washed ashore," he says. "And one of them is a woman."

They know. I look around frantically, wondering which way I can run. But my legs betray me; my knees buckle.

Father Bartholomew wraps a thick arm around my

shoulders, clamping his hand down like a vise. "I've got you, my lady," he says.

"If you would come this way," says Edward.

I nod—what else can I do?—and follow him back to the wagon. Father Bartholomew is still attached to me like a limpet.

What is the punishment for impersonating a noble lady? Will they show me the door? No, too easy. Whip me? Throw me in a dungeon to rot? The sword at Edward's waist swings with every step.

A small crowd has gathered and stands gazing solemnly at the back of the wagon. Several forms lie shrouded in cloth of a familiar dark green. The men used their capes to wrap the bodies.

Can I still plead my wounded head and say I didn't know I was an imposter? There are far too many men here for me to run, and the drawbridge is rattling back up. . . .

Edward reaches for the first body, lifting the cloak to reveal a face. A portly middle-aged man, so heavy with water, it's like he's still beneath the waves. A hole gapes where his nose should be.

I gasp, and Father Bartholomew tightens his hold.

"His name?" asks Edward.

I shake my head and whisper, "I don't know."

He nods, replaces the covering, then takes a step to
reach the other body. I'm holding my breath. He lifts a corner of the cloth slowly, watching my eyes the whole while.

It's her. It must be. Pale hair still wound in an elegant
braid. A weak chin, slightly buckteeth. Even death can't
hide her plainness. As plain as I thought when Beatrix said,
"Their descriptions didn't do you justice."

It's all over now. They know.

"As I assumed," says Edward. "Your lady-in-waiting."

I stare at him. "My—"

"We only need her name for the tomb, my lady, and then
we won't distress you any longer."

"Her . . . name?"

He nods.

I stare back down at the lifeless body, the skin bleached
pure white, and I find myself whispering, "Adelaide. That
was her name."

Church

The next day I'm dressed in a fine new gown of rose-colored silk and seated in a covered wagon with curtains on the sides. There's to be a memorial service for those lost in the storm, and it's too big and grand for the little chapel in the bailey. We're on our way to the church in town.

Beatrix insists on keeping the curtains closed—in respect for my grief, she says—as we rumble down the road, across the bridge, and through the narrow streets of town. We come to a stop, and I hear Edward say, "We have arrived, my lady."

I step down from the wagon, and Beatrix comes after. Villagers line the square, jostling one another to get a better look. Beatrix sees someone she knows and lifts her hand to wave, then remembers herself and pretends she was just adjusting her wimple. The men-at-arms form a human tunnel for me to walk the distance to the church door.

As I look out at the sea of expectant faces, I realize that whatever I'm feeling about this service, it isn't enough. I've seen dead bodies, shuddered as I touched them, but they were strangers to me. For Lady Matilda they were servants, companions, perhaps even friends. The way I look now should honor that.

Pious, I think. *And more than sad—on the verge of despair.*

I clasp my hands in front of me and raise my eyes to the church tower, sighing loudly. A surge of sighs flows back from the crowd in response. Like I'm living some part of life for everyone else.

I lower my head and walk slowly toward the arched door. The crowd breathes in rhythm to my steps, sharing my grief.

A priest comes forward, his hands outstretched in greeting. Behind me stands the rest of the party. We've brought almost the entire castle, with all of us dressed in bright new clothes. Someone has been sewing day and night to make the tunics and capes, my snug-fitting gown. We're showing our respect for the dead. And our importance. And me.

I feel everyone staring. As I walk through the door, the carved birds add their piercing, inquisitive gazes to the rest. Inside, I pause, adjusting to the darkness.

But where are the pews? The little table with its toppling stacks of historical brochures? The warm light? My steps are ringing out on a stone floor. There's no furniture to absorb the sound, just the altar. Candlelight flickers onto columns and arches before letting go again, so the ceiling drifts up like heaven's dome. Stripped of trappings, my little church is suddenly huge, immediate. Like God is looking right at me.

The priest begins the service, and soon he's intoning with the monotonous flatness of someone who knows every word without thinking. I strain to make out what he's saying over the low murmur in the room. *"Deus,"* I hear, and *"sanctum"*—it's all in Latin. I give up trying to understand.

Now the steady drone becomes a low roar in my ears, like the surf, and I start to remember things I'd rather not. How that limp arm felt in my hands. And the torso . . . the splintered boards . . . I think of bodies drifting to the bottom of the sea, and fish circling their blanching bones. Sailors, men-at-arms, ladies-in-waiting: the priest is saying prayers for all of them. All, except Lady Matilda. No one knows she's dead but me.

I picture that night: the boat tossing on raging waves, wind howling through the rigging, and Lady Matilda wide-eyed in terror, trying to hold on as the deck careened from side to side. A girl my age, on a journey to a new land. And never to arrive. Now I see the wagon in the bailey, that white, lifeless skin, the still-elegant braid. . . .

The priest chants a line, and everyone chants back. I move my mouth, pretending I know the words.

Pretending to be her.

Then guilt and sadness are washing over me so strong, I'm dizzy on my feet, grabbing Beatrix for support. No one else knows Lady Matilda is dead! No one is saying prayers for her soul! And here, in this church, does God see what I'm doing, the lie I'm stepping into?

As if in response, a circle of green light dances across my dress. I look up. A sunbeam pierces a stained glass window, blazing its picture bright: a girl, kneeling, stripped to the waist, and two men looming over her, their cudgels raised to strike. She lifts her clasped hands toward heaven. What has she done?

I'm keeping a dead girl's soul from its prayers.

I lift my hand to the glow, and my skin turns underwater green.

I plummet to my knees on the hard stone floor, clasping my hands before me like the girl in the window. I squeeze my eyes shut, and I pray with all my heart, as if my prayers alone can make up for each and every one of those Matilda is missing. I pray that her soul has found peace in heaven. And I pray that, if she sees me, she wants me to have this chance, to live the life that was ripped from her.

I feel tears running down my cheeks. And it's quiet. Too quiet. I open my eyes.

Everyone else is down on their knees, their hands raised in prayer. And their eyes—their eyes are on me.

I stand.

Everyone else stands with a clank and a swish and a rustle. Beatrix puts a hand on her lower back, leans into it, and sighs. There's more intoning, and some hailing this and that, and then the priest walks forward, clasps my hands, and stands with me as the others stream around us.

"It is hard," he says kindly. "I know it is hard. But the Lord does not give us a greater burden than we can bear."

I'm still speechless. He leads me to the door. The men are readying horses, preparing the wagon for Beatrix and me. I see her climbing up and arranging furs and cushions.

The priest is still holding my hands. "But life brings us joys to balance the pain," he says. "And when you next visit us, it will be a joyous occasion indeed."

That gets my attention. He's about to let go of my hands, but I clutch his tighter.

"My next visit?"

"Why, yes," he says. "We are honored indeed that it will be here."

"Honored?"

"Of course! Here, and not the cathedral! Quite a celebration, and the possibility of such eminent guests! Today the church supported us in our grief. When next we see you, it will be full of light for your wedding."

"My *wedding*?"

He leans forward. "And when does Sir Hugh return to take your hand?"

Beatrix has come back up and is bobbing and curtseying. I let her lead me back to the wagon. And it's a good thing, because I don't have a word to say.

Well, what did I *think* Lady Matilda was doing here? Would a lady come so far, bearing all her worldly goods, just for a visit? Would she be treated so fine, given the best room in the castle, and get bowed and groveled to just because of her noble blood? No, it's because she's—because I'm—to be lady of the house. Married to the lord.

A grand old lord with his grand old armor. And his grand old marriage bed.

And me who's never been kissed.

The wagon rumbles along the road. Beatrix looks at

my face and pulls the curtains shut around us.

"There now, my lady. That was too much for you, it was."

"Beatrix?"

"Yes, my lady? Oh, but your face is white. Do lie back and rest."

I look at my hands, still clenched together like the girl in the window awaiting her beating. "When . . ." I don't even want to say the words, but I need to know. "When am I to be wed?"

She tucks the fur in around me. "Well, let's see now. Sir Hugh is due back in a sennight, they say. Not long after that, once the other parties arrive."

"But, Beatrix, I'm fifteen!"

"Nothing to be embarrassed about," she says with a kindly look. "Not too old at all."

Back at the castle, everything feels different. We return to the great hall. This time I walk to the right seat. I sit. Everyone else sits. I hold my hands over the bowl for washing. I nod to the harpist. He strikes up a tune. Eustace actually gives me an approving glance. Everyone is looking at me, waiting for me to take the first bite, to show them what to do. Of course they are. I'm to be their lady.

Head and Heart

I peek out the curtains. Beatrix is asleep on her bench, her head flung back, snoring up a storm. Will she still sleep there when . . .

I shiver back under the furs and close my eyes, but there's no relief. I imagine a big, hairy hand creeping through the bed hangings: the lord of the castle, come to claim what's his. I can almost hear his rough, excited breathing. Now the fabric is like a cinema screen, and I see a girl walking down a corridor, a great globe of a belly distending her gown. It's me.

I sit up, ripping the curtains open, gasping for air. I'm not ready to marry!

Beatrix doesn't budge.

I run my fingers down the heavy embroidered hangings. In that moment of quiet, I hear a voice, clear as clear.

"Marrying the lord of the castle, what's so bad about that?"

It's my head talking to me.

"You've landed at the top, my girl. The real Lady Matilda can't come toss you out now, can she? This is everything you've always wanted in life. The richest clothes. The finest bites at table. Everyone groveling in respect. You couldn't do any better."

The voice is practical, yet that very practicality is seductive. I find myself listening.

"A dashing knight, all sparkling chain mail and bold striding," it says. "Not know him? Why, the real Lady Matilda most likely didn't know him, when she set sail. And you can be sure she hadn't kissed many lads yet, either. In this day, you're late to wed."

And then my heart cries, "Run!"

"Stay!" says my head. And now head and heart are battling it out.

"Your first kiss, on your wedding night, with a stranger," says my heart. "Is that truly what you want? To make a vow in church and come back to this cavernous bed—"

"Expensive bed," says my head.

"Bed," says my heart.

I feel cold, so cold. I pull the white furs higher.

But now my head brings out the one image it knows I can't argue against: Mum, sitting up late, so exhausted her eyes keep dropping closed, but she keeps stitching, stitching, mending my school dress one more time. Never enough money. Never any respect . . .

"She let her heart decide," says my head, as solemn as a death sentence.

And I hear, like the cawing of crows: *Who's your father then, Addy?*

That's what comes of love.

I pull those heavy curtains closed around me and lie back down under my fine fur covers. Doubts are for fools. This is my chance to be somebody. If I'm going to end up with a man, I'll end up with the right one. I clench my teeth until I stop shivering, until I feel as unbending as a double-starched collar. I'll do it, then. I'll marry the lord of the castle. I'll take his name. I'll share his bed. And no one will ever mock me again.

The Walk That Wasn't

❧

I pause for a moment just outside the door to the keep, looking down at the kennels and kitchens, the smithy, the mews. A cold wind snatches at my cloak with greedy fingers, and I pull the wool tighter as I start down the stairs. Today I'm going across the drawbridge, beyond the castle walls.

It's not that I changed my mind. I've decided to stay, marriage and all. But last night I dreamed that a fiery black horse galloped into the bailey, and on its back rode Sir Hugh. His face was hidden beneath a helmet, but he could see my face right enough, and what he saw, he didn't like. "Imposter!" he cried. And then I was fleeing toward the lift, with him galloping in pursuit, and those long-legged lymers baying, and the trails so tangled I couldn't see which way to go.

That's why I'm going for a walk through the woods this

morning, to find the quickest path to the lift in case I'm found out and have to run for it. It would be my only chance of escape. I couldn't hide in town, not after yesterday, with all those people lining the streets and staring. Even if I wore one of Beatrix's lumpy gowns, they'd know me in an instant, same as Mrs. Beale would recognize a cinema star if she met one on the train.

I walk across the bailey with my head held high, quite the proper lady. But the wind keeps trying to pull me astray, whipping my hair so wild, I almost wish it were braided again. I pull the strands back from my face as I near the massive doors. The barbican, that's what they call it. The drawbridge is up, the iron gate down, those dagger teeth clenched shut.

Two men-at-arms snap to attention.

"Open it, please," I say.

They stare at me. It must be the "please." Out of character. I make my voice lower, firmer. "Open it!"

But the only thing that opens is their mouths, gaping in astonishment. One of them finally stutters, "B-b-but where's your men, my lady?"

A head peers down from the walkway on top of the wall, eyes wide. And another.

"I don't need men," I say. "I'm just going for a walk."

The second guard lowers his head, backs off a few steps,

then hurries away. The remaining guard stays put, shifting from one foot to the other. "Not safe on your own, my lady."

I'm starting to feel exposed, aware of all the eyes on me. "Not safe?" I say. "Doesn't Sir Hugh own all this land?"

But the guard isn't looking at me, he's looking over my shoulder, and something makes him relax back on his wide-spread feet. I turn to find the second guard striding back with Eustace panting in his wake.

The steward takes a deep breath, letting it out as he sweeps one of his low bows. "My lady," he says, pulling his red face back up. "If I may have a moment . . ."

I'm back in my window seat, right where I started, staring down at the bailey. Apparently it isn't safe for a lady to wander around by herself. Especially a noble lady. Especially on foot. Another knight could come marauding along at any moment, hoping to catch the castle unawares and claim it for his own. It seems they attack each other all the time, and their spies could be skulking about, searching for weak spots in Berringstoke's defenses, delighted to find a valuable lady to hold for ransom.

All of which would be second nature to me, as instinctive as breath, if it weren't for the blow I suffered to my head, the wound so much deeper, alas, than it would seem by my healthy appearance. If I wish to go out, why, I have only to ask, with enough advance notice, and a proper contingent will be prepared, provided they can be spared from their other duties, though it's obviously too late to find the men today. But they're all at my beck and call, and my wish is their command, and my happiness their only concern. That, and of course, my safety.

Of course.

I struggle to put a name to the feelings muddling around inside me. There's frustration, and confusion. I'm their lady, am I not? With a seat at the high table, and the best room in the castle, and Beatrix to dress me and fetch for me, and a jeweled cross as heavy as a cobblestone. And yet here they are telling me what I can and cannot do. I thought I only had to say, "I want!" and they would leap to do my bidding. But I was as clear as could be, and still the doors stayed closed.

There are rules, it seems, even for a lady. And I'm only starting to learn them. I reach for my embroidery and try to make some of the fancy stitches Beatrix showed me.

And then, I don't want to admit it, but there's fear as well. Again I picture a steely knight, his finger pointed straight at my heart. Today must be the fifth day since I came. Ten more days the lift will be waiting in the field. When was it Beatrix said Sir Hugh returns?

I lean back against the wall. I want to stay! This life is a sight better than running into Caroline at the grocer's, or being shipped off as a scullery maid. All I want is a tiny dash of reassurance, no more than the few grains of nutmeg in a custard pie. Just a peek at the lift, is that too much to ask?

My embroidery slips to the floor. As I lean over to pick it up, I see two horses approaching the barbican: William and a sturdy dark-haired man, each with a falcon on his bent arm. The doors swing open, the iron gate lifts, the drawbridge lowers with a rattle and a clang. No one asks where they're going or tells them to wait. No one surrounds them with a battalion of soldiers. And it's not just because they're men. No, they ride through as easy as can be for their afternoon's hunting.

My mind starts turning as quickly as the numbers flipping past on the lift. I glance at the hanging with its hunters and horses and hounds. I think of the stag almost leaping off the tapestry into the great hall, and the prized pack of dogs in the kennels, and Father Bartholomew asking if I enjoy the hunt—such a noble sport, hunting! It seems to be valued above almost everything else here, except perhaps chapel and church. . . .

Then another picture comes into my mind, a picture so perfect, I laugh out loud. That's it! I jump up and start pacing the solar, brewing my plan like a heady cup of strong black tea.

Vision

>>>>>

I sit up with a start and jerk the bed curtain back. Sun streams in the window like a stage light, illuminating the bread and wine Beatrix left on the bench. How could I have slept so late? And today of all days?

I pull on my shift, grab the bread, and scoot into the window seat, where I can stare out at the morning hubbub. The dogs are barking in the kennels, the smith has his bellows going at the forge, and that looks like Oswald striding into the stables. And then, finally, there she is: Beatrix, walking back across the bailey with a purposeful step. I gulp down my last bite of bread and run to the door. It takes her forever to clomp her way to the top.

"Well?" I ask. "What did he say?"

She's breathing so hard from the stairs that I take her hand and lead her to the window seat. I pour her some wine.

She takes a hearty sip, then pants, "Never heard such a thing, says he"—she stops to fan her face—"but God wills it, and his father can spare him, and so be it, says he."

I jump up and pull my scarlet gown off its peg, holding it out to Beatrix, but she's still sitting there, one sturdy hand clutching the goblet, the other resting on her heart, and she's gazing at me with reverent eyes.

"Oh, do tell me where you were sitting when the vision came!" she begs.

I hang the gown back on its peg and walk to the center of the room, where it will make the most impact. "I wasn't sitting," I say. I drop to my knees and raise my clasped hands to my heart. "I was holding my cross, like this, and praying for a sign of what I'm meant to do here at Berringstoke."

Beatrix sighs deeply, contentedly. "Yes?"

"And then there was a blinding light, and a picture filled my head, as real as if it were right in front of me. I saw a field, and myself standing there, and a huge bird, lit up like an angel, flying to my arm. And a voice said, 'Go!'"

"Ahh!" sighs Beatrix.

"And I knew I was meant to find that place and see the holy falcon. Though what it may portend, I know not."

"Only Heaven knows what your vision foretells." Beatrix stands and takes down the dress, then waits while I rise from my knees to slip it on.

"And not too many people riding alongside you, no men-at-arms?" she says.

I nod. "That's how it was shown to me."

She snugs the ties. "Mayhap the bird will fly to your arm and come back to our mews."

"Mayhap," I say, pleased to have the word come so naturally. I remember to wait as she puts on my shoes. "I only know I must find that place."

"Indeed you must," she says, placing a cloak on my shoulders and fixing it with a jeweled pin.

I take a step toward the door. Beatrix follows.

"You needn't bother," I say. "I know my way to the mews."

She shakes her head. "You don't think I'd let you outside the walls alone!"

But that was exactly the point! I can't have everyone staring at the lift, wondering what it is, lugging it back to the castle for closer examination.

"I'm not going alone," I say. "William is taking me. After all, he was in the vision."

It's almost a knowing look she gives me then. "Then I must have been off at the side somewhere, under a tree," she says. "Because them in Heaven would surely know a lady can't go off alone with a young man, even a falconer's boy, and before she's wed at that."

I can feel myself blushing to the roots of my hair. I hadn't thought of it like that! But since she puts it that way . . .

"Very well," I say. "Let's go."

William is standing outside the mews, slim and tall. He steps forward and drops his head in a bow. The air is brisk and morning new.

He leads us across the bailey and stops in front of the stables. A gangly boy is bringing out three horses.

"Here we are," says William. "A pretty palfrey for you, my lady."

A white horse the size of an elephant dances from side to side. My breath is trapped in my throat. I hadn't thought about horses! Look at him, tossing his head; he'll buck me off and break every bone in my body.

"I thought we were going to walk," I say.

Beatrix looks at William, and William looks at the stableboy, and the stableboy looks at the horse, and the horse snorts loudly. They're none of them convinced.

I obviously need to pull out some ammunition. So I sigh and hang my head, aiming for a regretful air. "You see . . ." I pause, long and meaningful, as if the words are difficult for me to say. "I'm afraid I don't remember how to ride."

William strokes the monster's neck. "We don't know where it is, this place in your vision. We might be circling for hours before we find it."

I did say that to Beatrix, that I'll have to let the vision lead me. From what I remember of my breakneck ride with Edward, the trails are too twisted for me to even attempt going that way. I'll take us down to the bridge and then along the stream. Afterward, I'll ask William to show me the shortest way back.

I look at Beatrix; she's still catching her breath. It's different, with her coming.

"I suppose we could take the wagon," says William.

But a wagon won't fit along the stream. I take a deep breath, staring up at the horse's wide neck, his high haunches, and I pull my determination around me like armor. I learned to eat without a fork; I can learn to ride a horse.

"Beatrix, remind me how to get up, will you? It will come back to me soon enough."

"There's the spirit, my lady," she says.

My seat is already so sore, I won't be able to sit for a week. I'm bouncing around like a fool in spite of Beatrix's constant stream of advice to do this with my knees and that with my balance. Balance! How can I think about that when it's all I can do not to fall off? During a rare calm moment I hear

Beatrix murmuring to William, "Mayhap I'll ride Fidelius on the way back and give her old Bess here." Oh, I hear that perfectly well. And I see him nodding.

Mayhap? Not bloody likely! I clench my teeth. I may be sore, but I'll show them. I'll ride this beast there and back, even if I'm nothing but one big bruise when I'm done.

We clomp downhill for a while, following the well-worn way. It takes all my concentration just to stay upright. I don't even hear the stream until we come to the bridge. I pull the reins too sharply, and Fidelius skitters to a stop, tossing his head and snorting. I manage to hang on until he quiets down.

Then I close my eyes and assume a reverent expression, pretending I'm hearing a divine voice. "We must go here," I say. "Along this stream."

Riding down the embankment feels like careening off a cliff. My knuckles are white, one hand grasping the reins, the other tangled tight in the horse's mane. I sigh in relief when we reach the water's edge. It's easier now, on the flat. Once I realize I'm not going to fall off anytime soon, my breath quiets, and I become aware of birds singing in the trees, water murmuring around rocks, and sunlight filtering through the red and gold leaves. For a moment I almost feel I could come to enjoy this.

But we're nearing the field, and William and Beatrix mustn't see the lift. I have to go on from here by myself, just long enough to take a peek and make sure it's there, and then I'll come back and announce that my so-called vision was only a dream after all.

I stop, and they stop, watching me. Beatrix's eyes are bright with excitement.

I put on my listening look. Then, "I need to go on alone," I say.

"Not in the woods, my lady," says Beatrix.

"This is what I must do," I say in my most confident voice. "I'll be so close you can hear me."

I can almost see her thinking, *God wills it!* She sighs. "You call out every minute, then."

I nod, turning Fidelius through the trees, toward the opening and the light. I'm getting the hang of the reins, and as long as I don't tug too fast or too hard, Fidelius is surprisingly helpful. It's like he wants me to be in control, to tell him what to do. I go through the trees into the field. . . .

Where is it?

There's nothing here but long golden grass. Not a lift in sight.

My heart starts thumping around like a whisk beating in a bowl. Could I have the wrong place?

I turn Fidelius in a circle, my breath faster with every step. This is definitely where I came running out of the trees that day at sunset, though the leaves are already a deeper crimson.

The dead tree towers like a dark exclamation point. My eyes travel up the stripped trunk—

And there, on the jutting branch, sits a peregrine. A huge one, even bigger than Pilgrim. Just where I said it would be. And it's staring right at me.

I gasp, feeling dizzy. I made up that vision! How could it be coming true?

Fidelius senses my fear and whinnies.

"My lady?" Beatrix's voice rings through the trees. "Is everything all right? We're coming, we are!"

Then they're next to me, and William is reaching out an arm to steady me on the great horse's back, and Beatrix is gaping at the peregrine like it's the Virgin herself sitting up there on the branch. Suddenly—I don't believe this!—a ray of sun strikes the bird's feathers just like in a church picture, surrounding it with a circle of golden light.

Beatrix slides out of the saddle (it's lucky her horse is so much closer to the ground) and falls to her knees in the grass, clasping her hands to her chest. "It's a miracle!" she whispers. "A miracle!"

William stares at the falcon. At me. At the falcon again, as it spreads its striped wings wide and flaps from the branch, spiraling higher, and higher, until it's only a dot in the sky. Then even that is gone.

"Isn't it coming to the castle, then?" asks Beatrix.

I can't say anything. It was actually there, the peregrine, right when and where I said it would be! And that sunbeam, like a message from on high . . . I think of the bird—was this the same one?—that led me into town, and then to the shore, the shipwreck, Lady Matilda's jewels. . . . My heart is spinning and looping in great wide circles, like the bird's rising flight, and there's a space in my head so huge it scares me.

Beatrix is murmuring prayers. And William—William is glowing like there's a candle burning inside him.

"She was beautiful," he says, barely louder than a breath. Then he looks around the field and laughs so free and easy, it fills the big space in me, and I find myself leaning in relief against his strong arm, still there from when he reached over to keep me from falling.

"That's funny, that it was here," he says. "If you'd described that dead tree from your vision, I could have brought us in a third the time. I know this place well."

"You do?"

"A special place for me, this is."

He opens his mouth to say more, but all of a sudden he's staring at his hand on my shoulder, realizing it's still there. I become aware of the heat radiating from his touch, into my body, starting to flow through my blood. We startle and look up at the same time.

He pulls away, stepping his horse sideways until there's a gaping chasm between us. When he speaks again, his voice is short and clipped. "It's a good place for falcons. The brook. The open field."

The magic moment has passed. Now my mind starts to race again.

Where is that bloody lift? It should be here for nine more days yet! It can't have sidled off, now, can it? Grown little feet and gone traipsing into the trees?

The image is so ridiculous, I start to smile. But the more I think about it, the more it makes sense for the lift to disappear until the day dialed in for its return. You can't have people stumbling across a stray lift in a field, wondering what it is, messing about with the settings. Why would you even need a return dial if it just stayed?

That's it, of course! The lift is waiting back in the library. It will be here at sunset on the fifteenth day, and not a moment before. Relief washes over me, and now I can smell the grass again and hear the breeze rustling through the leaves.

"I'll take us back a faster way," says William.

Beatrix stops her murmuring and looks up. "Aren't we waiting for the bird to return?"

"No," I say. "It seems I was only meant to witness it, after all."

She clambers to her feet. William gets off his horse to help her back up on Bess.

"So much for having the mews become a holy place," she says.

"I do thank God for that," says William. "How would we care for his lordship's birds with townsfolk coming to stare?" His eyes roam the field. "No, this place is holy enough."

I follow his glance. I feel freer here, away from the castle's smoke and noise and careful manners. And I should make it a regular thing, going out through the gate. Customary, so no one is surprised if I come here the day the lift returns. And then there's William, and the way his hand felt on my shoulder. . . .

"It would please me to come back here with you," I say. "Hunting, and all."

"Hawking? As you please, your ladyship," he says carefully, though I think I see a bit of a spark in his eye. "We'll be flying Pilgrim off the creance soon. This is a good place for it, if you'd care to watch."

"Yes," I say. "I'd like that very much."

"And she's meant to work with the birds!" says Beatrix. "What else would her vision mean? It's a sign, that's what it is. Oh, wait until I tell Father Bartholomew!"

My lord, something terrible has occurred and I beg you to return with all possible haste. Lady Matilda is being sent visions from heaven. What is worse, they are coming true.

The lady was praying in the solar when she heard a divine voice, commanding her to find an angel in the guise of a peregrine falcon, bearing a halo of blinding gold. There is no doubt it was a holy vision and no mere dream, for on arriving at the place, all was as she had foreseen, as witnessed by her maidservant and the falconer's son.

Father Bartholomew, after deep prayer and study, has declared the lady destined, through her work with your lordship's falcons, to hear and spread the word of God. This profound connection to the divine has surprised many at Berringstoke, given the lady's lack of attendance at matins.

Perhaps we should have been forewarned by her tendency to exclaim, "My God!" as if expecting the holy presence.

I need hardly spell out the dangers that might ensue should the lady begin having visions on a regular basis. We had thought it sufficient to keep the document bearing your seal and that of Sir Giles under lock and key, but a lock would be worthless against divine revelation. Moreover, should the lady feel herself called to a life of contemplation in a convent before your marriage is found binding, then truly, my lord, disaster is upon us.

Yet even these reasons for your return pale beside the increased hostilities from Sir Giles. A skirmish near the territory in question wounded several men. I enclose a missive from your constable with more details. Each day your pledge remains unfilled, the threat to Berringstoke intensifies.

In spite of the danger, I raised no objection when Lady Matilda expressed a desire to work with your lordship's new peregrine, though it means leaving the safety of the castle walls. This noble activity indicates a welcome return to worldly concerns, and may distract her from unwelcome prying. The proposed field is safely centered in your demesne, and her ladyship will be with a falconer and maidservant at all times. Should you consider this insufficient, I will send a man-at-arms, but I need hardly remind you how dangerously undermanned the castle is at present.

I have succeeded, thus far, in keeping word of Sir Giles from Lady Matilda, impressing upon everyone the importance of preventing further anxiety in her weakened condition.

The cloth we purchased was delivered and cut in time for new garments to be worn to the memorial service. These will show Berringstoke in the best light for your wedding. I have also disbursed funds for lumber to make repairs in the bailey, in the hope that visitors of some importance might arrive for the nuptials.

Anxiously awaiting word of your arrival, I remain most loyally and fully dedicated to the furtherance of your estate,

Eustace, Steward of Berringstoke

From His
Glove to Mine

Everything is going gloriously well. After my so-called
vision, it's *my lady* this, and *my lady* that, and can I get you
more wine or another cushion perhaps, my lady? It's lovely.

Beatrix is still finishing up in my room as I head downstairs. Today I'm going back to the field.

William is standing outside the mews in the sun, the
peregrine perched on his fist. "Come meet Pilgrim properly,"
he says with a smile.

I come so close, I can see the outline of every feather.
Her back is the blue-gray of stormy ocean water, the feathers
rippling over one another like tiny waves. Her wing and tail
feathers are something different altogether: striped and long,
folded like the slats of a Japanese fan.

As I stare, Pilgrim stretches her wings to soak up the

morning sun. She gives a small flap, and the fan of her tail spreads wide, each feather distinct. She lifts her face to the bright light, drinking it in. Suddenly, she fluffs up; for a moment she looks as downy as a chick, but then she pulls her feathers in, even sleeker than before. Her breast shivers lightly.

"Is she cold?" I ask.

He laughs. "That's happiness, it is. She seems to like you."

Happy. That's how I feel, too. But it's something more. "What is it called," I ask, "when she fluffs up like that?"

"Rousing."

I feel like I'm rousing right now. Like a shiver of joy is running through me, making me open up suddenly and soak in the whole world. That's just how I feel.

William walks to the door of the mews and holds it open for me. "We'll gather our gear and let my father know we're ready."

Inside, birds stand quietly on their perches, most of them on one foot, the other foot tucked so far into their chest feathers, they look like a bunch of one-legged pirates. Along one wall there's a long narrow table with a hide sprawled across the wood, and a knife lies nearby, ready to cut the supple leather. Loops of polished leather and sturdy long gloves dangle from pegs on the wall. A door at the far end of the room reveals shelves laden with small pots, like an apothecary shop.

Everything, even the gravel spread on the floor, is spotlessly clean. The soft cooing of pigeons floats through the wall.

William's father looks up from the great white falcon standing on his wrist. It's the first time I've seen him so close, and I'm surprised to find father and son are nothing alike. Where William is fair and slim, Harold is a solid, broad-shouldered wall of a man with dark hair and eyes as brown as hazelnuts. There's a sense of command and confidence about him, the air of a man used to making quick decisions.

"Your ladyship," he says, with a brief bow of his head, and now I also see the kindness in his eyes.

I follow his glance back to the falcon on his glove. It's larger than Pilgrim, snow-white feathers flecked with black. A low brow and powerful neck make it look cross and regal at the same time.

Harold lifts up one of the falcon's bright yellow feet and peers closely. "Seems I'm staying here today," he says to William. "Since her ladyship's going to the field, she can hold Pilgrim on the glove."

"Bumblefoot?" asks William.

"Bumblefoot!" I laugh. "Is that the bird's name? Not very dignified, is it?"

But Harold doesn't smile. "Nothing funny about bumble-foot. 'Tis a disease that can kill a bird. No, this one's name is

Lightning. The king's own gyrfalcon, she is, and mewed at our expense. A great honor for us to be trusted with her care. But should any harm come to her . . . Well, let's just say the bird had best be healthy when the king arrives."

"The king?" I ask, trying to remember which king it would be. Henry I? No, too early. Richard the Lionhearted? Still too early. "When is he coming?"

The white falcon jerks her head in my direction, but Harold doesn't seem to hear a word I've said, he's looking so intently at those yellow feet. Then, to William: "A bruise. I need to make up some salve so it doesn't turn worse." He sets the bird on a perch, nods to me, and heads into the back room.

"I'm afraid it's just us and Beatrix, then," says William, picking up a leather coil and putting it into the bag draped over his shoulder. "More work for you, it turns out. Do you mind?"

I look up into his blue eyes. I don't mind one bit.

Beatrix is sitting against a tree trunk, sewing. The horses are grazing nearby. And I'm standing in a field of golden grass, so close to William, I can feel his breath.

The bell on Pilgrim's leg sings gaily as she steps from William's glove to mine. His fingers shape my hand, showing me how to hold the leather jesses fastened above her feet.

"Now the creance," he says, attaching a long line.

Then he turns and walks a distance away.

Pilgrim is much lighter than I expected. No need to brace my arm so tight. If I hold my upper arm close to my body and bend my elbow, like William showed me, I can stay with her on my wrist forever. I relax, and Pilgrim adjusts her feet easily on the glove.

"Are you ready?" calls William.

I nod, and he swings the lure in a circle before tossing it high in the air.

Pilgrim spreads her great wings wide, there's a rush of wind, and the next thing I know, she's standing on the ground near William, the lure firmly grasped in her talons. He motions me over.

"First time, and she came right off!" he says, looking at me like he realizes it could be a fine thing, having me along.

He pulls a strip of meat from his pouch and holds it out near Pilgrim, nudging it closer until she drops the lure and gets back on his glove to take the tidbit. He stands, murmuring to her, words of praise and affection. And then he whistles again, that same dancing phrase I heard the first day.

"Why is it always the same tune?" I ask.

"So she'll know it later, even from high in the air," he says. "It's her tune, to come back to."

And I realize I want one, too. A tune to come back to.

When it's time to go, I walk toward Fidelius, and he raises his head from the grass with a gentle nicker. I reach a hand to his side, feeling the strength and warmth of it. William makes a stirrup with his hands to boost me back up. Fidelius stays still while I settle. I pat his neck and lean over, whispering, "Thank you."

Now William helps Beatrix, and I wait, perfectly content. The sun sparkling on the leaves, the light wind teasing my hair, the warm look in William's eyes—it feels right, being here with him. As if I've been doing it all my life.

And then a cold current in the breeze whispers in my ear: *Like mother, like daughter.* Caroline's voice.

Fidelius takes a step sideways.

Who's your father, then, Addy?

But I'm not Addy anymore, I think fiercely, my hands tightening on the reins. I force the voice back into rustling leaves.

I glance at William. Pilgrim is perched on his left wrist; his right hand reaches to the saddle, and he swings up in a single supple movement before turning to me with an easy smile. Here, I get to do what I want.

Baudekin Cloth

Beatrix is rushing across the great hall clutching a bundle. When she sees me come through the door, she skitters to a stop.

"Oh, my lady!" she cries, bobbing a curtsey. "Such news!"

The bundle slips from her arms to the rushes, and she gapes, so horrified you'd think it was a baby. But as soon as she grabs it back up, she beams at me.

"Come see!" she says, hurrying to the table. "Over here!"

The great hall is especially gloomy today, the windows mere slivers of stone-gray sky. A few candles struggle to illuminate the cavernous space. Beatrix sets her armload down on the dark wood under the brightest candle. She pulls off the outer wrapping, and out tumbles a shimmering, sinuous river of golden fabric, the most beautiful I've ever seen.

I pick up a corner and lift it to my cheek. Oh, what Mum would say to work with stuff like this!

Beatrix gazes down with something like awe. "The king himself sent it for your wedding dress. Baudekin cloth, the finest silk with a warp of gold."

Of course! Only a king would have access to something so grand. I unroll a length of fabric and drape it around my shoulders like a luxurious shawl, hug it close, feel the flow and heft of it. And it's mine, I think, all smug. Me, the lady of the castle.

"I couldn't wait to find you and try the gold against your dark hair," says Beatrix. "I knew it. Perfect. The king himself! Imagine!" She sighs in contentment. "And that message he sent with it!"

"Message?" I ask, from somewhere in a dream.

"Yes! He sent it with the message that—"

"That he will indeed be honoring us with his presence," says Eustace, strutting in from the far door. His chest is a sail puffed full of wind. "What is more, His Majesty sent these to adorn the gown."

He produces a crimson pouch and tilts it over the cloth. Out pours a sparkling stream of pearls, and gems so green, they must be emeralds. They catch every ray of candlelight as they circle into a shimmering pool.

I gasp in pleasure. "For . . . me?"

Eustace nods. Beatrix beams like a proud new parent.

I gather up a handful of pearls and let them trickle through my fingers. Light swirls inside them like moonbeams.

"We had hoped His Majesty would come for the wedding," says Eustace, his eyes reflecting the emeralds' glint and shine. "But we couldn't be certain until now. He didn't do that for his other wards. You will be attired in a spectacular gown, his gift, as he witnesses the wedding he arranged, with everyone watching. Everyone."

There's a greedy joy to his voice, as if the jewels are all his, as if he's the one getting married.

"And I'm to sew the kirtle!" cries Beatrix. "I must get to work."

She starts to pick up the jewels, but Eustace holds out a cupped palm, his mouth narrowing into a tight line. "I'll keep an eye on those," he says briskly. "You may inform me when the gown is ready for adornment. Until then, they remain under lock and key."

He gathers up the rest of the gems and counts them twice before slipping them back into the pouch. Then he starts backing away, the treasure clutched to his chest. "And now, if you will pardon me, my lady, there are a great many preparations to be made for His Majesty's arrival. You may rest assured we will show Berringstoke to its best advantage."

I'm so caught up in the Midas spell of the golden cloth, I merely nod.

Beatrix starts to fold the fabric. "Baudekin cloth," she sighs in contentment. "Who would have thought it?"

"And sent by the king himself," I say.

And then, as if the words are still hanging in the air, I finally hear what Eustace said. "Beatrix, what does that mean, that I'm the king's ward?"

She makes that clucking, concerned sound of hers, the one that means *your poor hurt head*. "Of course," she says. "Let me remind you. Your parents died of the fever—naught but a small child you were, they say—and the king took control of your estate until you should wed."

Something tightens in my chest.

"He's the one arranged your marriage," she goes on. "Because our Sir Hugh has been such a help to him in his battles. If there's one thing that man can do, it's fight!"

But what if the king knows Lady Matilda? What if they were close? The questions start circling like a flock of ravens. What if someone else from her court comes for the wedding? What if—

My hand drifts down to stroke the silken cloth, and now it's as if the gold itself is speaking, reassuring me. *What if you make this work? What if you keep all this for your own?*

I can still feel those pearls in my palm, their cool, almost liquid weight.

Beatrix straightens, the Baudekin cloth once again secure in her arms. "How long a train to the kirtle, I wonder?"

"Quite long," I say.

She nods eagerly. "Oh, do let me do a first fitting!"

And together we hurry up the stairs to drape that dazzling fabric all over me.

Noble Blood Will Out

"How goes your work with the falcons, my lady?" asks Father Bartholomew as I pass him the salt.

"Very well, thank you," I say. "Today Pilgrim flew from my glove without the creance. Harold and William say she'll be hunting in no time."

Father Bartholomew nods. He picks up a chicken leg and takes a big bite, gulps it down, then leans forward confidentially and asks in a low, eager voice, "And was the angel bird there again today?"

I shake my head, wiping my mouth on the napkin before taking a sip from the goblet I share with Eustace, just like Beatrix taught me. I glance down to the lively throng at the trestle tables, half expecting to see her gazing up at me with approval. But the room is so full of talk and laughter and harp music, of platters brought and wine poured, of blazing fire and flickering candles, I give up and turn back to the chaplain.

"I don't think the bird is coming back," I say. "The vision was telling me to go out in the glory of God's creation and work with falcons, to learn from them. That's all."

Eustace leans forward from my other side. "Noble blood will out," he says to Father Bartholomew. "After the terrible blow Lady Matilda suffered, perhaps the Lord meant to reassure her, through her inborn talent with these regal birds, of the strength of her own noble blood."

Noble blood? If only they knew. I shift uncomfortably and take a good swig of the wine—damn! I forgot to wipe my mouth first that time. But Eustace is too intent on addressing Father Bartholomew to notice.

While they're going on about my pleasure in hawking and how noble that is, Timothy clears away the meat dish. He's the boy who was lugging rushes the day I came. Then the skinny boy I've seen at the well brings a dish of pears baked in wine. The warm scents of cinnamon and clove fill the air.

A stir from below draws my attention. People are looking up from their trenchers at three men who've just come in. They're washing their hands at the basin by the door, the one used by everyone but those of us at the high table. One of them, a burly man, only washes one hand; his other arm is strapped across his chest, swathed in bandages, and the linen is stained dark where blood seeped through. I've heard the clash of steel from outside the walls—training sessions, Eustace says. A shiver runs down my spine. Is that what happened to his arm?

As they walk to a table, others clear a space, murmuring and fussing over the wounded man. And then they're swallowed up in the hall's rambunctious calling and boasting, the boys rushing forward with trenchers and goblets, the dogs snuffling about hopefully in the rushes.

I pull my attention back to our table. The butler is filling my goblet. No common earthenware jug up here, but a silver ewer shaped like a dragon. Red wine pours from its mouth like flame.

Now Eustace and Father Bartholomew have moved on to debating the details for the plaque commemorating my holy vision, the one being carved for the church in town. Father Bartholomew feels it should be large enough to show the entire tree with an actual angel perched in its branches. Eustace is concerned about the cost. And me, I'm trying to figure out how to change the conversation. I have to admit I'm getting uncomfortable with the results of my made-up vision. I didn't think it would go this far, with everyone staring at me all reverent, and the pantler crossing himself each time he offers me more of his fine white bread. No, I'd rather talk about something else.

I glance over my shoulder at the huge empty chair against the tapestry, waiting for the arrival of Sir Hugh. My husband-to-be, I think, and I start to feel queasy. He should arrive in a matter of days. It's time I knew something more about him than his name. So when there's a gap in the conversation, I look at Father Bartholomew and ask, "What would Sir Hugh say about the carving?"

He guffaws, and a little bit of pear flies out of his mouth. He dabs apologetically with his napkin, then says, "Sir Hugh, care about a thing like that? He's never here! Leaves it all to Eustace!"

Eustace puts down the goblet. "Now, Father . . . "

"Likes the warrior's life, he does! Never happier than when he's off serving the king, raising that great bloody sword of his on the battlefield, lopping off heads left and right!"

Eustace raises his voice a bit, his eyes narrowing. "Father—"

"And when there's no war to please him, well, it's off to every tournament he can find. And not just for the racing and jousting and tilting and the like, the fine scrimmages on the field. No, it's for the drinking that goes on afterward, isn't it, Eustace?" He gives a hearty laugh. "Because, my, does our Sir Hugh enjoy his wine! Small wonder the buttery's so low on butts of wine all the time! Now, if he spent the time on farming he spends on—"

"You there!" cries Eustace, waving to the harpist. "Let's have another tune!" As the gay notes strike up, he calls to Timothy to clear away the last of the pears. Father Bartholomew pauses, befuddled.

Eustace bends toward me. "It is indeed my honor that Sir Hugh entrusts me with the management of the estate while he fulfills a knight's true destiny, defending the honor of the realm and serving the king."

"The king," I say. And suddenly it comes to me. "King Henry the Third! From 1216 to—"

Both men stop, staring. There's a long pause.

"What a . . . good . . . king," I say feebly, searching for words. They're still staring.

Eustace finally nods. "Indeed, my lady," he says, very slowly. He signals to the boy with the pitcher. "I believe Lady Matilda wishes to wash her hands."

I clamp my mouth shut, determined not to let another word sneak out. Instead of my ridiculous outburst, I should

have asked when Sir Hugh arrives. In only five days the lift will be here. I may well have to decide whether to take it without knowing if the lord of the castle has met his bride-to-be. That's the only thing that matters, isn't it? Whether I'm safe and can stay.

As for the rest of it? I hold my hands over the bowl, washing them in the thin stream of water. It seems Sir Hugh is a drinker, a fighter. What did I expect, a whist-playing fop? Here, marriage is obviously not a meeting of hearts, but a tactical alliance. I'm heading for one of the richest. And, provided I don't make too many more mistakes like my gaffe about the king, it's as good as mine.

The Lure

$\cancel{\text{≫}}$

William stands at the edge of the field and hands me my glove. Once I have it on, he holds his arm up to mine, and Pilgrim steps over. In the past few days she's flown from my glove to the lure with the creance, and then without. Today she'll soar free above us. She rouses, and joy flashes through my veins, as if it's me on the glove, knowing I'm about to sail into that limitless ocean of sky.

William reaches into his saddlebag for the lure and slips it into the pouch at his side. He sees the question in my eyes. "To call her back," he says.

"Won't she come back to you anyway?"

"Ah, it needs to be her choice." He smiles. "You're never a falcon's master; you're her equal. Not like herd animals. Dogs live to obey, and horses and men like to know who's in charge. But what cares a falcon if you approve or no?" He gazes down at Pilgrim. "She'll always be wild at heart." Then, softer: "You feel it. I know you do."

There's that flash of joy again. I catch my breath, glancing up at him, but he's already turning, walking toward the center of the field. I hurry to catch up. "The lure might help if something in the distance catches her eye," he says. "And we never fly when it's too warm, when gulls cross the sky without once flapping their wings. A soaring day, we call it. Hawks ride the rising air like a magic carpet."

We're in the open now, and he stops, gazing into the distance, his profile all high cheekbone and strong jaw. "She'd fill with the glory of it. And mayhap she'd never come back."

"You sound as if you know how it feels."

He takes a step closer. "And you," he says, lifting a gentle hand to stroke the back of Pilgrim's head. "Haven't you ever lost yourself in something you love?" And then he looks up into my eyes.

My heart stops. My head stops. Everything stops. There's just William looking at me, and nothing between us.

Suddenly, my heart is racing like it's never done before. Pilgrim bates, flapping and jumping backward off the glove. I clutch the cord tighter, trying to remember how calm flows through William when he holds her. I breathe deeply, soothing my own heart so I can soothe hers.

"There now," I say, as softly and confidently as I can. She settles back on the glove. I give William an embarrassed smile. "I must be too eager to see her fly."

"She's excited, too." He scans the sky. "We'll loose the creance. She'll stay on your glove. You'll be facing into the wind. When I tell you, step forward and drop your hand to cast off."

"Where is she, William? Is she gone?"

He laughs and points over the tops of some distant trees, and I pick it out again: a moving pinprick in a blue wilderness.

"She's spotted that kestrel," says William. Then he nods. "Good, she's not going to bother with it."

How can he see so much from here? I can't even keep my eyes on that dot! He must have a falcon's vision himself. He watches intently and then suddenly says, "There. She's making the turn."

He swings the lure overhead. Before I take my next breath, the speck in the sky is zooming toward us, closer, and bigger, and for a split second I see wings pressed in so tight, she's a raindrop, a bullet shooting toward the earth, and the sky sounds like it's ripping in two—

Pilgrim stands atop the lure on the ground, panting. She

starts tearing bits of flesh from it, trying to turn it over with a talon to get at the meat on the other side.

William pulls a tidbit from his pouch and kneels beside her, whistling those soft lilting notes. She looks over eagerly and steps to his glove. He stands, watching as she tears into the meat with focused contentment. Again he whistles that refrain, and something quivers in me, like those notes are a message calling from another world.

"What a stoop!" he says, all proud. "Did you see the height she had? You picked a good day to come."

Yes, I think, looking at Pilgrim, then back up at his glowing face. Yes, I did.

I'm running up the stairs to the keep when I remember, *Walk like a lady!* I slow to a dignified pace, glancing around anxiously, but no one seems to have noticed. They're all too busy with what I now know are wedding preparations, sprucing things up for His Majesty King Henry III.

I step inside, and the dark is so sudden, it feels like night. The skinny boy, Ralph, is only now starting to light the candles on their tall iron stands, as other lads pull out trestles to set up tables for dinner. There's a clinking from behind the curtained partitions at the back of the hall, where the butler and pantler and boys are always rushing during meals. My path to the stairs brings me closer. One of the red curtains draws back, and a man comes out with a rag; behind him I see dark wooden casks and a row of clay jugs. The silver dragon stands guard.

Wine, I think, flowing like water . . . like wind . . . and now it's the field I'm seeing, and William's face tilted upward, lit by the autumn sun, and his eyes as he follows Pilgrim's flight, as he turns to me—

Slap!

The sound of a hand striking flesh stops me cold.

Behind a closed curtain, someone draws a shuddering breath. My feet won't move. As if it's me who's been slapped. Me who's been discovered.

"Thought you could get away with it, did you?" The voice is so low and menacing, it takes me a moment to recognize the speaker: Eustace, all his studied charm stripped away.

"Please, sir!" cries a boy. I can hear the tears he's fighting back. "It won't happen again, I swear. On my life, I swear!"

"Your life? That will hardly be necessary," says Eustace. There's a strange undercurrent to his tone, a mix of threat and . . . pleasure. *He's enjoying this*. "But your hands, let's talk about those. Missing even one of them could be, shall we say, inconvenient."

The boy is sobbing openly now.

"I will not tolerate theft," says Eustace, hard and brusque. "Consider yourself warned."

Too late, I recognize the tone of finality. The curtain rips open, and suddenly Eustace is standing before me, his eyes small and brutal, his mouth a slash across his face. I flinch as the mouth curves up into a fawning smile.

"My lady," he says with a sweeping bow, as if nothing had happened. As if he'd only been doing his job. "May I be of some assistance?"

I shake my head, unable to say a word. He backs away respectfully, turning only when he reaches the door.

The curtain has closed again. I take a step, lift the edge— it's a pantry, with cutting boards and knives, and loaf after loaf of bread lined up, awaiting the meal. And staring out at me, a boy I've never seen before, no more than eight or nine years old, and so thin, he's little more than a skeleton with huge brown eyes. He clasps his hand to his cheek, trying to hide the flaming imprint of another, larger hand.

With a sob, he rushes past me, and something small and pale glances off his foot, like a mouse skittering away. It comes to a stop, and I stare in disbelief: a single piece of fine white bread, with one bite taken out of it. Could *this* be the reason Eustace was threatening to chop off his hand?

Someone needs to stand up for the boy! I know what it's like, being powerless, having to take what's handed out to you. I start walking toward the door Eustace went through. Behind it rises a second spiral stair, one I've never climbed. But no sooner do I start than a flicker of doubt slows my steps. What do I know of this world and its rules? I barely know the table manners. I've just learned to wipe my cup when I sip. . . .

And then I stop completely, as fear and caution chase my righteous anger away. If I tell Eustace this lady won't abide such injustice, he may start looking too closely at the lady in question. I'm not safe here yet myself.

In the end, it's my own stair I take, my stomach twisting with every turn, my face burning as if I'm the one bearing the mark of the steward's hand.

Came in a Box

At first I went to the field for the sake of the lift. But something is changing.

Each day when I rise, Beatrix brings me bread and wine and dresses me in a sturdy kirtle, good for riding. A quick visit to the castle chapel for matins, and then she and I meet William in the mews, and we're off to the field. Sun or rain or wind, it doesn't matter; rain beads up on Pilgrim's feathers like pearls, and as for wind, she prefers it, facing into a gale with a special alertness. As she stands on my wrist, I sense her excitement, and it starts to fill me, too.

Each day I count how much longer until the lift is in the field: only three more days now. And as for Sir Hugh arriving, it's clear that "sennight" of which Beatrix spoke in the wagon was just a guess. I'm used to time being something you count by the second, to people complaining if their train is five minutes late. Here there are no minutes, no clocks ticking away. Here there's breakfast and dinner and supper, there's matins in the morning and the sun high for noon. And days of the week? They'd rather talk of which saint's day it is. No one knows exactly when Sir Hugh will return. "Soon," they say. "Soon."

I wish it were never.

As I'm walking past the ovens in the bailey, I see the new boy feeding the chickens, the slap now a dull bruise across his cheek. A wave of shame washes over me. A cook has just pulled out a tray of little cakes scattered with walnuts. "May I have one?" I ask, and he practically falls over himself finding one that's cool enough to hold and hand over. I take a single bite, then walk to the boy.

"What is your name?"

His brown eyes get even larger. "They call me Tip, my lady."

"Well, Tip, I find I'm full and I don't want to waste this. Here."

I've been hungry before.

I enter the mews. William is settling Pilgrim on her perch. Harold comes in with Lightning and does the same. Two men, each with a great falcon, tying jesses with a one-handed knot. So smooth and easy it all is. As they step away, I follow them over to the table.

"That's why you're so good with them," I say to William, glancing from father to son. "It's in your blood."

Harold laughs, turning his head back to look at me. "Blood? Not likely. Came in a box, he did!"

William laughs, too, and his father claps an arm around his shoulders. It's clear they're enjoying an old familiar joke. Even the pigeons chortle and rustle on the other side of the wall. Everyone is in on this joke but me.

"A box?" I say.

They hang up their gloves. "Care to join us, my lady?" asks Harold. We're comfortable together, the three of us. He clears off a bench and nods at me, and once I sit, they sit and pull over some straps of leather and start oiling them, not needing a word between them.

"Well?" I finally ask. "Are you going to tell me or not? What box?"

"That's what he said at the time," says Harold, gazing with pride at the tall young man beside him. "Just you look at him, my lady. Thin as a heron's leg. Straight nose, as bold as the gyr's beak. Hair like sunlit sand, he has. He didn't get that from me, now, did he?"

I contemplate Harold's dark hair, his sturdy frame. "His looks must come from his mother, then," I say.

"God bless her soul," says Harold.

William looks up from the leather he's working into shining suppleness. "I never knew my mother," he says.

But he doesn't look sad, and there's no bitterness in his voice. And Harold is humming away under his breath, not at all like someone mourning a beloved wife.

"Tell me," I say.

Harold lays down his work, folds his hands on the table, and leans back as if preparing for a long tale.

"It was back in the old lord's day," he says. "I was flying Blackthorn. Now there was a peregrine for you! Faster than the wind, she was. It was near the stream, the one as what comes down from the lake, and Blackthorn brought down a fine fat mallard. I was running over when out he toddles from the undergrowth, this one. No taller than a brachet hound, with pudgy legs and eyes as round as a falcon's. All on his own. I called out for his people, but no one answered.

"Well, what was I to do? Got him up on the horse with me and tried to search, but I couldn't cover much ground balancing bird and boy and reins, so I brought him back to the castle. The whole time on horseback, the two of them were like a pair of eyases in the nest. Not a ruffled feather on Blackthorn, nor a peep from the lad. Amazing it was.

"Once we got back, the women swept up the lad and cosseted and cuddled him, and I went out again with the men. We searched everywhere. Asked in town. Never did find out what happened to his people. And him so plump, he must have been well cared for."

I glance at William's lanky frame. He catches my eye; I feel my cheeks flushing.

"Robbers killed them," he says, "and hid the bodies. That's what they thought."

Harold nods. "We kept asking the lad: 'Who are your folks? Where's your home? How did you get here?' And all he would say is he came in a box."

"They asked everyone who passed this way for months," says William. "No one knew of a missing child, a murdered family. So he kept me."

"How could I not?" asks Harold. "He kept escaping his nurse's watch. Slipped off, and every time, I'd come into the mews and here he'd be, sitting near Blackthorn, or watching the other birds, and boy and birds as comfortable as could be. Like family. Him and me, we decided we're family, too. Well, we're always together, aren't we? And him calling me Da from that first day. No, his way with birds isn't through my blood. But it's in *his* blood, right enough."

"And the box," I ask. "Was it a trunk? A wagon?"

"I don't remember," William says with a shrug. "And it doesn't matter to me. It brought me to this life."

I look at his sure, slim hands working the leather. Yes, this is the life he was born to live, even if he had to get lost to find it.

Wild

The next day, Beatrix heaves herself off the horse with a sigh. "Oh, my aching back! Can't do this all that much longer, my lady."

I wrap my arm around her and help her settle against a tree trunk at the field's edge. "Beatrix, you're the one who told me I can't come without you."

She pulls some needlework from her bag. "You'll have a proper lady-in-waiting when his lordship returns," she says. "Not that long now. One who's better on horseback."

"I'd rather you stay with me, Beatrix."

She smiles at me warmly and pats my hand. "But it's not quite proper, is it? For one of your position to have only a townswoman like me? You need more suitable female companionship." She glances over at William as he casts Pilgrim skyward. "Well, it's all coming soon enough, isn't it?"

She arranges the cloak around her shoulders and looks down to her needle. Before long, she's leaning back against the tree, mouth open, eyes closed.

As William and I walk about the field, he keeps glancing in her direction. Once she starts snoring, he calls Pilgrim down with the lure.

"There's something I want to show you," he says, settling the falcon on his wrist. "Because of the other day, when we talked about the wildness in Pilgrim. But we'd have to go alone, the two of us."

I glance at Beatrix, my pulse quickening. "She'll be fine here," I say.

He leads the way on foot into the woods, Pilgrim on his glove. Our steps are soft on the carpet of colored leaves. Each day, the branches are barer; more sideways light slants through. The forest is sparks of orange and red and gold, like stained glass. We walk upstream, and soon I see the glint of open water ahead.

William stops. "Promise you won't tell," he says, his voice low.

Where is he taking me? I look at his mouth, the hint of a smile on his broad lips, and my heart starts galloping like a runaway horse. I'm thankful Pilgrim is on his fist, not mine, or she'd flap and bate for sure.

"I promise."

He steps over a fallen tree trunk, then turns back to help me, his hand taking mine. I cross to his side, but somehow we both forget to let go, and I'm aware of the warmth of his skin as he leads me deeper, toward the stream's source. Finally, when we can see it flowing from the lake, singing and sparkling over shining gravel, he lets go and points. A peregrine perches on a branch overlooking the water. It's so wild and beautiful, I catch my breath.

William smiles. "I hoped he'd be here again today."

We sit near a bush so we're hidden by its crimson leaves. He leans closer. "I didn't tell my father. I couldn't bear to trap this one. I thought you'd understand."

I understand that he's trusting me with a dangerous secret: the son of the castle falconer, giving up the chance to own a valuable bird, so it can live wild. I understand the beauty of this lake, with the sun swirling through the last morning mist, a fish splashing, songbirds calling to one another in the trees. I understand that I'm sitting so close to his side, I feel him breathing.

The peregrine stretches his wings to the morning sun. An easy flap and he's circling the lake, swooping so close to the branches, the songbirds shriek in alarm, and a crow caws, "Hawk! Hawk!" Then the falcon spirals down to the graveled stream bank and plunges in, splashing up a shower of diamonds. I gasp, as if the freezing water is sharp on my own skin, as if those bright stones are tumbling under my feet.

The falcon flies back to the branch in the sun, and begins preening with beak and claw.

"There's a part of me loves the wildness in them best of all," William says softly. He pauses, as if trying to decide whether to tell me something. Then: "This spring I was climbing the cliffs and came on a scrape with three peregrine eyases. I sat and watched the tiercel bring back his kill, the falcon soar out to him, turning upside down in flight to grasp the prey. It was pure song. And as I watched"—his voice is almost a whisper now—"I heard them speaking, one to the other."

"Speaking?" I say, filled with the strangeness of it.

He leans closer, confiding, until his shoulder is touching mine. "Oh, it was bird tongue, chirrups and cries, but I swear they understand each other, the same as you and I. And I swear, yes, I swear they feel love, though the priests would call it sacrilege to say so." He looks at me, his blue eyes intense as flame. "How can love be sacrilege?"

Sacrilege. In this world, that means he's trusting me

with his life, to say such thoughts out loud. I shiver, and I don't know if it's because of his trust, or the danger, or the awareness of his body so close to mine.

I only say, "Did they fly free?"

He nods. "My father saw them then and hoped to catch them, but we never did. He would call it madness, not taking them when I could. And perhaps I am mad, for they were worth a fortune." He sees the doubt in my eyes. "Truly, a fortune. Say a peasant stole a peregrine eyas, tried to sell it on the sly for a purse of gold? He'd pay with his life. And as for a gyrfalcon, not even Sir Hugh, with all his lands and riches, could afford one such as Lightning."

The wild bird draws my eye with a rouse. The glistening feathers lie smooth to his body, as sleek as an otter's pelt. He lifts his head, tests the air with his wings, then rises with a few powerful strokes above the trees.

William stands and holds down his free hand to help me up. But Pilgrim's head turns sharply to the side, and William freezes. "Wait," he whispers, sinking back into a crouch. "Quiet."

A moment later, my ears catch the sound of horses riding through the woods. William must not want the men to see us without Beatrix. I nod and settle back down as still as can be.

But the four men who ride to the lake have blue tunics, not green, and the sun sparks off chain mail. These aren't Sir Hugh's men.

The horses lower their heads to drink. The riders don't say a word; their silence is tangible, almost solid, and their heads keep turning from side to side, looking, listening. There's a rustle in the trees, and to a man they reach for the hilts of their swords—but it's only a crow, hopping from branch to branch. William and I pull farther beneath the red leaves. His hand is tight around mine. On his other arm, Pilgrim is absolutely still.

When the horses are done drinking, one of the men raises his hand, motioning to the others, and they slip back into the trees, as stealthily as they came.

"William," I whisper, but he shakes his head, and I'm silent. Every part of him is aware, ready to spring, his face so alert, it frightens me. Finally, after a long minute, he stands and whispers, *"Go!"*

I wait until we reach the trail, and then I ask, "Who were they?"

"You don't know? They wear the blue of Sir Giles. His men, on Sir Hugh's land, and meaning no good, by the looks of them."

I breathe in, and the air is sharp with danger. Suddenly

I picture Beatrix, alone, asleep, completely vulnerable. "Hurry!" I cry, taking off down the trail.

William is close at my heels. "As soon as we have her, we'll gallop back to warn the castle," he says. "They'll send out a search party, put everyone on alert."

"No!" I stop, turning around to face him. "Don't tell!"

He stares at me in disbelief. "But there's danger about. We need to be prepared."

"Only four men. That's not enough for an attack, is it?"

He shakes his head. "But if it's a scouting party, more might come later."

"And they might not," I say urgently. "For God's sake, William, don't you see what will happen if you tell? I'll never get to come out here again. Never! I'll be trapped inside the castle walls, and there'll be no more flying Pilgrim. No more being here, with you."

We both glance at the trail ahead, and then we're running again, his hand holding mine as if to keep me safe. Along the stream, back to the edge of the field—

And there's Beatrix, snoring as safe as can be under her red and golden tree.

He turns to me, a question in his eyes.

"Let me be free," I whisper.

Slowly, very slowly, he nods, deciding to take the risk.

Fitting

꧁

I stand in my shift in the middle of the solar, the candles guttering on their stands, a cold wind howling outside the shuttered window. The fire in the hearth struggles to keep the chill at bay. Two more days and the lift will be standing in the field, and with no word of Sir Hugh arriving, it's clear I won't know by then whether I'm safe here or not. And now there's William. . . .

"Here you go then, my lady," says Beatrix. She holds the golden kirtle high so I can slip it over my head. There aren't any sleeves yet; this is only the second fitting. She fluffs the skirt out full around me and starts tugging at the waist to see how much tighter it should go.

There's a quick, easy confidence in the way she handles the fabric that reminds me of Mum. I never got that good.

Mum said it was all the time I spent on schooling and reading and the like. If I were at it twelve hours a day, then I'd
know my way around a dress, that's what she always said.

Suddenly, sadness takes hold of my heart and rips it
down the middle like a length of cloth. It should be Mum
sewing my wedding dress! Mum, who's probably sitting up
late right now, stitching; a cup of tea growing cold by her
side; no company to keep the silence at bay. I wish she were
here to see me wed.

Or do I?

I look down at the priceless fabric swirling about me,
and I start to feel embarrassed. Fabric sent by a king for my
marriage to a man I don't even know. When there's another,
a lad I know better all the time. I know the light in his eyes,
and the gentle knowledge in his voice, his hands. I know
how his face is alert when he's judging the wind, how it
softens when he gazes at me. How intently he kept me safe.

A shining circle appears on the cloth. Another, and
another.

"Tears?" says Beatrix. "Why, my lady! Whatever is the
matter?"

And then I'm sobbing, and Beatrix is wrapping her arm
around me and leading me to the window seat, replacing
the slinky silk with a thick, warm fur. She wraps me in a

comforting hug, not worried about my grand-ladyness at all.

"Now, now," she murmurs. "They say Sir Hugh is delayed again. It may be a good long while until he comes. And it's not so bad, is marriage. Not so bad at all."

Not a Lady

Beatrix says I might want to spend more time stitching, or learning how to oversee the castle's works and accounts. And the chapel. I might spend more time in the chapel. Not quite so much time in the mews, my lady, or out in the field. That's what she says.

But there's nowhere else I want to be. I'm only alive now when I'm with the falcons, with William. My brain keeps trying to remind me that Sir Hugh will be here before long, that the lift is about to arrive, that I must be prepared. . . .

And then my heart tells my brain to be quiet, so it can picture how William's eyes scan the sky, seeing everything, no matter how small; how his hands are strong and gentle at the same time, holding a bird, or tying that one-handed

falconer's knot, or grasping the pommel for the smooth
leap up to his horse's back; how the corners of his mouth
lift in that irresistible smile—and there's no room to think
of anything else. No room at all.

The dead tree stands like a sentinel at the edge of the field.
Tomorrow at sunset the lift will be waiting beneath that outstretched branch. I need to decide. But now the decision is
about so much more than merely whether I'm safe.

William and I are walking around the field as Pilgrim
circles overhead. Beatrix joined us at first, but soon stopped
and, murmuring an apology, settled down against her favorite tree. She wasn't awake for long.

When William decides Pilgrim is starting to loop too
wide, he pulls the lure from his pouch. This time, he hands
it to me. "When she turns downwind and sees you," he says.

I watch carefully, and at just the right time, I play out
the lure and swing it overhead. I see the sudden alertness in
Pilgrim's body, the tight-tucked wings. Then there's the split-
second brutal descent, and a raging wind roars past my head.

Pilgrim is on the ground, atop the lure, the proud
conqueror.

William pulls out a tidbit, but instead of giving it to her
himself, he hands it to me. So now I'm the one going up soft

and low to Pilgrim, tempting her to give up the lure for my glove. It's me standing with her on my fist.

I try to whistle her tune, and William laughs. "You've got it wrong," he says, and he whistles it softly, the right way, next to my ear. I try again, and this time I get it right.

With his easy stride, William walks to the trees and cuts a long, sturdy twig. He bends it into an arc and sticks both ends in the ground, making a perch. I kneel so Pilgrim can step over, and William kneels next to me, tying the one-handed knot. Laughing, leaning over . . .

And then we stop.

His face is a few inches from mine. His eyes are on my mouth, and his smile is replaced by something so intense, I feel it on my skin, like the air is electric. His hand reaches over and covers my bare hand on the ground. I hear his breath, and he's drawing closer, his lips brushing mine. . . .

He wrenches back. "What am I doing?" he cries, staring at his hands like they've betrayed him. "Forgive me, my lady. Forgive me!"

I lean so close, only a few inches separate us. "You want to kiss me," I whisper.

He breathes in sharply, staring at my mouth.

"So kiss me," I whisper again, so full of wanting, that's

all there is. And he feels the same, I know he does, it's thick in the air around us.

His face is all cheekbone and strong jaw. "But . . . you're to marry Sir Hugh."

My head is reeling, my heart flying. Is that all that stands between us?

"I've heard"—the next words come from deep inside me, from a place I don't recognize—"I've heard even married ladies sometimes kiss others."

"How can you think that's all it is?" His hands tighten into fists. "Don't make me say it."

"Don't make you say what?"

"That I don't deserve you!" he says, in a voice of pain and longing. "Me, who came wandering out of the woods and had to make a family from naught. An orphan! A mongrel! Do I have to make it any more clear? I'm not worthy of you."

"And if I weren't a lady," I whisper. "Would you kiss me then?"

His voice is low. "I would do more than kiss you, by God."

And there's nothing between us. Nothing but a title. *Lady*.

Suddenly, I want to tell him everything! How I came from another time, and found the wrecked ship, the jewel box. How I never bumped my head at all—me, a bastard maid, who was emptying rubbish bins and sweeping floors and curtseying to my betters! How there isn't a drop of noble blood in my body!

But then I remember last night, how I stood in the solar wearing that golden gown, Sir Hugh's wedding gown, knowing William had my heart. And suddenly I think, *I can have both, a name and love. I don't have to give up either one.*

I open my mouth, and the words that come out surprise me. "Just pretend," I whisper, lifting my hand to his cheek. "Pretend I'm not a lady."

I don't know if it's my words, or the touch of my hand, but his blue eyes get deeper, so I'm falling right into them, and his breath comes faster.

"By God's blood, I will," he says.

His hand reaches up and cradles the back of my head, pulling me closer, and closer, and then his lips are on mine. We melt together until I don't know where my mouth stops and his starts. His other hand is circling my waist, laying me gently on the grass, and my heart is beating in time with the heartbeat I feel pulsing through his tunic, and his skin is warm beneath the fabric, and—

"My lady!" calls Beatrix from a distance. "William! Wherever have you got to with that bird?"

We sit up with a jolt, staring at each other. I'm breathing too hard to answer.

"My lady!" she cries, a little louder.

I finally find my voice. "We'll be right there, Beatrix!"

But William doesn't let go yet. He presses close again for one more kiss, and then, very slowly, he pulls away. And smiles the most glorious sunlit smile I've ever seen.

Grass

I'm not walking across the bailey; I'm flying. I've never felt so free! It's all I can do to keep from grinning in the most unladylike way. Each time I glanced at William on the ride back, his eyes were on me, a smile playing at the corners of his mouth. When we got off our horses, Beatrix gave me a questioning look before bustling off. Does she suspect something? I laugh, because even if she does, she won't say anything. I know she won't!

I turn toward the walled garden so I can be alone. I want to sit on the bench beneath the pear tree and hug this feeling close, remembering William's lips on mine, the warmth of his breath.

A squat figure appears at the door to the keep, shielding his eyes with a hand as he peers from side to side: Eustace, searching for victims to find fault with, no doubt. I quicken my steps, praying he won't spot me. I couldn't stand to have him get in the way of this wonderful feeling.

I'm nearing the garden door when he calls, "Lady Matilda!"

I pretend not to hear him. I reach for the latch—

He calls again. "Lady Matilda! I beg a moment!"

Rapid footsteps scurry up behind me. I stop, sighing. There's nothing for it. Just let it be quick. I put on my gracious lady face and turn. "Good day, Eustace."

He sweeps one of his too-deep bows. "I have been searching for you everywhere, my lady," he says, rising. "I know you eagerly await his lordship, and would wish to be informed as soon as—"

Suddenly he stops, transfixed. He's staring at a spot above my left eyebrow. Whatever he sees there pulls his hand toward my temple, slowly, as if he were under a magician's spell. I'm so shocked by the idea of his touching me, I stand frozen. He reaches into my hair, then slowly pulls his hand back, clutching something between thumb and fingers.

We both stare down: three blades of brown, dried grass, crumpled from the weight of my head as I lay with William in the field.

We gasp at the same time. I look up with a start. His eyes are like a rat's eyes piercing the dark, a rat that has discovered a sack of grain and bares its teeth, ready to gnaw at the cloth that holds everything in, making a small hole, ripping it wider, and wider, until suddenly the grain spills out on the floor for everyone to see.

How could I have let my guard down? I force myself into my role, change my expression from shock to indignation. "How *dare* you!"

"What can I have been thinking?" he says. "I most humbly beg your pardon."

But he doesn't sound nearly humble enough for comfort. He's staring again at the grass, at me, at the mews, and his fingers are rolling the dried blades back and forth, back and forth. Again I hear the words, *But your hands . . . Missing even one of them could be . . . inconvenient.* And dallying with the lord's lady is a crime far worse than stealing a slice of bread. I need to pull his eyes away from the mews, now, before his thoughts can go any further.

Cloaking myself in the imperious tones Caroline's mother used at her back door, I throw my shoulders back as straight as they should have been from the moment we met. "You will *never* touch me again!" The scorn in my voice reaches him; I have his full attention now. "If the wind blows leaves and grass about, what concern could it be of yours? Are you in charge of my grooming now?"

He forces a tight smile, as if I were making a joke. "No, indeed, my lady."

"You had something you wished to tell me?"

Finally, the grass drops from his fingers to the ground. "It's . . . nothing, my lady. Forgive me. I fear I have inconvenienced you."

I incline my head slightly. "Now, if you will pardon me."

He bows. I turn toward the door, stepping on the blades of grass, grinding the evidence into dirt.

$\mathcal{B}$ath

A big wooden tub stands before a blazing fire, and Tip keeps running up the stairs with kettle after kettle of steaming water. I wait in my window seat, wrapped in a soft brown fur.

Today is the fifteenth day. And here I am. I'm staying.

Eustace never said another word about the grass in my hair. If he had any suspicions, they're obviously long gone.

Outside, the sun is setting. Beyond the gates, down the hill, beneath the dead tree, those last rays must be shining on the filigreed walls of the lift. I can practically see it there, the door slightly ajar, a sudden gust of wind swirling a few crimson leaves onto the floor. They'll ride back to the twentieth century, not me. Why would I leave? I love being a lady.

The door clicks shut; the tub is full, and Beatrix

sprinkles dried petals across the surface. The scent of roses fills the room.

Now, finally, everything is ready. And I haven't lifted a finger. Haven't heated the water, or lugged it to the tub, or tested the heat. It's everyone else's job to make it perfect for *me*.

Outside, a few clouds are glowing pink.

Beatrix helps me up the step, and I sigh in pleasure as I sink down into the hot perfumed water, my hair floating loose on the surface. The tub is lined with the thickest and softest of cloths, because we wouldn't want my noble skin— so delicate! so fine!—assaulted by rough splinters, now would we? Beatrix brings a little pot and pours a lavender-scented liquid on my head, working her strong, capable fingers through my hair—no, I'm not even expected to wash my own hair! I'm too grand for that. My eyes close, and I lean back into her hands, perfectly content.

I didn't try to sneak out the gates, or insist on a late-afternoon ride. After all my efforts to be sure I could reach the lift, I'm letting the day end without even seeing if it came. All my deciding is done. No more maids' caps and aprons and curtseying for *me*, thank you very much! I'm going to stay here for the rest of my life. I've learned my part to perfection. No one looks at me oddly anymore, wondering why I'm eating the trencher or staring around for a fork that doesn't exist. I've mastered the art of polite conversation and learned the graceful walk, all long neck, like a swan. I've convinced the castle I'm their lady.

As for Sir Hugh, I get the sense from people that he never did meet the real Lady Matilda. And now he's been delayed again. I wish he would keep being delayed forever. I try to remember the dates of the Crusades, rather hopeful that one is about to start and he'll be called away for years, leaving me here to wait. And I can wait very patiently indeed, with Will by my side.

Beatrix has long since finished rinsing my hair. I hear her padding out the door, closing it gently behind her.

The room is silent, except for the crackling fire. I lean back into the cloth cushioning the tub and I think once more of the field. But now I picture it in morning light, with Beatrix sleeping and Pilgrim standing on the perch. Will lays his cloak on the ground, and me on the cloak. Again I feel his lips soft on mine, then more insistent, and my mouth is just as eager, as hungry in return. Running my hands through his golden hair . . . hearing his breath . . .

I sink deeper into the water, thinking of tomorrow and tomorrow and tomorrow. It's like the embers of a fire are banked inside me, waiting to be sparked back into flame the next time I fall into those deep blue eyes.

Sir Giles

A few days later I'm walking across the bailey when there's a shout from the wall walk, and suddenly men-at-arms are pouring from the guardhouse. Edward strides over and says firmly, "I will see you inside the keep, my lady."

"What is it, Edward? What is happening?"

Then hoofbeats are pounding over the drawbridge, and Edward stops, every muscle tense, placing his body in front of me like a bulwark.

A man rides in on a powerful destrier. His brow is high, his chin juts forward like a prow, his blue-and-gold cloak is of the finest cloth. Two other riders flank him; I recognize one from the lake.

Sir Giles's men, Will said that day. *And meaning no good, by the looks of them.* This, then, must be Sir Giles himself.

He draws his horse up in the middle of the bailey and shouts, "I would have word with Sir Hugh!"

A soldier rushes into the keep. But if Sir Giles's men have been skulking about, he knows full well Sir Hugh is nowhere to be found. What game is he playing?

He turns his mount in a tight circle, surveying the bailey and all its men. His eyes light on me. "Well, well, well," he says with an unpleasant chuckle. "This must be the valuable young lady in question."

Part of me wants to retort, "And you must be the devious Sir Giles." But Edward's hand is hovering near the hilt of his sword, and I decide it would be wiser to keep my mouth closed.

Eustace appears at the door to the keep. "You wish to speak with me?" he calls, making no move to come down the stairs.

"Not with *you*," says Sir Giles, scornfully tossing down the words. "With your master."

"I talk for him until he returns," says Eustace.

"Talk!" Sir Giles gives a harsh laugh. "That seems to be all Sir Hugh will give me, talk and parchments and pasty-faced messengers. Then you tell him this: I will have the payment due me, and I will have it soon. In one form"—he pauses for emphasis, his eyes slashing across the bailey—"or another!"

He raises his hand. At the signal, the man behind him reaches for something at his saddle, and I hear the rattle of steel as every man-at-arms prepares to draw his sword. But it's not a weapon the man produces. He holds up a coarse sack, the kind you'd use to carry potatoes to market, making sure everyone sees it before he hurls it toward the steps. It rolls to a stop near Robert.

Robert picks up the sack, unties it, and looks inside. He blanches. Then he carries it up the stairs and holds it open for Eustace to peer in. Eustace whirls and shouts at Sir Giles, "Sir Hugh will hear of this!"

"My hope exactly," replies the knight, pulling on his reins. The destrier rears, the very picture of a battle steed. "You have had your warning!" he cries, wheeling to gallop from the bailey. His companions thunder close behind.

The moment they've crossed the drawbridge, it begins to rise. The iron gate descends.

Edward's hand finally comes away from the hilt of his sword.

I whirl toward him. "What was the meaning of that?"

But his face is closed, ever the professional soldier. "My lady, all your questions should be addressed to Eustace." He moves aside so I can pass.

As I walk toward the keep, everyone seems more aware

of me than usual. "Are you all right, my lady?" "Should I call Beatrix for you, my lady?" But I don't answer them as I should; I'm thinking of the men at the lake, and wondering if I made a mistake by not letting Will warn the castle. What was in that sack?

Only one person stands in the great hall, Tip, his face pale, a cleaning cloth gripped in white hands. I try to smile, hoping I can reassure him in spite of my own concern. He's too young to look so frightened.

"Have you seen Eustace?" I ask.

He nods toward the far door, the one that makes my chest feel tight whenever I look at it, the one I've never gone through. This time I force myself to keep walking.

The staircase is the twin of mine, every step and window slit identical. But the door at the top opens onto a long, deserted corridor, ill lit by a few flickering candles. Sets of dark curtains shroud the outer wall. I reach for an edge of nubby cloth, my heart pounding as if I'm about to unearth some terrible secret. But pulling it open only reveals a chilly room hollowed into the stones, big enough for its straw sleeping pallet, a stool, and little more. The next curtained space is the same, and the next.

Then I hear a rapid scratching sound. I follow it to the end of the hall, where a door is cracked ajar. I peer inside.

The steward sits at a table, quill in hand, scribbling furiously on a half-filled sheet of vellum. There's no fire, no tapestry warming the walls, so the room feels as cold as his eyes. A huge leather-bound book lies open on the table before him, baring a page full of columns and numbers.

Why should I have to feel I'm gathering my courage to speak with this man? Isn't he my servant, as well as Sir Hugh's?

I push open the door. "Pardon me, Eustace—"

He leaps to his feet, the quill still clutched in his hand.

"What was that about, just now in the bailey?" My voice isn't nearly as confident as I'd like.

His face may be drawn, but his eyes become sharper and more calculating than ever; his voice is strangely even. "Sir Giles? Why, he's only a neighboring knight, my lady, come to discuss a minor land dispute and nothing more. Pray, do not concern yourself."

"Eustace, he threatened the castle! What was in that sack?"

He ignores the question. "Threatened? No, not so much as all that. Such matters, as you must be aware, go on between knights all the time." The quill turns around and around in his fingers. "It hardly warrants your attention. Indeed, I expect the matter to be resolved quite soon."

But that's not how it felt in the bailey. The energy there was a spark only waiting for wind to blaze it into an inferno. And so I press on. "How soon? And what is it needs to be resolved?"

"Once Sir Hugh returns, this . . . *disagreement* will be settled. As for the specific details, forgive me, my lady, but I feel it is not my place to say. I am sure his lordship will give you all the answers you need." He holds a hand out toward the vellum. "I am writing him even now."

Urging him to come home, most likely. Now there's another feeling tangling up my thoughts. I'd like to know what's happening, but not at the cost of Sir Hugh's returning. I want things to go on as they've been.

Eustace walks around the table. With a respectful bow, he opens the door wider, suggesting I leave. "Is there anything you wish me to add to the letter, my lady?"

I shake my head.

"A land dispute and nothing more," he repeats.

I walk back down the stairs feeling I know even less than I did when I came. Is it true that Eustace must wait for Sir Hugh to tell me the details, or am I being intentionally misled? I'm angry at myself for not asking more, demanding more.

As I near the bottom of the stairs, I hear strange, gasping

noises from the other side of the door. I pause, listening, and now I make out stifled sobs and a low, guttural moan, far too deep for Tip. I open the door a few inches. It's Robert crying. Great, strong Robert, who helped bring me back from the shore. He sits splayed on a bench, his head thrown back against the wall, his eyes closed in raw pain. I'm so shocked to see him like this, his face drenched in tears, it takes me a moment to recognize the sack in his lap. His hands are cradling something half in, half out of the coarse fabric, something as large as a melon but covered in dark fur. A sob shakes his body, the sack slides down—that's not fur, it's hair. And those are Oswald's eyes staring blindly at me from his roughly severed head.

The floor gives way below me, and everything goes black.

To His Most Excellent Lord,
Sir Hugh of Berringstoke,
From His Faithful Servant Eustace

My lord, I am filled with a deep foreboding. If you do not return immediately, I fear you may lose Berringstoke. The severity of the threat forces me to be direct.

Firstly, Sir Giles himself rode to your very door, flinging down the bloody head of your messenger Oswald to show he will brook no further delay. Should he not be repaid with the utmost haste, he will take by force the lands you pledged as security for your debt.

Secondly, he spoke to Lady Matilda in a rude manner, as if he hoped the wedding would not take place at all. I suspect he would prefer the land to repayment, and hence is eager for battle.

Thirdly, Lady Matilda has become suspicious and is asking questions that may lead her to discover that these are the very lands you pledged as her marriage portion, a fact that, if brought to light, would render the marriage agreement void. In my attempt to assuage her ladyship's fears, I have called this a minor dispute, easily resolved. This prevents me from discontinuing her hawking forays, as I dare not speak of danger. And yet she is clearly at risk.

And fourthly, these hawking expeditions are comprised of so small and, dare I say, intimate a party, I fear it threatens to become unseemly.

Delay no longer, my lord. With profound apologies for the bluntness of this missive, and all due diligence in serving you and your estate, I remain, most faithfully,

Eustace, Steward of Berringstoke

On His Arm

"Are you sure it's wise to go out, my lady?" asks Beatrix, fixing the brooch on my cloak. "With your fainting? And Sir Giles, and all?"

"Eustace assures me it's only a minor dispute," I say, leading the way downstairs. "Something about land, and soon to be settled."

I don't blame her for the look of disbelief she gives me. Robert's anguished face, his hands cradling Oswald's head—I shudder at the memory. No sensible person would believe this is a minor matter. Leaving the castle feels dangerous, but it's a risk my heart insists that I take.

The gangly stable lad has Fidelius saddled, just as he does every day; neither he nor the stable master suggests I stay. And the guards lower the drawbridge for us without a word. Surely they'd refuse to open the gates or insist on coming along if they truly thought I was in peril. And wouldn't Will himself stop us if the threat were great enough?

I look over at him, riding alongside me. No, in truth, he'd never keep us from going out together. He needs my arms as much as I need his.

Beatrix is determined to stay awake today. She walks with us around the field for a good twenty minutes while Pilgrim circles overhead. But Will strides faster than usual to tire her out, and in time Beatrix says she's going to sit down for a moment to rest her feet. The next minute, her head has dropped against the tree trunk, and the sweet refrain of her snoring drifts through the air.

Will swings the lure wide to catch Pilgrim's eye. She plummets, but before Will lets her tag the lure, he gets a playful look and whips it in a circle right in front of me. For a glorious moment she's a tornado, passing so close, I feel the wind of her wings on my cheek.

And then she's standing on Will's glove. I run a finger down her back, the gray lapping waves of her feathers. "I wish it were me there, on your arm," I say, all soft.

He smiles that wonderful smile, his eyes deep and bright at the same time. "I think that can be arranged."

He settles Pilgrim on her perch. And then it's me resting on his arm, lying on the springy golden grass; and Will's other hand is gentling me, playing with my hair, running down my side.

"Matilda . . ." he starts to say, but I put a finger to his lips. It sounds wrong, that name: too sharp, too long and grand. "Call me Addy," I murmur. "For short. When it's just the two of us."

"Addy," he says with a smile. "I like that." And then he says it again, softer, "Addy," as he leans in to kiss me.

Later, I whisper, "I feel like a falcon you've tamed to your hand."

"Tame, you?" He laughs, stroking the hair back from my temple. "You're a wild one, that's what you are." His finger caresses my lips, my cheek, and then he's gazing down at me with love and sadness all mingled. "And the glove is not on my hand."

"If it were . . . ?"

The sadness disappears; his voice deepens into a warm rumble. "If it were, why, I'd loose your creance, like this." He pulls on the end of one of my laces, and his hand slips under the fabric. A shiver runs through me. "You'd rouse, like that," he whispers. "And I'd feel it in my own blood."

"Yes?" More a breath than a word.

"Why don't you tell me what happens next?"

I imagine the powerful stroke of wings lifting me into the clouds. And then, coming back to his hand; always coming back, the sound of his breath replacing the wind.

Let's Have a Look at You

A few days later, it happens.

I'm at the high table, reaching for the goblet, when there's a great hullabaloo from outside. Suddenly, a huge hulk of a man fills the door, blocking out the sunlight. His head nears the top of the frame; his shoulders fill it from side to side. Everyone leaps up, and the benches fall back from the trestle tables. There's silence, except for one great intake of breath, as if the whole room shared a single set of lungs.

Sir Hugh!

The goblet shakes in my hand, wine splashing over the rim, as I set it down and stand. He strides up to the dais, everyone's eyes on him, his eyes on me. In spite of the rushes, his feet pound as loud as a horse's hooves, carrying the great muscular girth of him.

Eustace signals to Timothy; together they lug the lord's great chair away from the wall, where it waited in his absence, and set it in pride of place at the high table. Next to me.

Eustace sinks into a bow. I, too, am on my feet, curtseying so deep, it's like I'm a maid again, about to get rebuked for something I've done wrong. My eyes are glued to the rushes. I'm so low, so low—I don't want to look up— and the great feet clomp over to me: dust-covered boots, muscled calves in tight leggings, the hem of an elegant tunic.

And then a broad hand swallows my shoulder blade, and he's pulling me up toward him. My heart crashes around like a hawk bating in the cage of my ribs.

Sir Hugh puts a finger under my chin, lifting it, so he can see my face. I look up into piercing gray eyes. Eyes used to commanding and being obeyed. They stare out from the craggy face of a man more than twice my age.

"Not bad!" His voice rattles my bones. "Why in God's name did they say you were ugly? Damn nice surprise!"

He hasn't met her, I think. I'm safe. I can stay. . . . So why do I feel like running for the door?

"Turn around," he says.

And I do. What choice do I have? I turn around, like a horse being examined for purchase. Is he going to ask to see my teeth next?

But when I come around to face him again, he's throwing his head back with a roaring laugh, and the butler himself is rushing forward with the best pitcher, the one shaped like a leaping silver stag, and he's pouring a goblet full to the brim as Sir Hugh flings himself into his chair—that great chair suddenly small with him filling it arm to arm—and the goblet is empty in a single gulp. The butler pours again. Sir Hugh lifts his drink with one hand and signals to the harpist with the other.

"Sit!" he calls to the throng, and they sit. "Eat!" he calls, and they eat. He takes a chunk of meat from the platter that's appeared before him, turns to me, and declares in what I believe is meant to be a softer tone, "And so we meet at last."

"My lord," I say, lowering my head.

"Young thing, aren't you?" His voice is thunder. "Not much more than a foal. I understand you had a rough go of it, getting here. Sorry to hear it."

"Thank you, my lord."

It's all the words I can find at the moment. No witty conversation for me. I'm too busy taking in that overmuscled, towering form, imagining that huge hand on my waist, my breast. . . . I shudder, and the wine goblet in my hand sloshes again.

Sir Hugh turns to Father Bartholomew. "Nervous filly,

isn't she?" he asks, loud enough for the entire room to hear. They all stare at me again.

I close my eyes, trying to calm my breath. I still have the dresses and jewels, I tell myself. I still have Will.

Different

I'm lying in the dark when the door creaks open. Footsteps
sneak across the room, stopping on the other side of the bed
curtains. Only a scrim of fabric separates me from the body
on the other side. I hear breathing, fast and heated; my own
breath speeds up to match it. He's not supposed to be here
yet! He's supposed to wait until we're married! I clutch the
furs to my neck, trying to cover every inch of my flesh. The
fabric trembles as a hand grasps it from the other side, and
suddenly the curtain is ripping open and I'm screaming at
the top of my lungs—

Beatrix tumbles backward with a shriek. My breakfast
flies out of her hands, and she lands sprawling on the floor.
Gasping for breath, she stares at the wine stains on her dress,
at the splatters across the room. At me.

"Oh, Beatrix! I'm so sorry! I thought—"

She gathers herself up, shaking her head, and tromps out the door, her footsteps heavy and hard done-by. She comes back with an armload of rags.

"And us with so much to get ready," she grumbles, wiping up the mess. Once the floor and bench are clean again, once she's scrubbed at her own kirtle—"That's the beauty of brown," she mutters, "hardly shows a thing"—she pulls my shift off the peg and carries it over to the bed. She slips it over my head, then pulls out my best kirtle, the Lincoln scarlet.

"Not that one, Beatrix. I'm going hawking this morning."

"Hawking!" she says, disapprovingly. "With Sir Hugh just arrived?"

Then she gets a good look at my face, and melts; she reaches for the blue kirtle instead and slips it over my head. But she laces the sides tighter than usual, so it hugs every curve of my body. She sits me on the bench, brushes my hair until it gleams. Finally, she clumps to the trunk in the corner. I hear her rummaging around, and then she returns with the ring I found on the beach, the one carved like a snarling bear.

It's too real. Everything is too real.

I stare at the ring like it's going to bite me. "It won't fit under Pilgrim's glove," I say.

"Then put it on your other hand. A nice gesture it will be, wearing the jewel he sent you."

I shove it on. The band cuts into the soft skin between my fingers.

"Ouch!"

Beatrix doesn't even seem to hear me. "I've a few things to get ready," she says. "Didn't think we'd be going out. I'll meet you in the mews."

Will looks up from Pilgrim's perch and takes in my eyes, tired with lack of sleep; the tight-laced kirtle; the ring.

"It's different now," he says softly.

I never imagined it could be this different. *I can have both*, isn't that what I said, so smug and sure? But that was when Sir Hugh was an idea. Now he's a man, and he smells like a man, and has a man's skin. I think of sharing a bed with that battle-hardened body, those demanding eyes, and the thought punches all the air out of me, like a fist in bread dough. I didn't think he'd ever really be here.

I need to feel Will's hands to put things right. "Hurry," I say. "Let's get out to the field, where we can talk freely."

A smile tugs at one corner of his mouth, and then he's walking to the pegs on the wall and his fine long fingers are gathering gear in his bag.

"I didn't know if we'd be going today," he says.

"Hurry! Shall I get Pilgrim? Beatrix will be here any moment."

And, indeed, steps are approaching the mews. But they're too broad, too heavy—

The door swings open, and Sir Hugh strides through.

"Lady Matilda. I heard you were here." His voice is as oversized as he is.

One of the birds bates in a jangle of bells, and Will is there instantly, calming, soothing it back to the perch. Sir Hugh doesn't even glance at Will. Of course not: Will is a servant. He's invisible.

I speak in a soft voice, hoping Sir Hugh will echo my quiet tone. "I have been hawking most mornings, my lord."

"Great stuff, hawking," he says, in an almost normal pitch. "I'll join you."

My heart sinks. I hadn't thought of him coming along. Not today. I glance over at the perches. Will is glaring at Sir Hugh with an expression that's far from respectful. His fist clenches at his side. The bird feels his anger and flaps again.

"There," Will whispers. "Quiet now." But he doesn't look like he's feeling so quiet himself. He's staring from Sir Hugh, to me, and back to Sir Hugh again.

The lord of the castle clasps his hands behind his back and starts walking around the mews, his bulk brushing into things as he goes. He passes the merlin with a nod, casts an approving eye over Pilgrim. When he gets to Lightning, he stops.

"Ah, so this is the gyrfalcon. Pure white. What a beauty." His voice is thick, as if with lust. He runs a finger down Lightning's sleek back. "I'll take this one today."

"Begging your pardon, my lord," says Will—how I hate to hear those words come from his mouth!—"but Lightning is the king's gyr."

Sir Hugh focuses on Will, seeing him for the first time. His eyes narrow.

"His Majesty will collect her when he comes," says Will. "She's not to fly until then."

"And you, boy, who are you to tell me what I can and cannot do?" It's a tone you'd use for a stray dog, good for nothing but kicking.

"William, at your service, my lord."

"Hardly my head falconer, are you, boy?"

"His son, my lord. Do you wish me to find him? He will tell you the same."

"What I bloody well wish is—"

But then there's another voice from the door. "Oh!

Begging your pardon, my lord," says Beatrix, bobbing one curtsey after another. "But your steward searches for you everywhere. Says it's of the greatest urgency, or I wouldn't disturb you, indeed, I wouldn't."

"God's bones," curses Sir Hugh. Then he smiles at me, actually smiles, as if the way he talked to Will weren't still lingering in the air. "It can't be helped, I'm afraid."

All I want is to be away, in the field, with Will. But I force myself to say, "Do you wish me to wait for you, my lord?"

"No, go ahead," he says, striding to the door. "No telling how long this will take. At dinner you can tell me all about your hunt."

I curtsey. I have to stop doing that! He brings it out in me.

As he leaves, he throws a parting word at Will. "And you, tell your father I'll be seeing him about the gyr."

The sky is the dark ocean gray of Pilgrim's back. A few leaves still fluttering on the trees make them look even more naked, all bare arms and reaching fingers. The air is different. The dry grass underfoot is different. It was always so easy before. There's nothing easy about it now.

"You can't look at Sir Hugh like that," I say, as Pilgrim soars overhead. "He'll notice next time, and then you'll be in for it. Just put on a different face. Just pretend."

He lifts his eyes to Pilgrim, and then to the trees, watching the wind in their swaying branches. His voice is low and intense. "I don't want to pretend."

The wind turns, and suddenly his words loosen a longing I didn't know I had. A longing that surges through me, filling my skin, my lungs, my veins, until it's more than I can hold. Like floodwaters gouging through rock, it opens up a space in me that wasn't there before.

Will stares at a flock of birds rising in the distance. "I thought I could do it the way you said. You with his lordship. You with me." His voice hardens. "But I can't. I think of his hands on you, his mouth. I can't."

But if I lose Will . . .

"Please!" I beg. "This is the only way!"

He takes a deep breath and turns, reaching for my hand. Where our skin touches, the heat spreads like fire. "There is another way," he says. "But I don't know if I can ask it of you. You, with so much to give up."

My voice is a whisper. "Ask."

"Run away with me, Addy! Tomorrow, before his lordship sees how we look at each other, before they can hold your wedding, before I have to see his hands on—"

But I don't need another word. I reach up, bringing his

face down to mine, and we kiss. Not the gentle, playful kiss of yesterday—my need, my hunger, frighten me. Thrill me.

His arms wrap around me, pulling me close. I feel his heart pounding as fast as mine. "You keep Beatrix from coming," he says. "I can do the rest. We'll say we're scouting good places for hawking with the royal party, and not to expect us for dinner. That will give us a day's start."

"And Pilgrim?" I ask.

He shakes his head. "Pilgrim stays. It's a different life we're going to." He lifts an errant lock of hair from my eyes. "You may even have to work with your hands."

"I can work with my hands."

"And no grand kirtles."

"I can do without grand kirtles."

"No guarantee of the next meal coming easy."

"I don't care."

"Are you *sure*?" His eyes are so close, that deep hypnotic blue.

The prestige, the riches, the respect—everything I thought I wanted when I came— "I don't have a doubt in the world," I say. "Tomorrow."

$\mathcal{A}$way

>))))

I pour the potion into the morning's wine. "You must be thirsty, Beatrix."

She nods. She's always ready for a good swig after tromping up all the stairs.

I got it from her last night. I said I was nervous about the wedding and needed something to help me sleep, like the concoction she gave me the first day I came. Her eyes were so full of concern, I almost felt guilty. Almost. But I pretended to drink the potion, and I set it aside, and now it's mixed with the dark red wine in the goblet I hold out to her.

"Go ahead, finish it," I say. "I've had enough."

She gulps the wine down eagerly before she even notices it tastes different. Her eyes open wide in sudden realization. "My lady! You wouldn't . . ."

Her words are already slurring, her shoulders slumping.
I barely get her over to the bench—the bed would be softer,
but it's too high to lift her—and I settle her down, covering
her gently with a blanket. I wait until she starts snoring.

The air coming through the window is warmer than
usual, but it's my sturdiest kirtle I put on, struggling to tie
the laces at my sides. I pull on my thickest stockings and
drape my fur-lined cloak over my shoulders. Today may feel
like summer again, but it will be winter soon enough, and
I'll need these clothes against the bitter cold to come.

I open the trunk to get my gloves, and there, staring at
me from atop the jewel box, is the mermaid, her two tails
pointing in different directions. My hand drifts down, then
stops, hovering in the air. I shouldn't take it, it's wrong. . . .
But I harden my heart. I've been poor, and there are no guar-
antees in life. I turn the clasp and lift the ivory lid. Before I
can hesitate again, I grab the jeweled cross on its heavy gold
chain and shove it into the purse at my side.

I'm taking too long! By the time I run down the stairs
and cross the bailey, the sun is already shining on the door
to the mews. I knock gently and enter.

Will lifts his head from Pilgrim's perch. He strokes the
bird's wing, saying farewell, then walks to the table and
grabs the biggest field bag.

"Beatrix?" he asks.

"She's asleep. And your father? Did you tell him we're going for longer than usual?"

"He won't stop us. Nor will Sir Hugh." There's a sharp edge to his voice. "His lordship came in at first light and said he'd take out the gyr or he'd have himself a new falconer. It wasn't so bad when they left, but now"—he looks out the window as if he could see far beyond the castle walls—"the air feels wrong. And we haven't been flying the gyr." He pulls his eyes back to the room and starts filling the bag: bread, cheese, strips of dried meat, apples. A sturdy, sharp knife. "But what's done is done."

"What if they see us?" I ask.

"Then we're only searching out good hawking for the king."

At the stables, the groom has three horses ready, like he does every morning. I tell him Beatrix won't be joining us because she isn't feeling well. As we ride toward the portcullis, a guard calls from above, "Why, where's your old nursemaid?"

"She's meeting us in the field shortly," I call back. "Good work, soldier." He puffs out his chest, proud to have been so alert. He'll be off duty before he has a chance to wonder.

And then we're away. The sun filters through the

branches, and we hold the horses to a steady walk, sashaying down the trail; but my pulse is racing as if whole armies were galloping after us. I glance at Will. He's not as relaxed as he'd have me believe. His mouth is more determined than I've ever seen, and his eyes are as alert as a falcon's, watching everywhere at once for any shiver of movement.

I throw my cloak back over my shoulders. Will sees me and stops.

"Go ahead, take it off," he says, removing his own cloak as he scans the sky. "The day is too warm. I don't like it."

"Better for us than storms," I say.

"Better for us; bad for my father. Look." He points up where a crow sails, high and buoyant. "Do you see that? No flapping, just riding the warm air. A soaring day, when a falcon can fly forever, never looking back at all."

"Never looking back," I say. "Like us."

"Like us," he echoes, suddenly smiling. And we're off again at our steady pace, into the thickness of the woods.

We've skirted the road to town, and now we're in the hills on trails I've never seen before. Will says there's another village down the coast, where there's little chance anyone will recognize us. He has coins in his purse. We'll buy passage on a boat and sail where they'll never find us, he says. We'll start a new life, the two of us. Together.

The air's stillness feels slow and heavy. I wish one of those wild autumn winds would come tugging and pushing, sending our horses flying as fast as they can go. Away from Sir Hugh, from Eustace and his prying eyes.

We've been riding for hours when Will pulls up in a glade and we dismount. He spreads his cloak and we sit.

"Not what you're used to for dinner," he says, cutting a slice of cheese. As he passes it to me, our hands touch. We pause, looking down where skin brushes against skin. Then he leans forward, and he kisses me, softly, sweetly, as if for the very first time. And in a way, it is. I barely recognize the person I am. Not a maid anymore, or a lady—just me, Addy, running off through the woods with the one I love.

"Can't stop too long," he says.

We gulp down the bread and salty cheese. Then we remount, and he leads us on, taking every turn without hesitation, pausing only to note the angle of the sun. I never came this far from home in my own time, and the countryside is as foreign to me as if we'd sailed across the ocean. I don't know this curve of hill, that crag, this last patch of crimson leaves clinging to a bush. It feels like wilderness.

Will keeps scanning the sky.

"What are you looking for?" I ask.

He shrugs. He's always looking, taking everything in.

It's how he is in the world, completely aware, all his senses alive. It's one of the things I love about him. And when we kiss, those senses are focused on nothing but me. I'm what he sees, hears, feels, smells, knows. I've never been so seen, so understood as me. . . .

Or who you pretend to be, says a little voice in my head.

But I'm not his lady anymore, am I? So what does it matter? We'll settle into a town, where he'll find work easily with those strong arms, that quick eye. And me . . .

Will pulls on his reins, coming to a sudden stop. His eyes have latched onto something, and I don't like the tension in his shoulders. What does he see? Harold and Sir Hugh? Men-at-arms in blue tunics? Robbers?

I follow his gaze to a wooded copse on the next hill. Something is jerking in a tangle of branches near the top of a tree. Something white. And then I hear the thin, clear chime of a bell.

"God's blood!" curses Will, kicking his horse. The next instant he's galloping over to the copse. Because it's Lightning up there, the king's gyrfalcon, her jesses snagged far above the ground, where the branches are thin and the twigs as tangled and knotted as briars.

But I don't move. I can barely breathe. How could Lightning be here, hours from the castle, on the very path we've taken? It's almost as if she were sent for us to find. Like the peregrine that greeted me in the field, led me to the shipwreck, made my lie of a vision become truth . . . I shiver. The lift that brought me here was science, not magic; but this feels like something beyond human ken.

Then I shake my head, hard, to clear it. What am I thinking? It's a coincidence, that's all. One huge, mad coincidence. I kick my horse into a gallop and race toward the copse.

By the time I pull the reins and leap off, Will is already scrambling from the broad lower branches to the thinner boughs above. Higher he climbs, and higher, until he reaches a bough that looks far too slender to hold him. He starts inching out, murmuring to the gyr in a low, soothing voice. A few inches more—I catch my breath as the limb swings wildly. It won't hold his weight! Will starts to shimmy back toward the trunk, cursing again.

Then he looks down and sees me unlacing the side of my kirtle.

"Addy, what are you—"

"I can't climb a tree in this heavy thing," I say. "My shift will be better."

"What?" He leaps down nimbly from branch to branch and lands at my side. "You're not going up there! You saw

how weak that limb is. It could break off beneath you, dash you to the ground!"

"I weigh less than you do."

I pull the kirtle off over my head. Will stops, staring at me in my shift.

I walk to the trunk and put my hands on its rough bark, trying to gauge the best way to climb. "Give me a boost to this first branch," I say. "I can make it from there."

"No. It's too dangerous."

I stare at him in disbelief. "More dangerous than you up there? More dangerous than running from Sir Hugh and his soldiers?" When he doesn't reply, I exclaim in exasperation, "Do you want to free Lightning, or no?"

At that he sets his jaw and comes over to make a stirrup of his hands, boosting me as easy as a feather. I pull myself up to the first branch, and it's steady and solid as the ground itself. Now I stand, one hand on the tree's great trunk, looking for handholds and footholds. It's just like climbing the castle ruins a lifetime ago, but instead of smooth stone, the bark is rough and biting, and bits of lichen flake off in my hand. The ground is soon very far below me.

The branches grow thinner and springier. I pause, waiting for one to stop bouncing beneath me.

"Watch your feet!" cries Will. "Slow down!"

And there I am, at the base of that slender bough. From the far end comes the silvery chime of Lightning's bell. I start scooting out. "There now," I murmur to the falcon. Closer I come, and closer. "Never you worry. I've got you." Once I would have been terrified to reach my hand toward that brutal beak, toward talons that pierce flesh as easily as a needle slides into silk. "Soft now," I say, reaching for the jesses.

"Don't try to unknot them!" shouts Will. "Jerk them free, shove the bird under your arm!"

And I grasp and jerk and shove all at the same time, just as there's an earsplitting *crack!* The limb is falling away beneath me, and I'm plunging through air, brushing past branches, rocketing downward so fast I think my last moment has come—but instead of a crash, there's a thud as Will catches me, and a second thud as we tumble together to the ground.

We lay there panting, our chests heaving up and down, splintered twigs and branches strewn about us in a rough carpet. We stare wide-eyed at each other, and at Lightning, still trapped under my arm. Then Will cracks a smile, and I follow, and the next moment we're laughing in relief and exhilaration.

Finally he says, "Give me the gyr."

Once I hand over the bird, I stand and turn around, making sure everything works: feet, legs, arms. I reach for my kirtle. Will's eyes linger on me as I slip it back over my head.

"Look to Lightning," I say, starting in on the laces.

He spreads her wings, starts fingering the long flight feathers. "You had her good and tight," he says. But when he examines the tail, his mouth narrows. "Two tail feathers broken. Too bad I can't imp them for her. I'm sure these are ones we have from the moult."

I look at his hands, so sure, almost instinctive. I look at his face, completely alive, connecting with Lightning like— what was it Harold said in the mews that day? *Like a pair of eyases in the nest.*

"I would have liked to leave her with something to eat," Will says. "But we've already lost too much time." He glances at the afternoon sun, three-quarters of the way across the sky.

A pair of eyases . . . I hear Harold's voice, easy, comfortable; I see him, his hands as quick and wise as Will's, his eyes warm, his arm wrapping around his son's shoulders.

"Will," I say quietly, and he turns at the new tone in my voice. "What happens if Lightning doesn't return to Berringstoke?"

A shadow crosses his face; he doesn't answer.

"That day at the lake, you said a man that harmed the

lord's falcon might pay with his life. That a gyrfalcon is the most valuable of all. And Lightning belongs to the king."

Will stands. "It's late," he says, hard as granite, not wanting to hear what I'm going to say. Already knowing what it is.

And I don't want to say it, either! I want to keep running! And it will be even more dangerous now, returning after we've been out this long, let alone trying to escape again, unseen, before the wedding.

"I'll cut off Lightning's jesses, and we'll be on our way," says Will.

But that bloody huge new space inside me has opened room for realizations that are bigger, far bigger, than I want to make. I find myself saying, "When the king arrives to collect his gyr, what happens if she's gone?"

There's a battle going on in his eyes.

"Someone will pay with his life for a loss like that," I say, forcing my voice to be firm. "Two men went out with the gyr: Sir Hugh and your father. You tell me which one will pay the price."

Before, when Eustace slapped Tip so hard it left the mark of his hand for days, I didn't say anything, do anything. But this time I realize I don't have that choice. I can't live with the knowledge that Harold's life was in my hands and I threw it away. And I could never do that to Will.

"I wouldn't go back for anything less," I say.

"Nor I," he says, deciding, his voice all gravel. "But tomorrow, or one more day at the very most, we'll get away. And nothing will stop us then."

It's twilight as we cross the familiar stream. Suddenly there's a shout, the pounding of hooves, and a dozen men are galloping toward us. "Are you all right, my lady?" asks Edward, with obvious relief. The men form a protective phalanx around us for the ride back to Berringstoke. Someone cries out from atop the wall walk, and then the portcullis is rising and the drawbridge coming down.

We trudge across, the sound of the horses' hooves as exhausted and heavy as my heart. We're not even through the barbican before we're caught up in a swirl of bodies and barking dogs, and Beatrix is clutching me and crying as if she were my mother—"We thought we'd lost you!"—and Sir Hugh strides up, his brows as low as storm clouds. But then he sees the gyr on Will's padded wrist, and all of a sudden he's throwing his head back and laughing in delight, so I doubt he even hears me explain how we were looking for good hawking sites when we saw the gyr soaring away;

how we decided to chase her down and bring her back safe, following the rising flocks of birds and straining our ears for the sound of her bell. Sir Hugh is as pleased and pigeon-chested as if he'd retrieved the bird himself, and Harold is grinning as Will hands him the gyr. But Eustace . . .

Eustace is staring only at me, his piercing eyes taking in my cloak, too warm for the weather; my heavy kirtle. His eyes widen when they reach my waist. I look down; hanging from the purse at my side are a few links of that heavy gold chain, the one that holds the costly cross. I lift my eyes. Now Eustace is staring at Will. At the horses. At me. I raise my hand unconsciously to my hair, as if it still held three crumpled blades of grass.

The Dungeon

I pull my bed hangings open, and light is streaming in through the window. It's later than usual.

"Beatrix?" No answer.

She'll need to come with us to the field today. It would look too odd if Will and I went out on our own again. She didn't seem to remember much about yesterday morning, but the whole time she was getting me ready for bed, she kept questioning me with her eyes. Does she guess? Is she angry? Is that why she's so late?

There's no time to wait. I'll find her downstairs. I pull on my shift, and then a kirtle: my blue, not the heavy one, so Eustace won't be suspicious. And I'll have to leave the gold cross behind. Not nearly as good as yesterday, but we've still got a chance, and we're going to take it.

I open the door and start down the stairs. Beatrix will fall asleep under her tree, like she always does; we'll leave Pilgrim with her, and this time we'll gallop like the wind. I wish there were a better way, one that didn't involve Beatrix, but we must leave today before Eustace has a chance to think.

As soon as I step into the bailey, I can tell something is wrong. Too many people are rushing around, and every face is drawn taut. Up on the wall walk, the sentries pace back and forth, staring into the distance; there isn't a slouched shoulder in the group. I draw in a sharp breath. Does this tension have something to do with Will and me? Did he say too much? Outside the stables, a dozen saddled horses are stamping and snorting in impatience. Will and I could leap on and gallop away— but no, the men-at-arms would race even faster in pursuit.

Father Bartholomew stands in the middle of the bailey, peering this way and that, excitement illuminating his round pink face. I hurry to his side.

"Father, pray tell, what is happening?"

"You haven't heard then, my lady?" His hands start kneading each other as if they were deep in bread dough. I wait anxiously, but he doesn't say any more, just gazes again at the great to-do.

I want to shout, *Of course I haven't heard! Why else would I be asking?* But I manage to keep my voice calm. "Why are the men in their chain mail?"

He opens his mouth to reply, but is distracted again as someone hurries by: a kitchen boy holding two great geese by their necks. Lord, I hope this doesn't have to do with yesterday!

I speak louder to get his attention. "Why are the horses saddled? Where is everyone going?"

"A spy!" he finally exclaims. "They've found a spy! And where there's a spy . . ." His words drift off again, his head swiveling around like he's watching a jolly pantomime show.

I sigh in relief. A spy! That's nothing to do with Will and me. But I still need to know if it could affect our plans. I step in front of the priest so he has to look at me. "Where there's a spy, *what*?"

His eyes work to focus on my face, and then they light up with sudden understanding. "Oh, of course! So sorry, Lady Matilda! For a moment I completely forgot how sorely you were wounded." He nods rapidly, leaning toward me in a confiding manner. "Edward and a few of the men went out this morning, and what did they see but tracks. Not horse tracks, mind you, but footprints, and starting out of thin air! Well, they thought, who would be on foot alone, so far from town? And the trail looping and twisting in the most surreptitious manner, don't you know? Not the trail of a poacher who knows the woods, but that of a lurker, someone new to the area, trying to disguise his path. They cleverly followed the trail, and there they found him, outfitted in a blue tunic far too splendid for a commoner."

Father Bartholomew stops to scratch his head, and gets distracted watching a clump of men gathered at the barbican.

"Go on," I urge.

"My lady, who travels the woods on his own, unless he's up to no good? And making no sense about whence he hails, nor able to explain what he's doing on Sir Hugh's land, except for rambling on about searching for someone. They even took him into town to see if anyone could speak up for him, and not a soul knew him. Not a soul!"

He stops, as if he'd explained the whole thing, and starts drifting toward the stables. I grab his arm. "But it's only one man. Why are they saddling so many horses?"

"One man, yes." He nods. "One man sent to sneak around and assess the castle's defenses, and report back to the army that may be just the other side of the next hill! Because where there's a spy, as likely as not there's an army nearby. But don't you fear, my lady."

Fear? No, I'm wondering how Will and I can get away, with everyone on such high alert, and teams of men roaming the countryside.

"No need for you to panic at all," he continues. "Battle is what our Sir Hugh does best! Happiest when he's hacking

and slashing with that great sword of his. The men will scour
the countryside. They'll assess any immediate threat we're
facing. And by the time they're back, we'll have burned and
stretched the truth out of that spy."

I look at him in disbelief. "Burned and—"

"Certainly! He's down in the dungeon right now, and as
soon as Sir Hugh is ready, they'll start in on him. Believe
me, by the time they're finished, they'll know whatever's
in his head, from battle plans to the name of his first puppy.
They tell you *everything*."

"You don't mean . . ."

He nods eagerly. "We may be a smallish castle, but Sir
Hugh made sure to have all the finest equipment. Even his
very own rack! And those work so much faster than just
hanging them by their wrists, don't you know? In fact, come
along. I'll show you."

Before I have time to protest, he takes my arm and steers
me over to the keep. But instead of going up the stairs, we
stop at a door I never paid attention to before. Now a guard
is standing watch.

"She wants to take a look at the prisoner," says Father
Bartholomew. The guard nods, and the heavy door swings
open. Father Bartholomew grabs a torch and leads the way
down a winding stair deep into the earth. With every step

it grows darker, colder, and damper; the bailey's smells of horse and smoke give way to a salty, mineral tang. Then there's a whiff of something else, putrid and rank. Suddenly unsteady, I reach out to the wall for support, only to touch something slimy and cold. I jerk back. But I want to know what lies at the bottom of the stairs, so I keep walking.

Another door opens, and a guard stands aside to let us in. "She wants to take a look at the prisoner," Father Bartholomew says again.

The guard nods toward the floor. "Watch your step."

The floor? Yes, there's an iron grate in the floor, opening into an even deeper, colder blackness. Father Bartholomew bends down. "Oh, my knees!" he groans, thrusting the torch through the bars so I can see into the gloom. "There, my lady. You see? You've no need to worry. He's already half caved in, by the looks of him. They'll have him telling the truth with one turn of the screw. It's easier when they're old, like this."

He waves the torch around until a faint beam finally reaches into the far corner of the cell. And there, blinking up at us in the sudden light—

"Mr. Greenwood!" I cry.

"Addy?" he croaks, trying to struggle to his feet in spite of the chains. And then his eyes roll up, and he collapses in a jangling heap.

Enough Truth

I grab the grating and jerk with all my might. It shrieks like nails on a chalkboard, until the lock stops me with a sudden clank.

"Oh, dear," mutters Father Bartholomew. "It's too much for her. I shouldn't have brought her down here." He turns to the guard. "Don't just stand there. Help me!"

The guard dashes forward, but not to open the grating. Instead, the two of them are seizing my arms and pulling me to my feet.

"To the stairs now," says Father Bartholomew, tugging me forward. "A bit of bad air, that's what's come over you, my lady. Damp and nasty down here. Oh, what can I have been thinking!" We're almost to the door. "We'll get you some fresh air in no time."

"No!" I cry, planting my feet and throwing off their hands. "You've got to get him out of there!"

They stare at me, agape. "The spy?" asks the guard in disbelief.

I need a reason, and I need it *now*.

I stand as rigid as a steel beam. "That is no spy," I announce, pointing one imperious finger toward the fetid hole in the floor. "You have wrongly imprisoned Sir Alec of Greenwood, come from my court for the wedding. And someone is going to pay for this!"

Father Bartholomew raises his hand to his mouth, and his lips pucker into a perfect little circle, like a boy caught surrounded by a pile of empty candy wrappers.

The guard doesn't waste any time. An immense black key appears in his hand. He shouts, and another man comes running down the stairs, sword drawn. The first guard is already kneeling at the lock. "He's from her court," he grunts, as he pulls up the massive grating. "Hurry! Grab that ladder!"

They hurl the ladder down and scramble into the gloom, coughing as they reach even moldier air. By the dim light of the torch, I see one of them throwing Mr. Greenwood's limp form over his shoulder, and then he's climbing back up, grunting under the weight. Then it's up the winding stair, with me close on their heels, praying with every step:

Please, don't let them have beaten him! Don't let that rotten air have settled in his chest! Don't let him be dead!

The sunlight hits me like a battering ram. I feel like I've just escaped from a season in hell.

Men come running. "Put him in the good bed, in the solar," I cry. "Find Beatrix, she knows about healing." I grab one of the men. "Ride into town, as fast as you can. Fetch a doctor."

"A doctor?" he says.

Father Bartholomew pants up. "The barber, man!" he says. "To bleed him. And grab the apothecary while you're at it. Oh, dear me." His voice grows fainter behind me as I rush after the men lugging Mr. Greenwood. "Dear, dear me."

Sir Hugh strides into the solar and stares down at the body in the bed. Mr. Greenwood is as pale as a corpse. I keep looking for the faint rise and fall of his chest.

"Alive anyway," declares Sir Hugh. "Damn fool way he had of getting here. What is it with you and your people? Shipwrecks. Roaming the hills like madmen."

Before, when he used that booming tone, I dropped into an automatic curtsey. But now I look at Mr. Greenwood lying there half dead, and all of a sudden I'm on my feet and glaring up into Sir Hugh's face.

"He's my man," I proclaim. "And *you* won't talk of him that way!"

To my amazement, he looks at me with something like admiration. "So," he says. "The filly has some spunk to her, after all."

He walks over to the wine, pours out a liberal dose, and downs it in a gulp. He wipes his mouth with the back of his hand. "How was I to know? Damned man sneaks around in the woods like he's got—"

"Sir Hugh!"

"All right, all right. But why couldn't he come with a retinue like any normal person? Or send word that he was on his way?"

He doesn't know the half of it! I have questions of my own. What on earth is Mr. Greenwood doing here? Was he looking for me, and why? Is it Mum, is she sick? And when did he set the lift to return? And how—I glance at the narrow window, toward the mews—how can I run away with Will when Mr. Greenwood lies here unconscious?

But I can't say any of that to Sir Hugh, and he's starting to shift from one foot to the other like an impatient bull. I must make sure he welcomes Mr. Greenwood, or it could be the dungeon again.

I take a deep breath and sit back on the stool so I'll look

touchingly small as I gaze up. Shaking my head sadly, I say, "Sir Alec always travels alone, in spite of the danger. It's a vow he took after the death of his young son." It's always good to toss in enough truth to give weight to your role. "He used to wander the woods on his own for days."

As if he thought he could still find the missing boy . . .

Sir Hugh crosses to the narrow window and gazes out into the bailey. "All that bother, getting the men ready," he says. "They seem to be out of practice."

"I didn't expect him." And *that's* certainly true enough. Like an electric shock, it was, seeing his face staring up at me from that hellhole. "He must have come for the wedding. We were always very close. He was . . ."

My voice drifts off as I think of Mr. Greenwood handing me yet another book, of our discussions over cake and tea. I think of his eyes, telling me I was somebody, in spite of the apron I wore, in spite of what others said. He believed in me. I know that now. Almost like—

"He was what?" asks Sir Hugh, turning.

My next words surprise me. "Like a father. The father I never had."

A wave of feelings swells inside me as I hear what I've just said. Me, who wanted a father more than anything in the world, I had one, after all. Not by birth, but by choice. If I'm the reason he's lying near death . . . I blink, trying to hold back tears, until I realize I can't afford to hold them back; I need to use them.

I lift my shining eyes to Sir Hugh. "My parents died when I was so very young," I say, as a single tear trickles down my cheek. Perfect.

A strange expression comes over his face. "That's not the worst thing that could happen."

His words nick me like a paring knife that's sliced too close. This man, with his noble lineage, what does *he* know of sneers and taunts, of people turning the other way when you enter a room?

"I wasn't born to be lord of this castle," he continues. "Why did you think I'm so late to wed? My older brother was to inherit it all. They taught him about the land and the people, how to watch the accounts." His bluster slips for a moment; his voice is raw. "Me? When my father looked my way, his eyes passed right through me, like I was the castle ghost."

That's my pain he's describing, a pain I could never wash away, no matter how many tears I cried into my pillow. My anger is turning to confusion.

"Now that they're dead . . ." He pauses, gives a bitter smile. "Now that they're dead and my brother's dead and

I'm lord of the castle—*now* I'm someone they would have bothered to find time for."

His face closes again so suddenly, it's like a helmet's visor crashing down. "But I've bored you." He pours himself more wine. "Don't worry about Sir Alec. I've seen enough men on the verge of death to know he's not of their company." He downs the drink. "Your man will live."

A Man's Very Life

I'm sitting vigil next to the bed when Mr. Greenwood's eyes flicker open. "Addy," he whispers.

Thank God! I grab his hand, hold it in both of mine, and lean close so I can hear. "Found your dress. No dust . . ." His voice trails off.

Beatrix looks up. "Ah, he's awake," she exclaims, bustling over. "And the rest has done him good. Nothing better than a deep sleep to heal body and soul."

"Along with a good bleeding," adds the barber, hurrying after her with his bowl and blade.

But if they hear him call me Addy . . . I squeeze his hand, hoping he'll understand. "Don't you know me, Sir Alec?" I cry. "Me, your Lady Matilda? You've come for my wedding." I look at Beatrix, shaking my head, and whisper, "He's as confused as I was when I came."

"Saw you'd gone," he gasps, staring at me. "Door open . . . no dust . . . didn't know . . ."

"Hush, Sir Alec. Don't tire yourself. There will be time enough to talk."

His eyes close; his hand is limp. I lay it back on the covers. He's asleep again.

Tears are streaming down my cheeks, I'm that relieved he's alive. And that moved by his words. *Found your dress—* he *did* come because of me. This man who always avoids people, who never changes a thing in his home or his life, he stepped into the lift because he was worried about me.

I feel a warm hand on my shoulder. Beatrix. I reach my hand up to cover hers, and we stay like that in silence, listening to the sound of his breath.

But now that Mr. Greenwood's life is out of danger, it's Will's hand I need on mine, his voice I need to hear. He'll be pacing the mews, desperate to know why I haven't been to see him since we brought back Lightning. He might even think I've changed my mind! And so I stand, wiping my tears away.

"I think I'll step out for some fresh air," I say.

"It will do you good," says Beatrix.

"Take care of Sir Alec for me."

"In faith, I don't think you need worry." She puts a capable hand on his brow. "The worst is over."

I pull my cloak from its peg; the air has turned chill with the promise of winter. At the bottom of the stairs I pause, peeking around the door into the great hall. I'm in luck; there's the usual bustle of boys, but neither Eustace nor Sir Hugh is anywhere to be seen. I hurry to the outer door. Standing half hidden by the windscreen, I search the bailey for the steward's mincing step, the lord's great stride. Again, nothing—nothing, that is, but the cooking and cleaning and pounding and provisioning of a castle preparing for the king's arrival, with all his party, for the marriage of his ward.

I hurry down the stairs and across the hard-packed earth. I'm halfway to the mews when I notice a shadow slipping from the stable wall, coming toward me. I shiver and quicken my pace. The shadow takes on color and form, like a blurry picture coming into focus, and suddenly it's Eustace, bearing down on me, angling his path to intersect with mine. My breath is coming short and fast. We haven't spoken since his eyes latched onto the gold chain dangling at my side.

"My lady, a word."

I stop, closing my eyes; I try to pull up some armor, but

I'm so drained by my watch over Mr. Greenwood, I find I
don't have the strength. So it's unprotected that I turn to face
the steward, unprotected that I plead, "Can't you just leave
me alone?"

"I'm afraid I can't do that, my lady."

Oh, the "my lady" is there, but with none of his usual
reverential tone. The change makes me suddenly alert, and
now I curse myself for letting him hear the frustration and
exhaustion in my voice. I scramble for the haughtiness to
put him in his place.

"And why not, pray tell?"

But I'm too late. "Let us stop playing games," he says,
as cold and sharp as an unsheathed blade. "There *will* be a
wedding."

"Why, of course there will."

But he's not fooled. He knows. We both know.

"The arrangements have been agreed upon," he continues. "Lands have been trothed. Dowries pledged. The king
himself arrives in four days."

Four days? So soon? My eyes dart to the mews. The
door has opened, and Will stands in the doorway, looking at
me too openly.

Eustace follows my gaze. Keeping his eyes on Will,
he says slowly, "If anything were to get in the way of that

wedding, I'd hate to see what might happen."

The menace in his voice sends another shiver through me; the blade has touched my skin. "What do you mean?"

"I regret that I could not, shall we say, guarantee the safety of anyone who might interfere with the pledging of faith between you and his lordship. Such a man's very life would be forfeit. No effort would be spared to hunt him down."

The door to the mews stands empty now, and Eustace turns to look at me, his face stark and brutal. "Do I make myself clear, my lady?"

I clench my jaws, not trusting myself to speak.

"I am forced to be so explicit only because of the . . . *blow* you suffered. Otherwise you would know the importance of your pledge to both your estate and Sir Hugh's. You would not act so rashly."

I breathe in sharply. Does he suspect that, too? That I'm not truly Matilda? I pull my cloak tighter, as if that will keep my disguise from slipping away.

"I care only for the survival and success of Berringstoke," he says. And now he bows deep, again the faithful servant, showing me he'll keep up with our usual pretense as long as I play by his rules. "I must see to the preparations. Allow me to escort you back to the keep, my lady."

A Dagger
at *My Throat*

~~~~

Back in the solar, the bed is empty.

"Oh, my lady," says Beatrix, wringing her hands. "I'm
so sorry, but what could I do? His lordship came in and saw
your man breathing easy. Then, 'Can't have that old fellow
in my marriage bed!' he cries, and the next thing I know
there are men tromping up the stairs with a litter to carry
Sir Alec off to another room. I tried to speak, indeed I did,
but you know Sir Hugh."

"But who's watching over him, Beatrix? Why didn't you
go along?"

"His lordship said it's my duty to care for you, and he'd
set the barber to watch over Sir Alec."

But I can't abandon Mr. Greenwood to someone whose
idea of healing is to slash him and drain his blood! And if

he should wake rambling about his maid, with Eustace so suspicious . . . I turn for the door.

"My lady, wherever are you going? Look at your face— you need rest!"

"No. I need to find Sir Alec."

I take the stairs two at a time. The great hall is empty. I search out Timothy, Tip, the butler, but nobody saw Mr. Greenwood, no one was called to prepare a room. Finally it comes to me. What an idiot I've been! They'll have put him in one of the curtained alcoves up the other staircase, the one I've no doubt been avoiding because it leads to the steward's lair.

My chest tightens as I open the door and start spiraling upward. I remember the only other time I climbed these stairs, the grisly sight of Oswald's head that met me on my return, and I have to set my shoulders firm before I can go on.

The corridor is deserted; guttering candles only deepen the gloom. The curtains in front of the hollowed rooms are closed as tight as a miser's heart. Not a soul sits outside keeping watch. Have they left Mr. Greenwood alone then, not caring if he turns worse? I walk to the first curtain and pull it back. A straw pallet waits in readiness for a visitor, a pile of blankets neatly folded at its foot. I walk to the next curtain, reach out—

Suddenly, a lion's roar shakes the very walls: *"GOD'S BONES!"*

It's Sir Hugh! A scream tries to burst out of me, but it gets tangled up with the desperate need to curtsey that's surging through my veins, and by the time I'm breathing again, I realize the roar wasn't aimed at me. It came from behind a door at the end of the hall, the cold room with its parchments and the leather-bound book of accounts.

"Allow me to read you his missive, my lord." That's Eustace. He clears his throat. "'Sir Hugh of Berringstoke having pledged said lands as security, and having refused to repay his debt,' et cetera, et cetera—ah, yes, this is the part. 'Should said debt not be repaid immediately, all means will be utilized to assure the transference—'"

"Stop your blathering, man, and tell me what it means."

"Repay him now or he seizes the land, and probably more, by force. We do not have the funds. And we are under-manned, my lord."

By force? Undermanned? I picture Sir Giles's horse rearing in the bailey, the sack rolling to a stop, the quill twirling in Eustace's hand as he speaks of a minor land dispute. *Minor?* Not likely, with their voices so urgent. Matters must be far worse than I guessed. And if they aren't going to tell me . . .

I'll have to wait a few minutes longer to find Mr. Greenwood. I can't miss this chance. I sneak closer, quietly, so I can hear every word.

"Pay him?" demands Sir Hugh. "Why should I pay the lousy dog? I've never run from a fight in my life. If we're shorthanded, round up the kitchen boys. They can pace the battlements in case anyone is looking from afar. And wield a sword, if need be. They'd at least blunt the attack."

He can't mean it! Timothy, untrained, facing battle-hardened men? And Tip is so slight, he'd struggle to even lift one of those swords—surely he's too young!

"But, my lord," says Eustace, speaking so softly now, I step closer to catch his words. "There's no need! Once Lady Matilda's dowry is in your coffers—"

And then my foot slips, making the smallest of sounds on the wooden floor.

In a heartbeat, the door is flung wide. Sir Hugh is a battering ram, a force of nature blasting toward me, and God help me, there's a dagger in his hand—at my throat—

For a moment we're all frozen as still as a photograph: my hands flung back in alarm; Sir Hugh pressing his cold blade against my skin; Eustace, a parchment clenched in his hands, his small eyes stretched as wide as they'll go.

"Why, Lady Matilda," says Sir Hugh, his voice courteous

as he takes a step back, sheathing the blade. "You surprised me, my dear."

I can't breathe, let alone speak.

"Perhaps her ladyship would care for a chair?" says Eustace, pushing one forward.

But I shake my head. They're staring at me, the room silent. I look at the books on the table, now closed, their secrets hidden beneath thick brown bindings. At the gray sky outside the narrow slit of a window. At the parchment in Eustace's hand. He sees me looking, then carefully rolls it from top to bottom, ties it with a ribbon, and sets it behind a pot of quills so I won't see what's written there.

Eustace, who threatened me in the bailey. Who ferrets out my secrets while keeping far worse secrets of his own. I realize just how angry I am.

"You were speaking of my dowry," I say, clipping each word short.

Sir Hugh, so quick with a blade, isn't quite as swift with his response. "Well, you see," he says, hemming and hawing. "It's like this—"

Eustace steps in. "Can your ladyship have forgotten our conversation so soon?"

Sir Hugh looks confused, and Eustace turns to address him. "I mentioned to Lady Matilda that certain transactions pertaining to the merging of your estates will take place at the time of your wedding."

"You didn't say Sir Giles was attacking!" I cry. "Or that you'd put the lives of innocent kitchen boys at risk!"

"Everyone here would willingly give his life for Berringstoke," says Eustace. "Kitchen boys. Peasants." He pauses. "Falconers."

William, he's saying. *Marry, or everyone pays the price.*

"I insist you tell me what this is about," I say. "I have come to care for the castle and its people. If I am to be their lady, I deserve to know."

Sir Hugh, at least, sees the sense in what I say. "I owe the man money. If I don't repay him, we lose land"— Eustace clears his throat; Sir Hugh glances at him before continuing—"that we cannot afford to lose. That I refuse to lose. But the moment we're wed, your dowry allows me to pay off the debt."

He places that huge arm around me. I preferred the knife.

"There's no need for you to worry," he says. "I enjoy a good fight. And it probably won't even come to that, not if we marry the moment the king arrives. Then Sir Giles is repaid; he's content; the problem is solved."

"My lord," says Eustace. "It might put her ladyship's mind at ease if I send a man at once to the church in town, telling the priest to be prepared at a moment's notice. Then there will be as little delay as possible."

"Excellent idea," says Sir Hugh. Then, to me: "You see? It is only days until we are wed." I feel his eyes running down my dress. He bends his head to rumble in my ear, "I, for one, can hardly wait."

I try not to flinch. He isn't talking about finances now.

I find Mr. Greenwood on the next floor, sleeping soundly under the watchful gaze of a kind-looking man. He doesn't need me right now. I walk back through the gloom to my solar, climb into bed, and pull the curtains closed, trying to shut out the words I just heard. The curtains aren't enough. I burrow under the white furs as if I could hide from the truth. As if life were still what it seemed a few days ago, when all I had to do was leap on a horse and ride away with the lad I love. But it's too late.

I think back to the day I ran from Caroline's door and climbed the castle ruins, how I thought such thick walls could withstand any assault. How young I was then! Now I can almost feel these stones shaking as boulders strike; smell the air bitter with smoke as flaming arrows set the thatch ablaze; see young boys running out the door with swords they've never been trained to use. Unless I marry Sir Hugh.

But it's only Will's hands I want. His whisper gentle in my ear: *Addy*.

I pull the covers tighter around me, trying to stop trembling.

When I was just Addy, no one's life hung on my actions. But I had to be a lady, didn't I? A very grand lady, with a pedigree and lands and a dowry. I got what I wanted, and now I know the price. It's only my dowry will keep the castle and its people safe. And that means I can't run away with Will. I have to share his lordship's bed.

The High Table

I've made a proper mess of my own life, but there's one thing I'm still hoping to do right: get Mr. Greenwood safely home again. I kept checking in on him yesterday, hoping to speak to him alone and find out if the lift is still coming, but he never woke. And now it seems I've missed my chance, because after Beatrix comes rushing up to find me—"My lady, you're late for dinner! They've started without you!"— I walk into the great hall to see him seated at the high table, Sir Hugh on his right and an empty place, mine, on his left. He looks wan and gray, the lines in his face etched deep, but he's surprisingly alert. In fact, he's saying something to Sir Hugh.

Oh, Lord! What has he given away? Has *he* been eating the plates? I force myself to walk, not run, to the dais.

"Pray, forgive my lateness," I say, slipping into my seat.

But they're none of them listening. Sir Hugh and Eustace are both leaning forward to catch Mr. Greenwood's every word. I strain to hear above the room's clamor.

"But of course you can do better than that," he's saying. "A plow can work eight- or ninescore acres a year."

"Impossible,' says Sir Hugh.

"Nowhere near that amount," says Eustace.

"Haven't you read Walter of Henley's *Husbandry*?" asks Mr. Greenwood, astounded. "Oh, that's right, that's probably not for decades yet."

Please, God, I'm praying.

"Well," he says. "A furlong is forty perches long and four wide; the king's perch is sixteen and one-half feet. Am I right?"

They nod.

"Hence an acre is sixty-six feet wide. If you go thirty-six times around in your plowing so the ridge is narrower . . ."

I don't believe it! He's teaching *them* medieval farming techniques. I think of those stacks of papers on his desk, the rows of leather-bound volumes lining his shelves; I remember our teas, and how he knew all those details about the past off the top of his head. And now Eustace and Sir Hugh are drinking up his words like the finest wine.

He finishes his description, and Eustace says to Sir Hugh, "We could take those young oxen, they're nearly grown, and . . ."

As the two of them start in, I grab my chance. Leaning close to Mr. Greenwood, I whisper, "Are you all right?"

"The library door was open," he whispers back. "Everything was too clean, including the contraption, so I looked inside—"

"I say!" exclaims Father Bartholomew from my left. "What a nice wine! And have you tried the partridge?"

"Yes, delicious," I say. "Please, Father, do take some more."

He occupies himself with searching for the perfect morsel.

Mr. Greenwood is lifting his goblet to drink. "Stop!" I hiss under my breath. "Wipe your mouth."

He smoothly lifts his napkin as if he meant to all along, then whispers, "I saw the dates had reset. I knew you'd gone back, and—"

"—other arrangements for the king's visit," says Eustace. "I instructed Harold to make sure all the bridges are in good repair for hawking with the royal company, and he assures me . . ."

"Hawking!" exclaims Father Bartholomew, placing a

tiny, clean-picked bone on the side of his trencher. "That reminds me, Sir Alec. Have you heard of our lady's holy vision? We're having a plaque carved for the church to commemorate—"

"I'll have more of that partridge," says Sir Hugh to Father Bartholemew.

"At first I didn't believe my eyes," whispers Mr. Greenwood. "The lift had never been used before."

I draw in a sharp breath. "You mean, you never—"

He shakes his head. "Some of the equations weren't coming out right, and I had concerns about the wiring. With my son depending on me, I couldn't take the risk. And once he disappeared . . ." His voice fades to a stop, and he sips from the goblet to steady himself. "I see now that I stopped trying, or caring," he says. "I damn near stopped living. I believe I was merely waiting to die, until you came."

"Right there in her solar!" exclaims Father Bartholomew, leaning toward Mr. Greenwood, sure his tale is the most fascinating thing our guest has ever heard. "And out they ride on horseback, her ladyship following the dulcet voice of the Virgin herself, to a spot where, exactly as her vision foretold, a peregrine perches: a bird of prodigious size and absolute perfection, a halo shining around its noble head, and a golden . . ."

Mr. Greenwood leans toward me again. "When I realized the lift had taken you to the past and left you stranded, I knew I had to—"

"You there!" Sir Hugh raises a hand for the butler to refill our goblets, and then continues, his voice still too loud. "And how many are accompanying the king?"

"Other than the soldiers, an intimate party, my lord," replies Eustace. "Only fifteen or so. Chambers are being prepared, though of course the noblewomen who are to remain with her ladyship as ladies-in-waiting will sleep in the—"

Father Bartholomew lets loose a massive belch, and conversation stops. "Oh, do pardon me!" says the priest, patting his mouth with his napkin. "As I was saying, I'm thinking of sending word of the vision to the pope. Though it would bring much more attention if she had been carried off then and there by the angel to . . ."

The droning resumes from both ends of the table, and Mr. Greenwood starts whispering so intently, I'm worried the others will notice. "I thought you'd need saving, Addy, but now I don't know what to do. Do you *want* to marry? You're only fifteen, and he's—"

I grasp his hand urgently. "It can't be helped. Just tell me when—"

"I'll take a look at the bridges myself," booms Sir Hugh.

"Organize a hawking party for us tomorrow, Eustace. Our guest will no doubt enjoy the sport." He turns our way. "Won't you, Sir Alec?"

At the word "hawking," Eustace goes as stiff as a broomstick. "I will tell the grooms to prepare for the two of you," he says to Sir Hugh. He looks at me, his eyes narrowing. "I very much doubt her ladyship would wish to accompany you. She will be resting in preparation for the king's arrival."

"She'll come," commands Sir Hugh, crashing his fist down on the table for emphasis. The goblets jump. "The fresh air will put some color in her cheeks. Indeed, Lady Matilda, do me the honor of flying Pilgrim tomorrow."

I give up trying to talk to Mr. Greenwood in this confusion. Tomorrow, when everyone is spread out on the trails, I'll ride alongside him and ask about the lift and figure out if we can get him home. And I'll finally have a chance to tell Will about the danger, the dowry, why I can no longer leave. He needs to know before he does something rash. . . .

I look up from my thoughts and see the steward seething at Sir Hugh's rebuke. I mustn't anger him any further. So I lower my head and say, in the meekest voice I can muster, "If it is your wish, my lord."

Hawking at the Brook

We leave so early, the sky is still pale and pink, the air sharp with autumn's chill. Fidelius nickers with pleasure as I approach; he nuzzles my hand for the piece of sweet bread he knows he'll find there. Mr. Greenwood watches how Sir Hugh mounts his horse, then follows suit on his own roan, as easily as if he'd been doing it every day of his life. But one person is missing.

As Harold hands me Pilgrim, I ask in a low voice, "Where is William?"

"He rode on ahead to find the best flocks, my lady. We'll meet him on the way."

And then we're all clattering across the drawbridge and down the trail. I try to angle in next to Mr. Greenwood, but the path is narrow, and Sir Hugh is stitched to his side as close as silk lining. He's telling our guest about the castle's construction, the many advantages of the cliff-top location. As we move into denser trees, the two men start discussing the amount of timber that can be harvested from what type of forest. I hang back a few horse lengths, wishing Mr. Greenwood weren't proving to be such a useful guest.

They only stop talking when we halt at the top of a rise. Harold rides alongside Sir Hugh and points down to an open stretch of marsh and ponds; a flock of mallards drifts peacefully like a sprinkling of colorful leaves. And there's Will, astride his horse, raising his hand to us in a signal.

Sir Hugh turns to Mr. Greenwood. "Now you're in for some good sport," he says. He leads the way, moving us to a better position. Is this going to be my chance to talk with Will? Will, who still thinks we're looking for any chance to run off, who might even be planning to try this very day—I hate what I have to tell him. Pilgrim, sensing my tension, shifts her feet on the glove.

But this isn't to be the moment. We've stopped, close enough for a good view, far enough not to frighten the flock. Will is dismounting. He hunches low and begins creeping toward the pond; two spaniels slink at his heels.

Sir Hugh looks at me and says, "Let's see what you've taught that peregrine."

I turn until Pilgrim and I are facing into the wind, and we're both alert to the weight of it, the speed and shift of it. I feel her excitement right through the glove. I hold out my arm, then drop it, casting her off. With forceful strokes, she spirals up into the cool morning air, quickly reaching her height. Now she waits-on directly above me, circling, watching. Ready.

The only sounds are the wind in the branches, the horses' breath, and Pilgrim's bell ringing bright and clear on high.

Then Will lifts a small drum—and the air explodes in drumbeats like a battle tattoo! And the spaniels are leaping, the mallards fleeing skyward in frantic confusion. We look up, and Pilgrim is already tucked tight as an arrow, a rocket, hurtling downward—a blur of speed—the sound as she slashes the sky—

She stands victorious atop her prey.

"Perfect!" exclaims Sir Hugh, nudging his mount.

We ride down through the damp grass as Will runs to Pilgrim, holds out the tidbit, and gets her back on his glove. He stands as we ride up alongside. The spaniels wag their muddy tails, panting with joy, and Sir Hugh looks as proud as if he had made the kill himself.

Will pulls out another bit of meat, and as he offers it to

Pilgrim, he whistles that lilting line of notes. Pilgrim's tune.

From beside me there's a sudden, harsh intake of breath. I look over in alarm. Mr. Greenwood is clutching his hand to his heart, staring at Will as if he'd seen a ghost. At Will's long, thin hands. At the angle of his cheeks. At his golden blond hair.

He'll draw too much attention to Will, the wrong kind of attention! I'm just about to suggest we move on when Mr. Greenwood opens his mouth and croaks out a thin thread of song:

"My sweetheart's the man in the moon . . ."

Suddenly something clicks in my head, and in that moment I see it, like the last piece of a jigsaw puzzle snapping into place. Now I know what tugged at my heart each time Will whistled Pilgrim's tune, why the notes always hung in the air, incandescent, like a magic spell.

"I'm going to marry him soon . . ."

In my mind I'm carrying the tea tray down the hall, hearing what I think is an old gramophone recording. I'm at the door to the drawing room, watching Mr. Greenwood gaze up at his wife's portrait, realizing the song is coming from him.

"Twould fill me with bliss just to give him one kiss,
But I know that a dozen I never would miss . . ."

The old tune his wife loved, the one she was always singing: it's Pilgrim's song.

Now both Pilgrim and Will lift their heads to stare at him. Pilgrim's eyes are as black and huge as night. And Will, his eyes—why didn't I see it before?—his eyes are the brilliant blue, the unusual blue, the remarkable blue, of the eyes gazing from the portrait of Mr. Greenwood's wife.

It's
Time I Told

Will. James. The falconer lad and the missing boy, they're one and the same. He must have toddled into the lift and bumped the door shut. And Mr. Greenwood never suspected because he thought the bloody thing didn't work.

Came in a box, he did.

For the rest of the day, as we ride from field to pond, from marsh to stream, my head is whirling. Mr. Greenwood's gaze keeps drifting to Will. He hums those notes again and again, and each time it sounds lighter, freer, as he lets go a weight he's carried for fifteen years. He's changing in front of my eyes. It's as if he'd been shrouded in ice, and now that ice is melting layer by layer. His eyes are bright and glowing. His face becomes a warmer pink.

"Wonderful hunting," he says with feeling. "Wonderful!"

That, of course, satisfies Sir Hugh; in his book, hunting is all it takes to move any man to rapture. "Let's head on," he says to Harold. "Across the upper bridge."

Mr. Greenwood rides in front of me, easy on his roan. And still the coat of ice keeps melting. A haze of joy shimmers around him, like mist rising from damp ground in a sudden burst of sunlight. His shoulders, which were always as stooped as an old man's, are straighter by the minute. It's like he's just been released from an evil spell.

As we near the bridge, he turns to stare at Will yet again, and this time his eyes meet mine. He says, so low only I can hear, "Don't tell him, Addy. Please."

And then he's swept up again by Sir Hugh.

Don't tell him? How can I not tell Will that he has two fathers? That he's just like me, a misfit from another time? How can Mr. Greenwood even stay on his horse, instead of running over and wrapping his son in an embrace big enough for all those years of longing?

Will has been lagging farther and farther behind. Now he cries, "By God's bones!"

I glance back; he's dismounting to pick up something he dropped—on purpose, because he's looking right at me, pleading, glaring. I know he's asking me to come join him and plan our escape. But now that I finally have my chance,

I do nothing but stare. He's starting to look bewildered.

I want to shout: You think *you're* confused? What am I to do—now that I know who you are, and Mr. Greenwood is floating along as light as an eiderdown feather, and people will die if I don't wed Sir Hugh, and the king is arriving; that's right, me, the wife-in-waiting—what am I to do?

And since I don't know the answer, don't know how to think past the tumult in my head, I turn and ride in the other direction.

By the end of the day we've bagged three mallards, two teal, and best of all, in Sir Hugh's opinion, a goose. Sir Hugh is as pleased as a cat with a pile of mice.

Stupid, I'm saying to myself as we ride back over the drawbridge. *Stupid, stupid, stupid. Why didn't I talk to Will when I had the chance?*

We dismount in the bailey. Mr. Greenwood walks over to Will and rests his hands on his son's shoulders, warmth beaming from his eyes. "That was a fine hunt, William," he says. "You're a remarkable young man."

How can he even call him William? Isn't he dying to say "James"? Will stands speechless at the surprising show of affection.

Sir Hugh strides over to his guest. "Come," he says. "We need a spot of wine after that. And I want to follow up on what you were saying about fertilization and crop yield." He wraps his arm around Mr. Greenwood's shoulders, steering him toward the keep.

As they pass me, Mr. Greenwood looks in my eyes. "Not a word," he whispers.

Sir Hugh, deep in the highlights of the hunt, doesn't hear him. And Will has already taken Pilgrim to the mews.

I glance around—stables, kennels, kitchens, the windows of the keep—and there's no sign of Eustace. I call toward Sir Hugh's departing back, "I'll be in shortly." He doesn't even turn, just waves a hand over his head.

I hurry to the mews, trying to be invisible to the people around me, like Will sneaking up on the ducks. *I shouldn't be doing this,* I think. *Not after Eustace made his threat so clear* . . . but I reach the door and slip inside, closing it silently behind me.

Will straightens from Pilgrim's perch. "God's breath, you had me scared!" he says, rushing over and grabbing my hand. "We leave tomorrow. It's our only chance; the king comes the day after. I heard Eustace and the cook planning your wedding feast."

"Will . . ."

"Twenty heron! Three oxen! Won't they be surprised when—"

"Will, we can't go."

He stares at me in disbelief. For three heartbeats there's silence. I see the anger building in his eyes. Then: "Why not?" And, long and sarcastic: *"My lady."*

When I don't answer right away, he turns and hurls his satchel on the table with such force, all the bits of metal on the wall jangle. His jaw is setting into stone. "I see. You want to marry his exalted lordship after all."

"No! Listen! Without my dowry—"

"I don't need to be a lady," he sneers. *"I'll work with my hands.* But then she starts to think better." He looks disgusted, whether with me or himself, I can't tell. "I should have known when you wouldn't come talk, me making it clear as clear, and you staying yoked to Sir Alec like an obedient beast."

"That's part of it. I can't leave him. Neither can you. He's—"

"Of course we can leave him! He's only a guest for your cursed wedding."

"No, he's not! He's—"

And then I hear Mr. Greenwood again, begging me not to say a word. I stop cold. If I can't tell Will who he really is, how can I explain what's happening? That there are three of us now with one foot in the future and one in the past. That I can't separate Mr. Greenwood from the son he's found after fifteen shrouded years.

Will is standing there waiting for an explanation. I take a deep breath, trying to pull my courage together. I have to start somewhere. And if I can't tell him the truth about his own life, at least I can tell him about mine.

"I don't come from here." The instant I say the words, I see it's the wrong way to start. I should have begun with Sir Giles and the dowry, or Eustace, his threats.

Bitterness sets in the corners of Will's mouth. "Tell me something I don't already know. You come from across the channel."

"No, I *really* don't come from here. I'm not even Lady Matilda."

"You tried that one on me already. *Just pretend.*" He crosses his arms, a barricade across his heart. "Go ahead, say it: you changed your mind. You want to be the lord's lady."

I finally explode. "Oh, shut up! Shut the bloody hell up, and don't say a single word until I've told you the whole thing, or I swear I'll strangle you with my own hands!"

That gets his attention. "Then talk."

And I do. I tell him I come not from a different place,

but from a different time, hundreds of years in the future. That I'm a bastard, and girls jeered at me and some boys whistled like I'd be easy pickings. That I was a maid, curtseying to my betters, and the man I worked for was Sir Alec. Mr. Greenwood.

As I speak, the anger leaves Will's eyes. It's replaced by confusion, and then, a moment later, by something like fear. But there's nothing for it but to plow ahead, even though I'm coming to the part that's hardest to believe. How I found the lift, and whirled back in time. How the peregrine led me to the shore and the wreck, and my new life as Lady Matilda.

I stop, hoping for some response from him. A look, a word . . . There's the strangest expression on his face.

"You think I've gone mad," I say.

When he doesn't answer, my heart plummets, a lead weight falling to the bottom of the sea. Why did I think he'd ever believe such a thing? And me with no proof. No proof at all . . . except . . .

"Don't you remember?" I cry, grabbing his hand. "When they found Sir Alec, they said his footprints sprang up out of nowhere. Everyone going on about how mysterious it was, and strange—don't you see? It's because he came from the same time I did! The start of his trail was almost seven hundred years in the future!"

I wait. Nothing.

"No," I say, letting go of his hand. "Why should you believe me?"

I turn away, unable to look at him. His glove is lying on the table; I pick it up, stroke the leather. "I just want you to understand," I say. "When I came here and they took me for their lady, *respected* me like a lady, oh, it tasted sweet! But then . . ." My voice catches. "Then I fell in love with you. And none of the rest of it mattered anymore."

Suddenly his hand is gentle on my shoulder, turning me around. I see it in his eyes, and I gasp, "You believe me!"

His arms are wrapping around me; his warmth flows through me like my own life's blood.

"You never belonged here," he says.

I shake my head.

"Then nothing holds you. Come away with me!" The urgency in his voice is at once a healing balm and an intoxicating drug. "While they're all tired and drinking, and no one is paying us any mind. Come, Addy. *Come!*"

Everything in me aches to say yes, to flee with him, leaving all the rest of it far behind. And so it is that I have to wrench out the next words. "I want to, Will, with my very soul. But there's more yet to tell you. I was climbing the far stair—"

The window darkens. We look up; there, filling the frame like a malevolent portrait, is Eustace, staring at us. And then the window is empty again.

A man's very life . . .

I'm leaping from Will's arms as the door swings open. The steward enters, closing the door firmly behind him. His fur-lined cloak brushes my side as he passes by me without a word. He stops in front of Will, reaches for the dagger at his waist, and raises the blade slowly, deliberately, until the point is almost touching a beautiful blue eye—

"No!" I cry.

"Oh, yes, my lady," says Eustace, his mouth cruel and excited. His hand moves forward again. But at the last moment there's the slightest of shifts and the blade kisses Will's temple. A thin crimson line rises, beads; a few thick drops begin to flow. Will stands motionless.

"There will be a wedding," says Eustace, wiping his blade.

"Yes," I say, answering him but meeting Will's eyes, seeing that he now understands. "A wedding, and my dowry, to do with as you will."

"Not as I will. As we must."

Another Door

≫≫≫

"The king may have the finest tailors in all of Christendom, but not one of them"—Beatrix notes where she's going to snug a seam tighter—"no, not *one* of them"—she shifts the girdle an inch lower on my hips—"not a single lace-loving one of them ever made a kirtle prettier than the one I've sewn for you."

And it must be true, because I look like a fairy princess stepped out from some book of enchantments. The gold weave of the Baudekin cloth sings in the solar's candle-light, and each pearl ripples in response. The emeralds sparkle like green stars. And it's not just the cloth and gems making me so magnificent. Beatrix has worked a miracle with the cut of the gown, so it hugs and drapes my curves at the same time. When I move, it's like the dress is another living thing, dancing with my body so we're entwined in a duet.

"It's the most beautiful kirtle ever made," I say.

She puts her hands on her round hips and sighs in exasperation. "Then why, by God's faith, do you look so miserable? A miracle from the neck down, you are; but from the neck up, why, you're as long-faced as a cat that's been doused with a bucket of water."

I fluff out the skirt, pasting on my best smile, but it doesn't fool Beatrix one bit. She shakes her head slowly.

I sigh, and all the boldness I was clutching flows out along with my breath. There's nothing to hold me up anymore but the heavy fabric of my gown.

Beatrix walks across the solar to grab a stool, lugs it back over, and, with a firm hand on my shoulder, sits me down.

"Most everyone marries," she says gently. "It's God's will."

"Are you married, Beatrix?" Why did it never occur to me to ask before?

She nods. "He's back in town. And making a great mess of things, I shouldn't wonder, while he waits for me to return."

"Return?"

"Of course." Another look at my face. "Why, my lady, you didn't think I could stay forever, did you? When the king comes tomorrow, he's bringing two proper ladies-in-waiting to live with you. As it should be. Everyone would think it strange if you only had one such as me for your companion. It wasn't even fitting for me to come hawking with all of you, so there you were, the only lady with all those men!"

"That doesn't matter to me."

"It does to others. I hear one of your ladies is a widow, a bit older, but good on horseback. Not so likely to fall asleep when you're out training that bird of yours."

I grab her hand. Beatrix, all kindness and practicality, who treats me more like a daughter than a lady . . . My shoulders sag; tears start flowing down my face.

"Why, what's this, my lady?" she asks in concern. "It's what you came here for, isn't it? To be lady of Berringstoke?"

"But I'm not—" The words catch in my throat with the pain of losing her, losing Will, and all at once I'm sobbing. I try to stop, but it only makes the sobs stronger, and rougher, until they're tossing me back and forth like a gale at sea. I draw in a ragged breath. "I'm not even—" But my words are snatched away by the storm. Will! To see him every day, but never again be able to touch him. And his whisper warm in my ear, his hand in the small of my back as he pulls me closer—lost! All lost.

Beatrix is sitting beside me, wrapping me in her arms, trying to shelter me through the crashing waves of my grief.

I've lost him forever, and all because of this golden gown. A gown that's not even rightly mine, because—the words finally burst from my lips—"I'm not even Lady Matilda!"

"Ah," says Beatrix, "I wondered."

I'm so shocked, I stop sobbing and sit up, staring at her face. *"You knew?"*

"I wouldn't say I knew, but from that day when I saw you making your bed, I wondered how a lady had such knowledge in her hands. The way you crisped those covers!"

Somehow I've come to my feet, and there I am, standing in front of her in my grand gold gown. And her still sitting, as she'd never do with a real lady.

"And you so friendly with me," she goes on. "Well, you must have learned faster than anything, because it was no time until I was sure I'd been mistaken. God's faith, it's a bold chance you took!"

"You're not angry?"

"By the Virgin! Why should I be angry?"

"I'm an imposter. And a thief. I've stolen Lady Matilda's name, her money—her *life!*"

Beatrix shakes her head. "And what good are they doing her, down at the bottom of the deep blue sea? And her guardian, the king: surely he has enough gold already without claiming her lands back again."

"But you're always saying, 'It's God's will.' Beatrix, I've taken someone else's place, not what God gave me!"

"And isn't it Himself showed you the door in the first place, a door that was standing wide open?" Her voice is warm and sure. "Are you so meek then, or yet so proud, that you'd scorn to walk through?"

"But look what's come of it. Forced to marry Sir Hugh, bear his children . . . and lose the one I love."

Beatrix nods. "I wondered that, too," she says softly.

I run my hands along the front of my gown, each gem an obstacle. "Riches," I say, with a shuddering breath. "A fancy name. Once I thought they'd make me happy. And now that's all I'll ever have."

I expect to see compassion on her face. But she gets a quick, insightful look, all alert, like Will when he's sensing the shape of the wind.

"All you'll ever have?" she says slowly, making me listen to each word.

"There's no escaping this marriage! Unless Sir Hugh gets Lady Matilda's dowry, people will die. Don't you see? I have no choice. I can't run away."

"There's running away," she says. "And then there's looking to see if another door stands open."

How can she sound so confident? A castle maid—no, not even that, a townswoman, hired for a month—and yet there's a strength to her like an oak. It's me in my pearl-studded gown who feels trapped.

She stands. "You're all done in. You need sleep."

"But the king comes tomorrow! And the very next day, I wed."

"The king comes whether you sleep or not," she says, starting to unlace my gown. "And you might as well have a head on your shoulders when it comes to facing the morning."

Loud snores saw through my bed hangings. I pull the heavy cloth aside and peer through the dark at Beatrix, her chest rising and falling with each rattling surge. I can't sleep. Worry weighs on me heavier than the furs piled atop my bed. The marriage bed. The birthing bed.

Everything is so tangled in my mind, I can't follow one thread straight through. I start thinking about how Beatrix knows I'm not Lady Matilda, and then about Will, the red line beading on his brow. I think of the lift—I still don't know if it's coming back—and getting Mr. Greenwood home. Except now it seems he wants to stay here with Will. No, it's *me* wishes I could step in the lift and close that door behind me one last time, but I can't, not with the debt, and Will's two fathers . . . and Sir Hugh . . . and the king. . . .

I must have fallen asleep, finally, in the darkest hour of night, because suddenly I'm in my wedding dress in the middle of an oddly deserted bailey, standing atop a pedestal like a statue.

A fanfare of trumpets shatters the air. The drawbridge lowers, and the portcullis creaks open like a gaping maw, baring its long metal fangs.

"His Majesty the King!" booms a voice that's too big, like a salesman hawking some indispensable object. The king strides through the gate like he owns the world, a large man draped in red velvet, sporting a golden crown and carrying a scepter.

"Lady Matilda!" he exclaims. "My favorite ward! It's been years."

Then we're standing face-to-face, the same height in spite of my pedestal. I stare straight ahead, unblinking, an expensive possession on display.

Lines furrow his brow; his eyes grow puzzled. "What have

you done with your hair?" he demands. "It's supposed to be gold, like the coins in my coffers. Not brown as a chestnut."

I raise an alabaster finger to my lips. "Shh," I whisper. "Please, Your Majesty, don't tell anyone. It's only a woman's vanity. I dyed my hair."

He peers at me, leaning so close I smell the wine on his breath. Then he growls, low and menacing like a guard dog. "You may be able to change your hair," he says. *"But you can't change the color of your eyes!"*

He swings around, bellowing, "Guards!"

I leap off the pedestal and start running toward the gate-house. I'm not fast enough! The iron teeth are descending, inch by gnashing inch. A hand grabs at my skirt, rips off a strip of golden cloth, and then a gust of wind sweeps it up into the sky, sparkling in the sun—

"Imposter!" screams the king. "What have you done with my favorite ward? We'll soon have the truth out of you! To the dungeons! All the latest equipment!"

My feet are pounding and I'm screaming and an arm grabs mine—

It's morning. Beatrix is shaking me, hard. "Wake up, my lady!"

I sit bolt upright, my chest heaving.

"You were having a nightmare," she says.

I grasp her hand. "Beatrix, how quickly can you sew me a veil?"

"If I can find a scrap of sheer cloth, then no time at all." She leans closer and peers at me. "By my faith, you've thought of something, haven't you?"

"It's been staring me right in the face." I scramble from bed and reach for my kirtle. "The castle needs my dowry so there won't be bloodshed, but—"

"Yes?" she says, helping pull down the kirtle and starting in on the laces.

"But it doesn't need *me*," I say, turning to jerk the bed curtains closed behind me.

The
Jester's Cap

Beatrix has been turning the trunks inside out, searching for cloth for my veil. Finally, I run down the stairs, through the great hall—where Timothy and Ralph have already set up the last trestle table and are pulling out benches—and out the armored door. And there, thank God, is Mr. Greenwood, walking out of the stables with Eustace.

"Sir Alec," I call. "A word!"

I'm in luck, because Eustace gives a little bow and heads back into the stables. Mr. Greenwood comes bounding up the stairs.

"Addy," he says fervently, "I've been hoping for a moment."

We find a spot in the hall where we're out of the way and the boys can't hear us. Before I can speak, he grabs my hands and says, his voice deep with feeling, "How can I ever thank you? I would never have come here if it weren't for you, never have known James—I mean, William—is alive! And not just alive, but a fine young man, with skill in his hands and passion in his heart."

The intensity of his joy pulls so strong, I find myself asking, "Why don't you want him to know? To look at you and say, 'Father'?"

He shakes his head, and a touch of sadness comes into his eyes. "He's got a father. And a good one. Did you see the look on Harold's face as he watched William during the hunt? There was pride there, and affection, and love. How could I rip my son away from that, from a father who raised him so well?"

Timothy and Ralph are setting out napkins. Soon the room will be filling with people.

"I don't need to own him," says Mr. Greenwood. "I see him growing into a good man, with a rewarding life. It's enough for me to be near him."

"Near him," I say, grabbing my chance. "You won't be near him if you go back to our time. *Could* you go back? Has the lift—"

"Go back?" He shakes his head. "There's nothing for me there. Indeed, I'm glad to tell you Sir Hugh has asked me to stay on at Berringstoke, and I have accepted. There's so much to be done here. Addy, you've given me back my life." He squeezes my hands; there are tears in his eyes. "Now the question is, what do you wish to do with yours? I sense you don't enjoy Sir Hugh's company quite as much as I do."

As he speaks, people are flowing around us, washing their hands, gathering by the tables. I haven't much time! "The lift," I say, urgently. "When did you set it to—"

"There you are!" booms a voice from across the hall. I look up. Sir Hugh is rapidly closing in with his seven-league strides.

"—to come back and get you? Has it left or is—"

But his lordship is already here, taking Mr. Greenwood's arm, leading him to the dais. "I've rearranged our seats to put you between Eustace and myself," he says. "Now, as we were saying about crop rotation . . ."

I bite my tongue and follow. The high table gleams with polished silver; neatly cut trenchers wait obediently; the dragon ewer stands guard. I take my seat between Sir Hugh and Father Bartholomew, feeling miles away from Mr. Greenwood. The meal begins, but I have no appetite; I'm too anxious to know about the lift. Did it already appear in the field, only to return as empty as it came? Or is there still a chance for a miracle? I need to go through with the wedding, but after that . . .

I bring my attention back to the hubbub at the table. Sir
Hugh is asking about new developments in cattle breeding.
Cattle breeding! I can't wait any longer. I lean in front of
him, cutting him off mid-sentence, and ask, "How long are
you planning to stay with us, Sir Alec?"

"What kind of question is that to ask a guest?" says
Sir Hugh, stabbing a piece of meat from the platter. Before
Mr. Greenwood can answer me, Eustace starts in on dairy
conditions, and now the three of them are back in lively
discussion.

I can't help but admire Mr. Greenwood, so vibrant and
engaged. As I sit watching him, I realize his transformation is
about more than finding his son. Before, he tried to reach this
time through paper and ink; now it's in his senses: the clamor
of the great hall, the scent of the fresh-turned soil. He's living
the life he was meant for, using his head and heart to their
fullest. He should stay here. But not me. No, not me.

Capon, venison, eels: dish after dish is served, eaten, and
cleared. And I still haven't found a way to ask Mr. Greenwood
about the lift. The meal is drawing to a close. The king is on
his way.

Father Bartholomew passes a tray of marzipan sweets,
breaking into my thoughts. "And for you, my lady?"

The almond paste is shaped into elegant little figures: a

miniature castle, a prancing horse, a flower. And then I see a jester's cap, its bells picked out with bits of candied peel. A hat for an actor. That's what I've been doing here, I think, as I pick it up: playing a part, and playing it so well, I'm about to be trapped in it forever.

"Go ahead, eat it!" urges Father Bartholomew.

There's only one hope for me now, and words like *slow* and *quiet* and *remember your place* aren't going to get me there. I lean right across Sir Hugh's blather, catch Mr. Greenwood's eye, and say in a piercing tone, "When *would* you have gone home, had you been going?"

He realizes what I'm asking. "Tomorrow," he says, as clear as Pilgrim's bell. "At sunset."

Sunset. After the king arrives, after the ceremony at the church, but before night brings the curtains closing around the marriage bed. Could it work?

I bite into the marzipan. As its sweetness bursts into my mouth, there's a rush at the door and a man-at-arms hurries to the dais, begging his lordship's ear. "King's messenger," I hear him murmur. ". . . inform us . . . not far now . . . just before dusk."

A Veil of Mist

Gray clouds darken the horizon, low and heavy with the threat of rain. The king's party must be almost here, with their land-granting parchments, their ladies-in-waiting, their purses of gold. But I'm staying in my solar as long as I can.

I thought the bailey was busy before, but now I look down on a world swarming like an anthill under siege. All the ovens are going full blaze, and the spit strains under an ox so massive, the boy struggles to turn the handle. There's Timothy toting more rushes, and the pantler's boy at a full run, and one of the kitchen lads at the well for the fourth time. Eustace seems to be everywhere at once: in the stables, at the kennels, striding out of the guardhouse, marching up the stairs to the keep, and down again, as tireless as a mechanical windup toy. A wagon clatters over the drawbridge and unloads a pyramid of barrels; Eustace counts each one as it's lugged into the keep. That should last Sir Hugh another day or two.

"Almost finished," says Beatrix, her voice pulling me back into the room. She turns the veil and starts stitching on the final bit of gold trim with rapid-fire flicks of her needle.

I think how an actress steps onstage and the audience sees her for the first time. They take in how she's dressed, how she stands, the tilt of her head. In that split second they decide who it is that they see. It will be like that when I don this veil and appear before the king.

"It's about making an entrance," I say out loud.

"It's about hiding your face, is what it is," Beatrix says in her no-nonsense way. She bites off her thread and holds the veil up proudly. "There!"

It's perfect. Nothing more than a floating wisp of innocent white with a sparkle of noble gold.

Beatrix sits me back on the stool to braid and coil my hair. Then she floats the gauzy shimmer of cloth over my head. It's so light, like wearing a bit of mist. She pulls out a thin circlet woven around with golden ribbon, and settles it atop the veil, the thinnest of crowns.

She nods, pleased with her work. "Though I miss your bright eyes already," she says. "And so help me, I wonder what Sir Hugh will say. He's the type of man to snatch it off if he has a mind to."

"Then I'll have to make sure he hasn't the mind to," I say, thinking of those impulsive hands. It's going to take something big to stop him, more important than he is, higher up the ladder. . . . Of course! I smile at Beatrix. "And he won't dare. Not once he knows God wills it."

"God wills it?" She tilts her head sideways, looking for all the world like a plump, curious chicken. "And what do you mean by that?"

"I believe I feel another vision coming on."

"Believe you feel . . ." Her voice drifts off.

"Oh, Beatrix, you didn't think I *really* had a holy vision that first time, did you?"

She crosses her arms in front of her chest. "By my faith," she says, looking all disgruntled.

"I'll say I was praying again here in the solar, and suddenly I knew I had to honor my holy experience by wearing a veil until after I wed."

Her eyes have that look I remember from Mum, the one that's all steel and certainty. She uncrosses her arms and walks to the center of the solar, to the exact place where I demonstrated my so-called vision.

"If you're going to say you did it, you might as well do

it," she says. "Heaven knows you need all the help you can get." With that she sinks to her knees and closes her eyes.

Something like peace seems to flow from the spot where she's kneeling. Not a miracle. Nothing worthy of a letter to the pope or even a carved plaque for the church. No, it's something simple calls to me, as bright and clear as birdsong.

So I walk over and sink to my knees beside her. I close my eyes. I don't even pray. I just kneel there on the wooden floor, my head strangely free of thought. And then there's the warmth of her rough, calloused hand holding mine.

Trumpets burst out in a bold brass fanfare, and my eyes fly open. I jump to my feet and run to the window. The drawbridge is lowering, and it looks like everyone in the entire castle is rushing into place in the bailey. Sir Hugh, all green and yellow in his finest, is striding to the front of the gathering crowd. Not far behind come Eustace with his mincing steps, and Mr. Greenwood, his new green cloak flapping in the rising wind. I search until, at the back of the crowd, I make out Will's golden hair.

Sir Hugh turns this way and that, then lifts his head and stares straight up at my window. Even from here I can see the impatience on his face.

It's time.

I walk down the stairs, Beatrix close after; across the sweet-smelling rushes newly laid on the great hall's floor, through the door held wide by the fancy-dressed guard, down the stairs, and through the parting crowd to Sir Hugh's side. I hear a low rumble from beyond the walls as wagons and riders approach. Tension traces currents around Sir Hugh's shoulders, down his arms to his clenched, ring-laden hands. The lord of the castle, awaiting his lord.

"About time," he grumbles. Then he does a double take. "What's that for?" he demands, staring at my veil.

Before I can answer, the trumpets blare again, and the clatter of hooves and creak of wheels are suddenly huge in the air, amplified by the walls into a riot of noise. A bold white stallion prances through the gate, reins and saddle glittering all in gold, and on its back, clad in a richly embroidered burgundy cloak, rides King Henry himself.

The master of the horse runs forward to take the reins as the king dismounts. Sir Hugh sweeps into a bow. At his side I curtsey, deeper and lower than ever before. But there's nothing low inside me; my mind and heart are too busy racing, readying for the next step.

The king takes my hand, and I rise. He's not a giant after all, but a man of medium height, and much younger than

I expected. His build is slight and his face not particularly strong; one of his eyes seems to droop.

"My, how you've grown," he says.

So, he *did* know her. I thank God for the dream, and my veil.

"Your Majesty." Not a curtsey this time, I think. I lower my head.

When I look up again, his hand is reaching toward the corner of my veil. I gasp, barely keeping myself from taking a step back; but he only fingers the floating fabric briefly.

"What's this, then?" he asks.

Sir Hugh has moved to his side, so he's facing me as well. "I wondered the same, Your Majesty. Why should she hide that beautiful face?"

At the word *beautiful*, an amused look sparkles in the king's eyes. But they're both waiting. It's time to deliver my lines, in a way that radiates both confident nobility and sweet, pure innocence. I stand taller.

"I wear it to honor this important moment, Your Majesty. This step I am taking into a new world." I lower my head a fraction of an inch, the modest maiden. "After I marry, the veil will be removed from my eyes."

The king turns to Sir Hugh, more amused all the time.

"She'll be losing more than the veil, if this man has anything to say about it!" And then they both give those hearty laughs that are always barreling out of pub doors. If the king weren't so noble, I bet he'd be elbowing Sir Hugh with a nudge and a wink.

I breathe again.

A gust of wind swirls dead leaves through the gate, and in their wake rolls a canopied wagon with gaily painted sides. The air smells damp; the sky grows darker.

"The ladies," says King Henry. "I shall introduce you." As we walk toward the wagon, I hear him whisper to Sir Hugh, "If I remember her looks, you might encourage her to keep the veil on!"

Sir Hugh turns a confused face his way, but luckily the king is already focused on the first woman being helped from the wagon. This must be the widow. She's a woman of thirty or so, the elegance of her kirtle and wimple only emphasizing a certain grim set to her thin lips. "The Lady Winifred," says the king.

As we curtsey to each other, her eyes are busy appraising the value of my kirtle.

"Welcome to Berringstoke, Lady Winifred," I say.

"His Majesty tells me there is good hawking in these parts," she says. "I am an excellent huntswoman."

The next woman to step down is something different altogether. Nearing twenty, I'd say, with rose-flushed cheeks, her golden hair still worn loose and flowing over a more than ample chest. There's an intake of breath next to me; Sir Hugh's eyes are dancing over her figure with obvious pleasure.

"My ward the Lady Hildegard," says the king. "She'll be pleased to be part of your household until I figure out whom she's to wed."

"You are most welcome, Lady Hildegard," I say.

"Indeed!" says Sir Hugh, a little too fervently. Clearly the man inhales buxom women as eagerly as he inhales his wine.

I turn to the ladies. "You must be exhausted. Do come to the solar and rest from your difficult journey."

Lady Hildegard grabs my hand. "I hear the wedding is tomorrow!" she exclaims, as excited as a schoolgirl. "So soon! Can we see your kirtle?"

We all walk to the great hall, and the men reach for their wine and worldcraft as I lead the ladies up the winding stair. It's time to tell them about the veil and my vision. If all goes as I've planned, they're the ones who will spread the news and prepare everyone for the miracle yet to come.

After they've oohed and aahed over my wedding dress—well, Lady Hildegard oohed and aahed; Lady Winifred just gave a stingy nod of approval as she fingered the needlework, pausing over the pearls—after they've settled down comfortably and made serious inroads into the wine, I announce, "I believe I shall bear my peregrine on my arm tomorrow."

"You have a peregrine?" exclaims Lady Hildegard, pouring her third goblet. "That will look wonderful. Especially with those pearls. What is its name?"

"Pilgrim."

"A pilgrim to a church; how fitting," says Lady Winifred, still thin-lipped in spite of the wine. "I wonder if His Majesty will carry his gyrfalcon. Now *that* would be grand."

"I suppose I should speak with the falconer before the ceremony," I say. "To work out the details. I'd ask you to join me, but you must be exhausted."

Lady Winifred closes her eyes and sighs, showing how wearying the journey has been. Beatrix pours the very rosy-cheeked Hildegard yet another goblet.

"Allow me to accompany you, my lady," she says, setting down the pitcher and then walking to open the door for me.

"Yes, you shall accompany me. While the ladies rest."

When I told Beatrix about my plan, and the lift that,

God willing, will sweep me away, she accepted it easily, one more miracle in a world where miracles are expected to happen. But now, as she closes the door behind us, I can feel her anxiety sharp in the air.

"Are you sure this is wise?" she hisses. "If they're still in the hall, we'll never get to the door. . . ." But the royal party is no longer in the hall; the boys are plumping hay for their beds by the fire as we slip to the door. "And if Eustace should see you in the bailey . . ." But they're not in the bailey, and the men at the stables pay us no heed as we hurry across to the mews. "Do pull your hood closer," she urges. "That veil is brighter than a moonbeam. By the Virgin, I should have made you another in dark fabric—"

"Beatrix," I say. "Hush."

A candle shines from the window of the mews. Will and Harold sit at the table, deep in conversation. As we enter, they stand abruptly; I can tell by the concern etched on Harold's face that he knows everything. But he simply bows his head in greeting and walks to the door.

"I'd best check in with John at the kennels," he says, slipping out.

Neither Will nor I move while Beatrix goes around blowing out candles. Once the room is dark enough for her liking, she goes into the room lined with apothecary jars.

"Be quick, my lady," she says, as she shuts the door. "It isn't safe."

Alone. For the last time, we're alone.

Will takes my hand and leads me near the wall, where no one can see us through the window. There's nothing now of last time's anger. His arms circle me, and I feel the warmth of his body through his tunic. He lifts the veil back over my head, then lets go the fabric to run his hand up my neck. He leans down, his other arm pulling me closer, and our lips, our souls, meet.

How can I live without this? How can I leave him behind?

The kiss ends, but before I have time to miss it, he kisses my lips again, quick and sweet, three times more. There's a kiss on each of my eyelids, so soft, it's like the touch of a butterfly's wing.

I open my eyes, and he's gazing at me like a parched man reaching for water.

"You're leaving," he says softly.

I draw in my breath. "You know!"

He lets go and turns toward the table. "I've been thinking. Ever since you told me where you come from." He reaches to the table and picks up a white gyrfalcon feather, running a finger down the edge so each filament ripples along the feather's spine. "You're a wild one at heart," he says.

How can this be so easy for him? I thought he'd shout, fight, storm against my going!

Outside the window, legions of black clouds are scudding across the sky, so heavy, what should be twilight is become night.

But why should I wish him pain, when he's only accepting what has to be? And I don't have much time. If Eustace finds me here . . .

"It's tomorrow," I say. "I need your help."

He turns back to me, his arms again gathering my waist. "Of course I'll help." His voice confuses me; it's low and intimate, more suited for murmuring love than plotting my escape.

"Listen, Will. I have to wed so the castle gets my dowry. I'm bringing Pilgrim to church. You'll come to hold her during the ceremony."

"Mmm." He's nuzzling the side of my neck.

"Listen! After the ceremony, we need to get to the field, our field. The lift will be there at sunset. And no one but you and Beatrix can see me leave; they'd call it witchcraft, or worse, and then what would happen to the dowry? No, we have to give them a miracle."

I sketch out the plan. Then: "I don't want to go, but it will be worse if I stay. . . ."

Beatrix calls through the door, "It's late, my lady!"

One last time my mouth finds his; one last time, his kiss flows through my veins like the sweetest water.

"Good-bye, Will," I whisper.

"Good-bye?" He looks surprised. "I'm coming with you."

The Storm

The wind is singing in earnest now. The last light fled like a terrified child, and only flickering candles and the fire illuminate our faces as we sit stitching in the solar. There's Lady Winifred, her handwork a masterpiece of intricate detail; and Lady Hildegard, taking one stitch for each sip of wine, almost as if she were the nervous one about to marry and share that bed; and then there's me, pretending to embroider, but in truth playing Will's words over and over in my mind.

I'm coming with you. That's what he said. I should have told him no—I was going to say no—but then he was kissing me again, and I didn't want him to stop. Even when Beatrix came through the door, he kissed me. As if he didn't care any longer who knew.

Lady Winifred looks at the fabric in my lap as if she

can't believe the crooked castle she sees stitched there. She can't restrain herself any longer. "If you'd take off that veil, you could see what you're doing," she snaps.

A gust of wind surges through the window, carrying the sweet scent of rain and damp earth.

"I can't," I say. "Because of my vision."

"My point exactly." She pulls a pair of stork-shaped scissors from her needle case and snips off a thread. "No one could see properly through that thing."

Another gust, stronger: the candles dance wildly, blow out. The embers from the fireplace tint the room red. Suddenly there's a deafening crash, and we jump in our seats—thunder, shaking the walls like a battering ram.

"Ouch!" cries Lady Hildegard, looking at a drop of blood on her finger.

"You won't marry tomorrow if this keeps up," says Lady Winifred. She's nothing but a dark outline in front of the glowing fire.

I lift my head sharply. "What do you mean?"

Beatrix relights the first candle; it shines on one side of the widow's face, so she looks at me from one cold eye and speaks with half a disapproving mouth. "His Majesty is recovering from a cold. He will not go out in weather like this."

"But it *must* be tomorrow," I say. The wedding, the dowry, the miracle: everything has to go like clockwork.

"Nonsense," says Lady Winifred with a sniff. "One day is as good as another." She glances at the bed. "I should think you wouldn't mind the delay."

Lady Hildegard, sucking her finger, follows our eyes. "Lady Matilda might well mind," she giggles, all blushing pink cheeks.

Setting down my embroidery, I step up into the window seat and reach to close the shutter, as if I could wish the storm away. But the wind has other ideas—it punches the panel from my hand, flinging it back against the wall with a resounding *crack*!—and I'm staring at broken wood, useless now against the wind and rain.

I turn back to face the others. Lady Winifred is looking with chilly disapproval at my rain-spattered gown. "There will be no sleeping here, I see," she says, coming to her feet. "Kindly have your woman show me to another chamber. You will join me, Lady Hildegard?"

"Oh, no!" exclaims Lady Hildegard. "I'm sleeping here. I think the storm is exciting!"

Not long after, she climbs into the bed, pulls the covers to her chin, and falls into a peaceful slumber. Beatrix encourages me to join her. But how can I sleep knowing this storm might keep me from the church, the field, the lift?

"I'm sure I don't see how you'll face the morrow if you catch your death," says Beatrix, shaking her head. But when she sees there's no budging me, she wraps me in furs, satisfies herself I'm far enough back to be out of the rain, and only then makes her bench into a bed. Her snores are soon rumbling along with the thunder.

In the dark, pictures flash in front of my eyes like leaves swirling past in the storm: Sir Giles on his stallion—Oswald's severed head—the lift in the golden field—Will's eyes—

I'm coming with you, he said.

And I want him to come! We'd step in the lift together and land with a welcoming rattle and clank in the library. I'd teach him the ways of my time: how to dress, and stand, and talk, whether with a shopkeeper or a gentleman. . . .

There's a blinding blaze of light—an instant of pure white brilliance—and suddenly I see what I didn't want to. Teach Will how to stand, to talk—what was I thinking? As if I'd want to teach him his *place*! To be submissive, a lackey, properly trained! I shudder, appalled at myself.

This world of his, with its knights and peasants, believes in rank as something parceled out by God. But here, with his skill so valued, Will somehow exists outside it. Even when

Eustace held that blade as if to blind him, there was no subservience in Will's eyes.

Another flash of lightning, and now it's the field I see, and Will watching the peregrine's flight, the confidence in his shoulders, the tilt of his head as he judges how the wind will shift a moment before the wind itself realizes what it's going to do. I hear his words again. *You're never a falcon's master; you're her equal. Not like herd animals. Dogs live to obey, and horses and men like to know who's in charge. But what cares a falcon if you approve or no? She'll always be wild at heart.*

Like Will himself . . .

Now I try to picture him making a living in my day, trapped in a gardener's trousers, a spade in those fine long fingers. Or in a shop boy's apron, delivering parcels from the grocer's. How would those bright blue eyes keep their spark then?

As thunder growls into the distance, I finally understand why Mr. Greenwood whispered, *Don't tell him.* He couldn't bear to rip Will from the life he was meant to live. Can I?

A Matter of Timing

~~~))>

When Beatrix wakes, I'm still huddled in the window seat, staring out at a low gray dawn. The thunder has long since passed on; the rain is a drizzle.

"That won't keep the king indoors, will it?" I ask, slipping on my shift. Beatrix only shrugs as she holds up my Lincoln scarlet. I look at her in surprise. "Why, what about my wedding kirtle?"

"Not until we know when you're leaving for town." She adjusts the veil over my face. "And do speak softly; Lady Hildegard is still sleeping like a babe."

Down in the great hall, Lady Winifred sits at the high table, so alert, she's probably been up for hours. Slowly, too slowly, the others drift downstairs. From the bailey comes a hullabaloo of shouting, hammering, and dragging as people clean up from the storm.

"Everything is blown about!" says Father Bartholomew. "Great branches crashed down in the forest, I hear. Edward has taken a contingent to see if the roads are clear enough for travel."

"Of course they'll be clear," says Mr. Greenwood, trying to reassure me. But the certainty of his voice isn't reaching his eyes.

"What matters the condition of the roads?" says the widow. "His Majesty will not ride in the rain."

Footsteps pound like drumbeats down the stairs, and then Sir Hugh's bulk is filling the seat beside me. "Last time I sleep up there," he says, with a smile that sends ice through my veins. "Today is the day."

Father Bartholomew chuckles. "You mean tonight is the night!"

Someone offers me bread and wine, but I shake my head; the mere sight of them makes me feel ill.

"Tonight will *not* be the night," says Lady Winifred, dripping disapproval. "His Majesty won't ride to town in the rain. There will be no wedding. Not unless . . . Of course!" She turns to Father Bartholomew. "You could conduct the ceremony here. Then none of us need leave these walls, and the marriage may be consummated."

"No!" I say so loudly that they look at me in surprise. I lower my voice. "I must wed at the church in town."

Sir Hugh leans toward me. "The church or the castle, what does it matter, so long as we're wed?"

There's a flurry of movement at the door. Eustace enters, shaking rain from his cloak like a wet hound. "Severe damage to the dovecot," he says, joining us at the table. "The fletcher's shed blew over. We'll need to replace thatching on most of the outbuildings. Still, it's better than I expected."

"And the road to town?" I ask anxiously.

"How many times must I tell you?" says Lady Thin-lips, as if speaking to a willful child. "It doesn't matter if the roads are clear. His Majesty won't ride in the rain."

"She's right, you know," comes a voice from the far stairs. We all leap to our feet as King Henry enters the room. "I was in bed for seven days with that cold."

"But it's no more than a sprinkle!" I cry. "A mist, that's all."

There's a common intake of breath as everyone stares at me. I've dared to contradict the king!

But he waves his hand in the air as if clearing away smoke. "My ward may say what she pleases on her wedding day. And this may yet be the day." He lifts his golden goblet. "If the rain clears."

Minute follows minute, hour follows hour. And still the raindrops fall.

I'm stuck in purgatory: making small talk with Lady Winifred and, when she finally comes downstairs, Lady Hildegard; feigning interest as Sir Hugh and the king play endless games of chess; straining my ears for sounds of change from the bailey. I try to stay in my seat, but time after time I cross the rushes to peer out the door. The sky lightens from charcoal to silver. Then the rain is no more than a shimmer. Finally the clouds are as light as a stage scrim, revealing a hazy sun directly overhead— Midday! Only half a day left to ride into town, be married, and reach the field by sunset. Half a day to carry out a miracle . . . or spend my life bearing Sir Hugh's children.

Please, let me go home.

From outside comes a clatter of hooves, and then feet are running up the stairs. We all turn as Edward and Robert stride into the hall and sweep their deep, respectful bows.

"Well?" demands Sir Hugh.

Edward steps forward. "My lord, the road to town is clear and the rain has abated."

I leap to my feet.

There's a hearty chuckle from the table. "I've never

seen a maid so eager to wed," says the king. He turns to Edward. "Merely abated, or ceased?"

"As good as ceased, Your Majesty, the clouds grown so sparse, the sun begins to shine through."

The king pushes back the great chair and stands. "Well, then. To church!"

"Edward, ride to town," commands Sir Hugh, once more the brisk leader preparing for battle. "Tell the priest to expect us anon. Robert, have them ready the horses and the ladies' wagon. I'll ride my destrier. Make sure to use the gilded saddle." He looks at me; his eyes sparkle. "And you, my dear, might wish to change."

I look down with a gasp—my wedding dress! I run toward the stairs as the room fills with laughter behind me.

Married

The church is ablaze with stained-glass rainbows and the rippling light of hundreds of candles. Ribbons of incense waft up to the arched ceiling, where they mingle with the priest's last mumbled phrases. For a moment, the only sounds are the rustle of capes and the clink of swords. And then, from somewhere in the crowd behind me, I hear the silver jingle of Pilgrim's bell as she shifts on Will's glove. Will, who just heard me say, "I do."

"That's it?" says Sir Hugh. The priest looks confused. "We're married?"

The priest nods. "Why, certainly."

Sir Hugh turns to me. "Now you can take off that veil," he says with a leer, as if he's undressing me right there in church. "Or perhaps you're waiting for your husband to help

you." The men around him snicker as he reaches up a hand.

I step back out of his reach. I may be married, but the king still mustn't see my face, not if the castle is to keep my dowry.

"But, my lord, don't you remember my vision?"

"The angel? How could I forget?" He looks at the king with a wry smile. "For a while we actually feared she was convent bound."

"Then you wouldn't have had *that*," says the king, glancing at Eustace, who clutches a parchment as if his life depended upon it. And indeed, it probably does; those are the dowry papers, now signed, with the king's seal shining a brilliant blood red at the bottom of the page.

"Nor *that*," says Sir Hugh under his breath, his eyes running up and down the curves of my golden gown.

Each time he speaks my chest feels tighter, but I manage to keep my voice steady. "My lord, I must remove this veil at the very spot where I saw the angel, and nowhere else." Turning slightly to face the cross on the altar, I tinge my words with the slightest hint of fear. "I dare not do otherwise."

There's a collective sigh from the crowd behind me.

"Let us be off, then," says Sir Hugh, suddenly gruff and impatient.

The king starts toward the door. I try not to flinch as

Sir Hugh takes my arm in his, leading me after. I search the crowd for Will, but he's nowhere to be seen.

Outside, long shadows reach out to me from the tombstones. Not long now until sunset. Everything in me longs to run, to leap on Fidelius and gallop to the field—*faster*, I think, *faster!*—but I force myself to breathe calmly as Sir Hugh leads me to my horse, sees me into my richly embroidered saddle. He heads off to find his destrier, but he's stopping to speak with Eustace. . . . And the sun sinks lower.

Here, at last, is Will, come to give me Pilgrim. He rides up close, pressing against my leg—oh, I'm right not to stay! He puts himself at risk each time he's near me!—and I lean over to whisper a word. At that moment Sir Hugh trots alongside on his fine black steed.

"My lady," he says, and there's a new sound of ownership in the words.

I straighten, settling Pilgrim on my wrist, arranging my golden skirts across the saddle; I crane my neck, trying to see the sun as it disappears behind thatched rooftops. We can't delay much longer, or this wedding dress will seal my fate and I'll be Lady Matilda forever. I see her again, the real Matilda, limp in the back of the wagon—the sodden braid, the bleached skin—and suddenly I can't breathe. I'm the one who's drowning.

The church slips into shadow; the air is suddenly chill.

Finally, the king mounts his steed. Finally, he raises a regal hand, and the crowd erupts in frenzied cheers. Finally, our unwieldy column snakes through the narrow streets, past the half-timbered houses, through the town gates and onto the road.

All That Remains

We trudge along, too slowly, more like a small army than a wedding party. Fidelius senses my urge to gallop, and I have to rein him in. King Henry, Sir Hugh, Eustace, and Mr. Greenwood ride near me, followed by Beatrix and Will because, as I explained to the disapproving Lady Winifred, they were with me when my vision came true and so must be there as I pay it homage. Father Bartholomew is rolling along with the ladies in the wagon, and a long line of men-at-arms brings up the rear.

The sun is so low, its rays are almost horizontal, tinting the world pink. The bare trees are robed in a rosy glow, and even the stones sparkle like jewels. This road has never been so beautiful, or so long.

Mr. Greenwood keeps glancing at me uneasily, all too

aware how close we are to sunset. Then he rides alongside me and whispers, "I could create a diversion so you can gallop ahead."

But even as he says it, we're rounding the last curve. There's the familiar bridge, the oak tree, the winding stream.

I trot up alongside Sir Hugh. "This is the place," I say.

"Halt!" he calls, in a voice so commanding, everyone freezes. Not even a strand of a horse's tail twitches.

Trying for my holiest expression, I start the speech I rehearsed. "Your Majesty, my lord, I go down here to honor the vision I was granted and leave my—"

But Sir Hugh is already turning his horse, clattering down the stream bank.

"My lord!" I cry, urging Fidelius after. "I'm afraid you can't come."

"Nonsense," says the king, following in our wake. "You can't deprive a man of watching his own wife's deveiling." From somewhere behind us comes a chortle of amusement.

Now all three of us are crowded by the water's edge. I can't stop and argue; the sun is too low. I'll have to convince them along the way. The wagon waits on the road with most of the men-at-arms, so it's a much smaller group that winds the narrow path upstream.

I take up my case with Sir Hugh again. "Before, my lord,

it was only my maidservant and the falconer lad who came with me, because that was how I foresaw it in my vision." The path disappears, and we lead our horses splashing up the shallow stream. I speak louder. "The three of us who saw the angel must enter the field alone. But only for the very first moments. And then, indeed, I wish you all come witness how I have left this veil behind."

We're almost there. I stop, and they all stop with me. There are so few leaves remaining, I glance ahead anxiously to see if the lift shows through the branches. But the copse is tangled enough that the field is blocked from view.

"I pray you, wait here," I say.

To my immense relief, the king answers for him. "Hurry along, then. I'm ready for that wedding feast."

He waves toward Will and Beatrix, commanding them on, and—oh!—Beatrix's eyes are rounder than platters as her little horse trots in front of His Majesty's mighty steed.

The three of us round the last tangle of bushes, break into the field—

"By God's breath!" exclaims Beatrix, staring agape at the lift. Its filigreed sides are aglow in a last moment of sun.

The top of the dead tree is lit as bright as a match, but much of the field already lies deep in shadow. We leap off our mounts, and Will takes Pilgrim. I tear off my veil and tie it around one of her legs, lightly, so it will flutter off as she flies.

"Hurry," says Beatrix.

Will pulls out his knife and cuts off Pilgrim's jesses. "She's not coming back," he says. "And nor are we."

My heart twists. The gardener's gloves, the shop boy's apron—

"You belong here," I whisper, not wanting to say it.

"It's with you I belong."

And I'm so tempted . . .

"Hurry," pleads Beatrix. "The *miracle*."

And then, suddenly, I see what to do, how to make it all work. I put a hand on Will's arm. "You can't come now," I say urgently. "They'd think we ran off together. It's only if I go alone they'll have their miracle."

"And not dare take back the dowry," says Beatrix.

"I'll send the lift back for you in ten days, Will," I say, stepping inside, turning to face him. As I start to close the door, a sudden chill makes me shiver. "Ten days to make sure you'd have no regrets. And you must tell Sir Alec—"

He sees my hand on the door and realizes what I'm doing. With a fierce look, he drops the knife and reaches out, just as the latch catches. There's a click, the sound of finality. Now Will is dropping his other arm, casting Pilgrim off so he can free his hand, grab the door—but it's locked. The lift begins to shake.

Pilgrim is trained to rise high, and rise she does, above the trees, into the last rays of the setting sun. "Oh, the light!" screams Beatrix, so piercing, everyone will hear, will look. "Up in the sky! My faith! It's a miracle!" And the shafts of light are arrows fanned across the sky, arrows that strike the gold-trimmed veil, blazing it into a circle of light. A halo.

A wisp of radiant fabric drifts down from the sky, slowly, toward the king, all that remains of Lady Matilda. . . .

The rattling and shaking are reaching their pitch, and Beatrix is screaming—"She was carried aloft with that bird! She's been taken!"—and the numbers are whipping past in a blur. I reach toward Will, his hand outstretched toward mine, and then he, too, is spinning away on the other side of the lift, and the world turns black.

Home

The rattling stops and everything is wrong. The library smells of smoke. My eyes fly open. Orange flames are devouring the control panel, the dial that says RETURN.

"No!"

I wrench the door open, leaping out to grab something—anything!—to suffocate the fire, but I only see papers, brittle and crinkled with age; and there's no time, the blaze is growing, so I reach for the only thing I have, the wedding gown draped on my body. Lifting as much as I can of the skirt, the long train, I plunge back into the booth and pound the golden fabric against the flames, again and again, the heat blasting my skin, the smoke and stench of scorched cloth choking my lungs—

And then I realize that I'm still pounding, but the fire is

gone. I stop with a shuddering breath, my arms falling to my sides. The air is charred and thick. Dials dangle from half-melted wire. The numbers that once flipped by so briskly are nothing but ash. The control panel gapes outward, and I pry off the cover; inside is a ravaged wasteland, all signposts for rebuilding gone. I touch one of the knobs, and it falls off in my hand.

I'll send the lift back for you in ten days. Ten days to make sure you'd have no regrets . . .

I see his fierce eyes, hear the certainty in his voice: *It's with you I belong.*

I stumble from the lift, fall to my knees, and then not even my knees will hold me. Sobs rip through me, as jagged as shards of glass. I sob as if I could wrench my breaking heart from my body, as if my tears could carry him back to my side. Will! He'll be standing in the field, waiting for a lift that never comes. And as the days pass, he'll think I'm the one had second thoughts. . . .

In time I feel the pain stabbing my palm, and I unclench my fist. A cracked knob rolls from my hand to the floor.

Later, much later, when I've opened the windows to let out the reek of smoke and charred fabric, when I've washed my face and changed into the navy blue dress I left lying there a lifetime ago, when I've walked like a ghost through the village streets, I open my own front door.

Mum reaches for the teapot. "How was your day?" she says.

My day. I look back outside; the trees are only beginning to turn gold. It's the same day I left. Somehow Mr. Greenwood managed to do that for me, too.

Mum is setting the teapot down again, peering at me with concern. "You look all done in," she says, walking to where I'm hanging my apron on the hook. "Why, what's this? Have you been crying?"

Then I'm sobbing again, and my grief is a flood, wiping out everything in its path. I'm drowning, unable to catch a breath, to lift my head above the torrent.

"Addy, what is it?" says Mum, sitting me in a chair. "It can't be as bad as all that, now. Whatever it is, we'll fix it."

"There's no fixing it," I say, wrenching out one aching word at a time.

"Tell me, then," she says, her hand on my shoulder.

But I can't tell her where I've been. Who I've been. What I've lost. I can't even say Will's name.

"Sometimes," she murmurs, "when you think all doors are closed to you, there's another one stands open."

I startle, looking up at her. I've heard those words before.

In time, my sobs crest and then lessen. I picture the

burned lift in the library, and I know I have to tell her something, in words that she'll understand. That the whole town will understand. And so I say that I was out doing errands, and when I came back, the house reeked of smoke. There had been a fire in the library, and Mr. Greenwood was nowhere to be found. I say that I waited and waited, but he didn't come home.

"We'd best see the constable," she says.

They search for Mr. Greenwood for weeks. I feel terrible for their efforts, knowing they'll never find him. At first, the paper is full of stories of the mysterious fire, the strange contraption in the library, the disappearance of the man whose son disappeared so many years ago. And then the attention begins to fade.

Neither Mum nor I mention my leaving to be a live-in. I sit at home helping with her stitching, and I cry for Mr. Greenwood, who loved me enough to risk his life because he thought I needed saving. And he was right. I did need saving, after all.

But mostly I cry for Will, and the brightness in his eyes, the touch of his hands, the warmth of his mouth on mine. I cry for knowing I'll never see him again. So I stitch, watering the furrows of my seams with tears.

Then a day comes when I realize I have to go on. That's all I can do, take one step at a time, like climbing the castle ruins, hoping each time I place a foot there'll be stone enough to hold me.

I knot off a thread, draw a deep breath, and look up at Mum. "I'm going back to school," I say. I see the doubt looking back at me, but I keep going. "There'll be enough to live on, you'll see. At night I'll do your hemming, learn to help with the cutting and fitting, so you can take on more work. But I'm going back to school."

I watch her face. There's a long pause as she struggles, and then something shifts and she sighs. "All right then. One more chance."

A Necessary Prompt

~~~~~>>>>

I enter the classroom, and there's still an empty desk. Every head turns as I walk over and set my satchel down. Miss Rowland stands at the board, a piece of chalk frozen in her upraised hand.

"I've come back," I say.

A smile brightens her face. "That's wonderful, Addy. Please be seated." She brings over a textbook. "We've moved on to this one." As she gives it to me, her hand presses mine.

And then she's all brisk again at the board. I've missed more than a month, so I just listen and read, catching my place. It feels different, and not only because I was so long away. I can't put my finger on it. A new intensity, a new kind of wanting.

When the bell rings and I'm gathering my books, and

the others are starting to file out around me, Miss Rowland says, "Addy, would you mind waiting for a moment?"

Caroline sashays past. Without turning her head, she whispers, "Don't forget your mop and bucket!"

How long has it been for her since we met at the grocer's? Two weeks, three? Her words feel so little now; she still thinks she's heading a great army, but behind her trails nothing more than a flock of harmless yellow chicks.

When everyone else has left, Miss Rowland sits in the desk beside mine and sets down a slim volume. I look up from its title in surprise.

"The play," I say.

"That's right. It's still two weeks until we go on. I'm afraid the role you had is taken, though we are having some"—she pauses, searching for the right word—"some *challenges* with that role at the moment. But there is a part open, one I cut from the script when I had nobody to play it. Putting it back in makes the play much stronger."

I'm surprised at the excitement I feel as I think of working with lines, finding a character, bringing her to life. "What is the part?"

"The nursemaid."

The part Caroline had before she became queen.

"A nice, solid role," says Miss Rowland. "A no-nonsense

woman with a big heart and a good dose of humor."

I know just the person to model her on. "I'd be honored," I say.

She walks to her desk and scribbles a note. "Give this to Mrs. Murchie at the theatrical society, and she'll find you a costume."

I have to wait for a moment in the street. The door to the theatrical society is wide open, but it's blocked by two burly men trying to fit an overlarge ornate chair inside. They turn it, and tilt it, and then with a stubborn push—and a small *snap*—they're through. One of the chair's gilded feet lies on the step behind them.

I pick it up on my way in and hand it to one of the men.

"Bloody thrones," he says.

I walk downstairs. The door to the costume room is ajar. I look around, wondering which dress they've put Caroline in, what the old woman thought when she couldn't find the red and gold gown.

There are footsteps on the stairs, slow and careful, and then the old woman appears at the door. "Oh, it's you," she says in her scratchy voice.

"Mrs. Murchie?" I hand her the note.

"Hmm," she says, reading. "A nursemaid. I have

several that might work. This is Miss Rowland's production. Medieval, yes?"

I nod.

"Then we'll need the one with the wimple. It's brown, if I remember correctly. You search through that side, and I'll begin over here."

The rack is crowded with costumes waiting to be brought to life. I go through them more slowly than I should, running my hand across this sturdy homespun, that elegant lace. It makes me think of the last time I was here, how I found the glove. . . . I look down, and my heart stops. There it is, right where I left it. A falconer's glove.

I pick it up, and as I touch the well-worn leather, I feel a changing wind blowing my hair back once more. I smell the field, the trees, the dried grass. I slide my left hand into the glove, bending my arm as if Pilgrim stood there.

"Here we are!" exclaims Mrs. Murchie, turning to me with an armful of brown wool. She stops when she sees the glove on my hand. "That old thing! I never could figure out what it's for. Sometimes I think this room needs a good sorting out."

I'm remembering how Will took my hand that first time, how he shaped my fingers with his, showing me how to hold the jesses. . . .

Mrs. Murchie holds the kirtle up against me to measure the length. "Far too big," she sighs, shaking her head. "And heaven knows when I'll find time to alter it."

"I can do it," I say. "If you don't mind my taking it home."

"Well, if you're sure." She rummages around in a corner and comes back with a wimple. "Do you know how this goes on?" I nod. She puts the costume in a sack and holds it out to me, waiting.

But the glove doesn't want to leave my hand. I see Will, reaching out to me, to the door of the lift. . . . "Please," I say. "May I take this glove as well?"

"Not for your costume, surely?"

"No, I just—I just need it. I'll pay you, of course."

"Take it," she says. "I never could figure out why there was just the one. One glove! What good does that do you? And you're doing my work with the alterations."

She pulls the glove from my hand, tosses it into the bag with the rest, and offers it all to me.

The rehearsals have already moved to the stage. I have to work quickly to learn my blocking, and the others have to remember to wait for me to speak, since they're used to doing it without me. Jane, as a glamorous lady-in-waiting, keeps stepping right on top of my lines; each time, she throws up her hands in exasperation, everything grinds to a halt, and we have to start all over again.

But the biggest problem isn't lines. It's Caroline, the queen, the center of the play. With all her natural haughtiness, she should be perfect for the role. But the moment she takes the stage, she looks down as if she's searching for her lines on the floor; she speaks so softly, at times it feels like she's actually shrinking.

There's part of me doesn't mind one bit, watching her struggle, seeing her face as Miss Rowland tells her to take a line again and again. But she's not the only one who will pay the price for a bad performance. The entire cast will suffer. Miss Rowland has worked so hard to give us this chance with real costumes and a real stage—and not a soul in the audience will be able to bear it.

"Again," says Miss Rowland. "From 'Bring me my cloak.'"

Caroline clasps her hands in front of her like a good little girl. "Bring me my cloak," she says, all flat.

Ah! It's enough to drive me mad! And finally it must, because all of a sudden, as I bring up her cloak, I find myself whispering, "Is *that* all you can do?"

I see her shoulders tighten. I place the cloak around

them and lean up close. "You hate me," I whisper in her ear. "Then use it. Use it like a grand lady!"

She whirls around to face me—which is right, she should be turning toward the door—and for once there's fire in her eyes. Under her breath, she threatens, "Why, you . . ."

"You're a queen," I whisper, my back to Miss Rowland. "To you, I'm nothing. You rule the world! God put you there!"

"Who do you think you are, telling me—"

"That's it," I whisper, backing away, seeing her blazing eyes, her shoulders thrown back, hearing the disdain in her voice. "Now do it with your next lines."

She flings back her cloak and says her next line in a voice that would make her mother proud at the back door, a voice as disdainful and cold as Lady Winifred's thin lips.

Miss Rowland stands, applauding. "I think we're getting somewhere!" she exclaims.

Caroline does what helps Caroline. By the time practice is over, she realizes I've been useful to her. Over the course of the rehearsals, she listens as I whisper asides to her about how to hold her head when she addresses her lady-in-waiting, how to adjust her stance when she speaks to the king, where to pause in her lines, when to strike a pose.

And by the night of the performance, as I peer out from

the wings at the audience filing into the theater, taking their places in the plush red seats; as I see Mum coming in, and the grocer, and the women from Mrs. Miller's shop, and even a man from the local paper; as the house lights dim and a hush comes over the room and Caroline strides out on the stage, I know we'll do all right.

A Visitor

〰〰⋙

Another month goes by. One morning I'm clearing our tea things from the table when there's a knock at the door. I open it to a man in a city suit.

"Miss Adelaide Morrow?" I nod in surprise. "Bertram P. Halliburton, Esquire, at your service." He hands me his card. "I am, that is to say, I was, Mr. Greenwood's solicitor."

I step back, staring at the card, dumbstruck. What could he be doing here?

Mum waits for a moment, but when I don't speak, she comes to the door. "Won't you come in, Mr. Halliburton?" she says. She offers him a seat at the table. They both look at me, and I realize I'm to join them, so I pull up a stool.

The solicitor sets his attaché case on the table. He opens the clasps, pulls out a sheet of thick ivory paper, and hands it to me with a flourish. "Please read it, Miss Morrow," he says.

Wondering why he's giving it to me instead of Mum, I start reading aloud. "I, Alec Greenwood, being of sound mind and body—"

It's his last will and testament. My voice catches; the paper blurs.

Mum, seeing I can't go on, gently takes the paper from my hand and reads the rest. "—being of sound mind and body, do hereby bequeath my worldly goods, including my house and all its contents, to Miss Adelaide Morrow of Little Pembleton, in thanks for the friendship and warmth she brought to an old man's life."

"I won't take it," I say.

Mum's eyes go wide with shock. "But, Addy, you'll live in comfort! You'll never have to work again."

"I won't take it. He may still be coming back."

They both look at me so sadly, I almost start crying again. The solicitor shakes his head. "I'm afraid that is highly unlikely, Miss Morrow. Months have passed with no sign or word of him. I'm sorry." But when he sees I won't change my mind, he closes his case and stands. "The estate will be held in trust for you, in case you change your mind."

What good would they do me, his house, his money? They won't bring back Mr. Greenwood. They won't give me Will.

The Bridge

≫≫≫

There is a part of me that always seems to be waiting. That will be waiting my entire life for something I can never have again. Like a fool, I wander the churchyard, trying to make out the names on the oldest stones, to see if his is there, because then I would know.

One day I pull aside vines on a stone and find a carving of a tree in full leaf, and soaring above the tree, a bird, and fluttering below the bird, something that might well be a veil. But the words underneath are eaten away by time, and I can't make them out.

The stone doesn't show the rest of them. The king and his knight staring in astonishment at the miracle taking place before their very eyes. Or the dear woman whose ringing shouts pierce the air like a falcon's cry. Or the lad with his

arms outstretched, trying to grasp the empty air: *It's with you I belong.*

It's only in memory now I can feel his breath warm on my cheek, hear his voice murmuring low and sweet in my ear.

And so, once again, I start up the road toward the castle ruins, to pace out the distance from the keep to the spot where the mews stood centuries ago. That's where I sit these days when I reach the top of the cliff, not in the window seat, but on a pile of stones in what was once the bailey.

He's so strong in my mind today, I barely see the shops along Market Street, or notice when they disappear and trees take their place. But as I pass the edge of the village and the road begins to climb uphill, I hear rapid footsteps coming up behind me. I pause to let them pass, so I can be alone.

Mrs. Miller and several of her plump friends scurry by, their hats bent toward one another in eager argument.

"Yes, a prank," says one. "Why else use it to block the bridge?"

"Nonsense. It fell off a wagon."

"And landed upright? And not a twig broken?"

Their strange conversation makes me aware, again, of the world around me. Now I notice a bunch of children running up the road ahead, as excited as if it were a holiday, and glancing back, I see a swagger of lads coming from town.

What could be pulling them from their tasks this time of day?

When I round the curve, I can't even see the bridge, there's such a cluster of people around it. It makes me think of the crowd I pushed my way into so long ago at the fair, to discover the bear dancing on its hind legs. Intrigued, I walk to the edge of the crowd and stand on tiptoe, craning to see, but the women's hats bob like oversized flowers, blocking my view.

"That's a door, it is," says a man. "You're meant to go in it."

"When it's crafted so strange?" says another. "More like a house for a forest creature."

"—blocking the road!" comes a haughty voice. "I demand—"

I edge past Mrs. Miller and her friends, nudge several men aside, slip around a group of lads, until I reach the front of the crowd.

And now my heart starts pounding, because I can see something none of the rest of them have figured out. It's exactly the size and shape of a lift. But no lift you ever saw; no, it's more like a fairy creation. The bottom half is carefully fitted planks, and the folding door is lighter slats, but the top half is woven of curving willow branches, strong and light.

I reach out a hand and push in the folding door.

"Careful!" cries a woman. "It could be an anarchist's trap, meant to blow us all sky high!"

I see why she'd think that. There's a panel on the side wall, with the most elaborate maze of wiring you ever saw, like a labyrinth. And no ordinary wire: this has been hammered out by hand, leaving bits of thick and thin, round and flat, just like the texture of chain mail.

It couldn't be. And yet here it stands in the middle of the bridge, the one place he'd be sure no tree had grown. . . .

I turn to a man beside me and ask, "Has anyone new been seen about since it came?"

"Only the toff," he says, nodding toward a man in a motoring suit. "Demanding we make way for his precious motorcar."

I stare at every face in the crowd, hoping against hope. It couldn't be! How could Mr. Greenwood make another lift from twigs and bits of hand-pounded metal? But as much as my brain is refusing to believe, my heart is pulling me past the lift and out the other side of the crowd.

I was heading for the castle, Sir Hugh's castle. But if it is Will, if by some miracle he's come, he won't have gone there.

A special place for me, this is.

The field! It isn't a field any longer, but the land around Mr. Greenwood's house, and Will won't know of the new road leading to the door. . . . I edge back from the crowd, slip down to the stream, and I start to run.

The path is so much more tangled now than it was in the past, barely a path at all, and I'm weaving between tree trunks and bushes, leaping from stone to stone in the middle of the stream. The sounds of the crowd disappear behind me, replaced by the slap of my feet, the water's vibrant song. Every part of me—my heart, my mind, my skin, my very blood—is burning with the most unreasonable of hopes.

The stream curves; there's a slight rise. And then I hear it, each note incandescent in the air: a whistled fragment of a tune. Pilgrim's tune. And the longing in me, the need, the fear that I'm dreaming, the strangeness, all make me walk slowly now, silently, toward the source of the music.

That's how I come to see him before he sees me. He's leaning against a tree, like part of the forest himself in his green tunic, his brown leather boots. As I watch, he closes his eyes as if summoning some inner power, and he whistles again. But it's no falcon he's whistling down; there's no glove upon his hand. No, he's calling to me.

I step into the open. "That's what I always wanted," I say softly. "A song to come back to."

And then his arms are around me; his lips, those fine broad lips, are on mine; his hand is in my hair and mine in his as if we could pull each other even closer. And our hearts are beating together, as they must. As they always will.

We're sitting on a flat rock by the bank, watching the stream's dance. I lean back into the shelter of his arms. There are words, and they flow as easily as the water—about my life now, and Mum, and school; and getting him clothes and how he should come into town—our talk is light with the feeling it will all work out somehow.

And then, "You didn't tell me I had two fathers," he says with a smile in his voice.

"That wasn't mine to tell." My heart speeds up. "Did Mr. Greenwood come?"

"Neither one of them," he says. "I've my own life to live, is what I told them. A new life to make."

I've heard those words before. But now I know that a new life doesn't mean erasing who you were. It means finding the strength in it, like a tree drawing moisture from the earth.

Like a falcon facing into the wind.

AUTHOR'S NOTE

I love entering another time, or another world, and that's one of the reasons I love research. But once I'm in that world, I have no qualms about taking liberties with the facts for the sake of my story. Addy would have had to speak French, not English, in Sir Hugh's castle. Falcons would have been hooded much of the time. And so on.

One of the best things about being a writer is that it forces you to be brave, in life as well as on the page. Because of Addy's story, I met some amazing people and birds. I heard a gyrfalcon slash through a crisp blue sky. I saw a falconer sneak low through wet grass, his dogs silent at his side, toward a pond of ducks, while a peregrine circled overhead. The relationship I witnessed between a volunteer and a rescued wild falcon informed Will's feelings about wild birds in this book. Sharing these experiences was such a gift.

The church in Little Pembleton is based on the Church of St. Mary the Virgin in Iffley, England. There are wonderful pictures online, showing those rows of watchful bird heads carved around the door (http://www.iffley.co.uk/, http://www.sacred-destinations.com/england/oxford-iffley-church). Eustace's letters were inspired by those of Simon de Senliz, a thirteenth-century steward to Ralph de Nevill, who was a bishop and chancellor to King Henry III (W. H. Blaauw in *Sussex Archaeological Collections Illustrating the History and Antiquities of the County*, v. III, 1850, pp. 35–76). Eustace, the wily fellow, may have lifted several phrases from these letters for his own use. Pilgrim is named after one of Henry III's peregrines. Mr. Greenwood's song, "My Sweetheart's the Man in the Moon" (words and music by James Thornton) was a hit in England in 1892, several years before Will was born. Pamela Horn's wonderful book on domestic service, *Life Below Stairs in the 20th Century* (Stroud, U.K.: Sutton Publishing, 2001), makes clear how opportunities for women changed with the First World War, shortly after Addy's return at the end of my novel.

~~ACKNOWLEDGMENTS~~

My heartfelt thanks to everyone who gave so generously of their time, knowledge, wisdom, and support as I wrote *Wildwing*. Falconer Randy Carnahan took me hawking with his peregrine and goshawk, and answered innumerable questions with a depth of knowledge and sense of humor that made research a joy. Many thanks to Cascades Raptor Center, volunteer Jean Daugherty, and Leia the peregrine; to Bob Welle for a day with gyrfalcons, and for making sure I heard a falcon's descent ripping the air; to Austin Moller for the horses; and to Susan Fletcher, who said, "I know a falconer," and whose *Flight of the Dragon Kyn* planted a seed for my interest. Thanks to Michael Faletra, Medievalist extraordinaire, for showing me the castle of my dreams and for looking at drafts for historical inconsistencies. All errors (whether hawking or historical), as well as willful deviations made for the sake of the story, are mine and mine alone.

My thanks to Susan Blackaby, Susan Fletcher, Eileen Pettycrew, and Linda Zuckerman for invaluable feedback and insight on various drafts. Words can't express my appreciation to Elisabeth Benfey for helping me figure out both story and life. To my daughter, Kate Whitman, one of the most perceptive readers I know: You see right to the heart of things and help me get there. Thank you.

It is a gift to work with all the good people of Greenwillow, who care so deeply about making great books. Special thanks to my editor, Steve Geck, whose vision, enthusiasm, and trust mean the world to me; to Lois Adams, for her sharp eye and kind heart; and to Sylvie Le Floc'h, for a cover that blows my socks off. And many thanks to my wonderful agent, Nancy Gallt, for a nudge at the right time to the right ending.

Most of all, thank you, my dearest Richard, Sam, and Kate. I love you.